"All characters and events and situations are purely fictional, a personal thank you to all the terrible British soaps and sitcoms that inspired this book, I may hate you, but I love you all the same"

Our story commences where many a good British tale often does, inside a pub. Not a great nor grand building by any means but small and quaint inside, white walls with glimpses of darker shades where the paint barely hides the slowly building disaster of damp eating the mortar behind, the walls no higher than the tallest man, its base met by dark and stained carpet, blotches of beer and what seems to be passed evidences of a good night spilling from guts to ground, the smell of vomit long gone yet the remains in small dark marks filling the floor with blotches on a dusty carpet. The ceilings the giveaway to the buildings age, for long black painted beams run along dividing the white with time defining purpose, sixteenth century most would guess at a glance of the black wood, and those who guessed were often near right. Like any pub it is filled with chairs and tables, a long back room filled with strange red tiles nearer orange from wear and age line the floor, unpainted beams and a dividing wall gives this place its restaurant , a small kitchen often filled with the clatter of pans and the beating of hammers onto steak and the chopping sound of blade slicing lettuce, the usual, a small kitchen.

But of course all that defines a pub, which every thirsty and weary journeymen eyes first see, is the bar itself, and in this pub, known by its great sign above its door outside as the griffin, the bar takes centre place, grand dark and varnished oak, rumoured to be near the same age as the pub itself, although it is often a conversation for discussion, a solid answer rarely reached on the matter, regardless its age, it is impressing to see, for it runs around the centre of the pub, all manner of pumps and different ales for thirsty eyes to see. Lagers, ciders real ales and stouts, all clear and easy to choose, and if nothing takes the fancy of a particular palate then near twenty bottles of spirits of varying taste and make sit ready to greet you on a shelf, as well as two large fridges of bottles of different sorts, party pops of varying colours, beers and light ales from different countries, all is there for a great night. A pool table at the end of the pub, the green stained and fluffy through years of play, a dart board with more holes than cork yet all is there, even a duke box, even a large tv to show the sports, even a slot machine. And yet, on a Friday night where we find ourselves, the pub is quiet, four men at the pool table, one at the bar, and one outside at the smoking area, it is nine o'clock on a Friday, and there is better movement at the local graveyard than here, where now we begin our story.

Of the four men taking turns to take there shots on the pool table, one stands out from the rest, leather waist coats on all four, tattoos and long hair and muscle on all too, one with a large moustache, known as "stripper", a name obtained apparently for his love of the art form, a past life it is rumoured, he still smiles to remember. His brother beside him, a hulk of a form, muscle where many would believe it shouldn't be, a man known as "crusher", for good reason too, his brother beside him laughing as stripper misses his shot, the mans laughter shrill and slightly jarring, tattoos everywhere, skulls and knives all about his skin, a well deserved name of "ripper" identifies him, indeed all three are easily identified, for upon the leather waistcoats above there left breast, each has there name, ripper, stripper and crusher sewn to the dark material, with stripper having the word "president" above his name, for all three had upon there backs a set of rockers, "VigilanteS" top, "England" bottom, the centre a large golden letter of v, blood specks painted on the sharp point of the v.

As for the fourth, the one who stands out, "scooter" was his name, and all that marked his colours was the word in giant upon his back, "prospect", thinner than the other three but still well built in comparison to most, his eyes watching the shot on the pool table, as ripper takes his turn, the three laughing as he misses, the mans menacing eyes looking to bare into scooters soul, "hell you laughing at student?" he smiles, the prospect quickly stopping his chuckle, "beers empty" ripper says gesturing to his empty lager bottle, "make yourself useful", "yes ripper" the young man replies, "four more?" he asks, the others nodding and chuckling, the prospect swiftly walking to the bar. The bartender being nowhere to be seen, as scooter reaches the bar, his hands nervously searching his pocket for his wallet, coming to stand next to a sitting man, a skinny rag of a soul, curly hair and a ragged beer, his demeanour slightly scared, of the muscle man now standing beside him,

"the hells pete?" scooter asks, "dying of thirst here" he groans, looking at the man on the chair beside him, a man called matt meadows, an orange top and black trousers and a nervous slight shake to his hand as he picks up and sips his beer, "gone for a fag" he replies nervously, "wont be long" he shrugs slightly, quickly putting his pint down, fumbling in his pocket and pulling out a pouch of tobacco, nervously rolling a quick smoke, "only five of us in here" Scooter groans, "still gotta wait for drink" he sighs, looking at matt, his eyes very carefully looking him up and down, "names Scooter" he says holding out a hand, "he knows who you are you twit" a loud voice laughs as a packet of pork scratchings hits him in the back of the head, the feint noise making matt jump and scooter rub the back of his head, turning to look at Ripper, "hes in here every friday" he says slightly mockingly, "probably met a hundred times"

"really?" scooter says, looking back to matt, "sorry mate not got a good memory for faces" he says in a half effort of an apology, "its fine mate" matt says standing up, walking away towards the back door, his smoke hanging in his lips, scooter turning to pick up the pork scratchings and throw them at ripper as matt leaves the bar area, coming to a small outside landing with the toilets to his left, a large glass door to his front, wide open and leading to a large car park, where sits four large bikes, and a large bench, with two sat smoking and chatting, "hey pete you got people waiting" matt says nervously, the young man in a white shirt standing up and stubbing out his smoke, "cheers mate" he says as he quickly walks passed him, brushing against him slightly before re-entering the pub, a brief sound of cheer erupting in a mocking tone as he enters, leaving matt to stand in the car park, pulling a lighter out and sparking his smoke, the man at the bench barely acknowledging him, playing a game on his phone, casting a quick glance at matt, "alright?" he asks,

"not bad" replies matt, "how you been harv?", "same as ever" Harvey replies, "bored, and sick of seeing them every day" he says, gesturing to the bikes in the car park, "still" he says, stubbing out his smoke, "breathing as always so there's that" he chuckles lightly, "scooter just tired to introduce himself to me" matt says nervously, a slight smile on his lips, "what a tool" Harvey scoffs, "never mind, should be off shortly, busy with there patrols soon id say" he smiles, "have a game once they grant us permission too?" he asks, "sure" matt replies, "haven't got to be home anytime soon" he sighs slightly, taking a draw on his smoke, "where's the wife and kid this evening?" Harvey asks, "kims out with some friends and I'm paying Anne until eleven" matt replies, the smoke coming softly from his lips, "needed an evening off, hows Mary?" he asks, "pleasuring some other mug id imagine" he laughs, tapping his phone as his game blares a warning at him that his battery is about to run out, Harvey muttering as he closes his game and puts the mobile away, turning his head to look fully at matt, "broke it off with her" he says darkly,

"sorry mate" matt says with a genuine tone, "she was a good one too" his comment making Harvey scoff with a dark chuckle, "a good one" he says sarcastically, "sure stripper in there would agree", his comment making matt shake a little as he draws another smoke, "pete saw them kissing the other night, then she told me more happened this morning" Harvey laughs, "must be a biker thing, brings out the slut in a princess" his eyes taught and his voice slightly angry, "mary and stripper?" matt asks, harvey looking and nodding, "mate im sorry" "so am I" Harvey says, "three friends in this boring village, and I end up dating and blowing it with one of them, just leaves you and pete I guess" he says finding another cigarette from a packet laying on the bench beside him, lighting it up, "mate you haven't come to talk to stripper about it have you?" matt says nervously, looking towards the door, "no, no" Harvey says quickly, "came to smoke and drink, the fool being inside is why I'm outside, besides, I basically drove mary to his dick anyway" he says taking a drag, the smoke coming from him, "accused her of cheating so many times I might as well have plonked her on that big bikers shaft myself" he sighs, "were going to brake up soon enough without our neighbourhood super hero"

"damn mate" matt sighs, taking another drag, "sounds like you need a drink" he says pointing at Harveys empty glass, "in a bit mate," Harvey replies, "wait until the neighbourhood watch go for there patrol" "course mate" matt replies, "cant face them at the minute, cant face the same bullsh..." Harvey stops quickly as pete comes back out, carrying a pint with him, placing it down in front of Harvey, "here you go bud" he says slapping his mate on the back, "didn't think you'd want come get one yourself" "cheers mate" Harvey says, taking the pint, "you hear?" pete asks, looking at Matt, "yeah he was just saying" he replies, "bloody vigilantes" pete says, sounding slightly jealous, walking back to the door, "make a place boring and have all the sex they want" he scoffs, his frown turning to a forced smile as he re-enters the pub, the door closing behind him, "how's it been going with kim and the little un?" Harvey asks, his tone and look of face making it clear his need to change the subject, matt stepping to the bench and sitting beside his friend, taking a final draw of his smoke and stubbing it out in the ash tray, his voice coming slightly sadly, "okay I guess"

"that bad huh?" Harvey smiles, "thought you were getting on better now", "we were, a few days last week were good," matt shrugs meekly, "watching tv together on the sofa, but…" he trails off, "she still doesn't think much of you" his friend replies, "told you before, you can do better mate" "I try to please her, got a job for a couple of days" matt says exhaustedly, "selling crap at a shop" Harvey laughing gently as he picks

up his pint and taking a sip, "longest you lasted in a job, your getting better" "I tired mate, really I did, but…I woke on the Wednesday and couldn't get up.." he shrugs, "you got no motivation matt" Harvey says, "we all suffer with the big d sometimes, just gotta get up and.." "I know" matt sighs, "I know, but every time I think I'm managing" he shakes his head, "it's just…you know" "its kim mate" Harvey says, "a soul sucker like that in your bed, told you before she's no good for you"
Matt shakes his head, "her and the kid are the only thing keeping me going mate" he says, "she isn't the problem,"

  "so out of work again? Bet the dole officer gonna enjoy another story why your signing on again" Harvey says softly, looking at his friend, "sorry mate" he says snapping out of his light smile, "with everything going on just good to know I'm not the worst in this hell hole at relationships" he says playfully slapping Matts back, "its alright mate, shouldn't be talking about it, not with you and mary breaking up, sorry" matt replies, shaking his head, "so how's Todd?, haven't seen him for a while" Harvey says changing the conversation again, "still after that channel?", the question making Matt laugh, "all he bloody talks about, told him we cant afford twenty pound a month for one blooming channel, can barely afford to eat" "well that's kids mate" Harvey smiles, "go round each others houses and want what there friends have, be happy its not a console, proper money there mate" he laughs, "oh he wants one of them as well, but a tv for his room and the channel subscription is all he wants for his birthday, sure the console question will be saved for Christmas" he smiles, "you coming Monday for it?"

  "yeah I'll be there bud, cant miss my best mates boys tenth birthday" Harvey replies, taking a drag on his smoke and grabbing his beer for a long sip, "so what you get him in the end?" he asks, Matt shaking his head, "box of chocolate and a card" he says slightly ashamedly, "all I can afford", "christ mate" Harvey says, pulling a wallet out of his pocket, "here, get him a toy he likes or something" he says holding a twenty pound note, "I appreciate it mate" Matt says, holding his hand out and brushing the hand gently aside, "but I don't need the money, Todd needs to learn to make do as his family does" he says honestly, "cant afford to pay you back any way", "take it as a gift" Harvey says, "sorry mate, I can't" matt replies, "ah its your pride getting in the way again" Harvey sighs, putting the money back in his wallet, "I'll use it to get something nice for Todd from me then" he says softly, "prides all I got mate" matt sighs, "nothing to put it in but it all I got for now"

  "sorry mate, had a few drinks, didn't mean to be so obnoxious" Harvey says lightly, "I know you like your son needing you for things, what dad doesn't" he says gently, "where'd you get twenty quid anyway?" Matt asks, changing the subject quickly, "your just as broke as me", Harvey shrugging the question aside swiftly, "your not dealing again?" he asks seeing his friends reaction, "Harv?" he asks, quickly hushing his voice, nervously looking at the door of the pub, "oh come on you idiot!" he says slapping his friends head, harv quickly stubbing his cigarette out, looking firmly at Matt, "why not?" he asks stubbornly, "just a bit of puff" "oh for christ sake harv come on!" matt says in a harsh and hushed voice, "you know what they will do if they find out?" he says pointing at the bikes,

"there not going to find out" Harvey says defensively, "anyway don't much care if they do, think they bleeding own the village" "they do own the village!" Matt says quickly, "who in the hell was stupid enough to buy from you in the first place!?" he asks shocked, "people who don't give a damn about no vigilantes!" Harvey says stubbornly, "its just a bit of puff matt" he shrugs, "should try some once in a while, might help you keep a job down" "oh please" matt says dismissively, "I might be a dosser to most but I aint that far dropped from society to sit a smoke weed all day" his comment making his friend smile and laugh again, "what else is there to do in this mud bucket of a village" he says, seeing his friend tense up, his tone relaxing and his laughter stopping, "was just this once matt, needed something to keep me out of the red this month"

"well make sure it is" Matt warns, "you know what they do to dealers" he says nervously, "you'll be drinking soup for years" "at least it'd be free" Harvey sighs, "promise me mate" Matt says seriously, "no more dealing, if you need money talk to the dole officer, must be something he can do". Harvey puts his hands softly in the air, "no more mate, promise" "my only mate being put in a hospital ward recovering from a broken spine would just be the nail mate" Matt says shaking his head, quickly coming to a silence as the pub door swings open, the four bikers walking out, scooter saying "see ya later" as he walks passed, stripper coming to a stop, looking at Harvey, "alright harv?" he asks, his voice strong and husky, his eyes glaring at the seated man, "sorry to hear about Mary", he says, Harvey quickly tensing, Matt starting to shake and look down at the floor, "she's a slut mate" Harvey replies with a careful shrug, "not your fault,"

"alright" stripper smiles, stepping away, "so no problems then" he says gesturing for his waiting brothers to leave, the three men mounting the motorcycles and strapping there helmets on , "see you Monday Matt" he says smiling, the shaking man looking at him confused, "Todds birthday, kim invited me" Stripper says, "six o'clock yeah?", "umm yeah mate…six" Matt replies, "I'll get something nice" Stripper says, stepping away and mounting his bike, taking his helmet and slowly strapping it on, "have a safe night, remember if you need us just call" he shouts through his helmet, starting the bike his brothers do the same, pulling the clutch and hitting the gear he kicks the side stand up and pulls away, "and remember we are always watching" a loud voice shouts from Crushers helmet, as the three follow the president and leave the car park, leaving matt and Harvey to nervously look at each other.

"always watching" Harvey spits, standing up, his figure showing a slightly scared form, "watch this" he says flicking up two fingers in the direction of the car park exit, picking up his beer and walking for the door, "fancy a game now?" he asks, Matt looking at him, "he's coming to my house?" he asks slightly shocked, "kim invited him?" his friend shaking his head, "told you mate, kim aint no good" he says walking through the door, Matt quickly following him, "but they don't even really know each other....do they?" he asks confused, walking through the door after his friend, Harvey going over to the pool table, "Pete you drink down the sun" Harvey says as he walks passed the barman, "kim know stripper?", "hell yeah they're always drinking together" Pete says, looking at Matt, "come on mate she goes out every night to that pub, course they know each other" Harvey adds, Matt looking at him confused, "no…but" he says not understanding, his mind racing, suddenly Harvey and Pete laughing, "sorry mate" pete says, "too easy"

"you guys are arses" he snaps, "sorry mate" Harvey smiles, "inappropriate joke" he admits, "come on rack up mate" he says putting a coin in the pool table, the balls dropping and tumbling to the collection hole, Matt grabbing his beer from the bar, "but he still knows her" he says, taking a sip and putting it back on the bar nearer the pool table, "they had a drink the other night" Pete says pouring himself a pint, "down the sun", "why do you drink at that pub anyway you traitor? You work here" Harvey says laughing, watching Matt rack up the pool balls, "its on the way home" Pete says defensively, "besides aren't no sides when it comes to drinking"

"just the pub they use as a club house" Harvey says mockingly, "hoping they might notice you and let you prospect", "screw you harv" pete says finishing pouring his pint, taking a sip, "love em about as much as you two, come in here as part of there patrol, making sure the other half of the village they don't drink in is behaving" he says mockingly, "so kim didn't say anything about stripper then?" Harvey asks looking at Matt, "nope" he replies, lining the cue and breaking the balls apart, a yellow one dropping into a pocket, "just another thing she wont talk to me about" he sighs, stepping round the table and lining his next shot, "you coming to the party Monday pete?" Harvey asks, looking at his friend, "cant mate sorry, working" pete replies, "we never hang out anymore you know that" Matt says as he takes his shot, "that's cause hes always licking bikers bum and kim keeps you prisoner mate" Harvey says with a chuckle, "I don't lick bottoms" pete huffs, "im not a prisoner" Matt says, making Harvey laugh "oh please, when's the last time you got out, week ago?

Long time for a dole dosser mate" "I get every Friday night to myself"
matt says defensively, Pete laughing at the pitiful defence, "blimey mate
time to get your balls back"

"kim goes to work during the day, she needs her time in the evenings"
Matt says quickly, "means I get to spend time with todd each night,"
"house husband" Harvey says nodding his head, "you are a poor abused
house husband" he laughs, "and your girlfriend was finger flicked by a
vigilante" Matt snaps, instantly regretting his words, a weird and strange
silence filling the pub with awkwardness, instantly shattered by pete and
Harvey laughing, "I'll give you that" Harvey says, "good comeback", he
says slapping his friends back, stepping to the table and lining his shot,
"though kim might be riding them fingers too if you think about it" he
winks, pete smiling as a large lady walks through the front door, "evening
Marge" he says politely, "evening Pete, rose wine and cheese and onion
my darling" she says removing her large leopard skin coat and hanging it
up, "evening boys" she says with a large smile,

"hey marge" Harvey says, "ooh I was sad to hear about mary darling"
she says sitting down at the bar, watching pete pour a rose wine into a
glass, "is what it is" Harvey says, taking his shot, "well if ever your
lonely you come see me for a good supper" she says, "thanks…"he says,
slightly rolling his eyes, "last man to do that was never seen again" he
says quietly to matt, making him smile, "so how are you Matt?" Marge
asks, taking the glass of wine from pete and taking a bag of cheese and
onion, placing a five pound note on the bar, pete taking it and opening the
till, "not bad" he says watching the missed shot, the white ball rolling and
hitting his own colour, "two shots" Harv sighs, standing up straight and
walking away from the table, "here your kim is down the sun, had a few I
would say" Marge says, taking a long sip from her glass, "left her singing
sweet home Alabama on the karaoke"

"sounds about right, had to get out of there did you?" Pete asks with a
smile, returning the change and putting the coins on the bar, "na the
cavalry finished there patrol and took over the place again" she sighs,
"lovely bunch but bloody loud," she says softly, "keep forgetting to get
out of there by ten", "thought you loved them marge, saviours you called
them" Harvey says mockingly though not horribly, "the brass of your
nuts Harv" marge says defensively, "they are saviours, you'd do well
remember that"

"Vigilantes marge, says so on there backs, not saviours" he says, causing
Pete to roll his eyes,. "all I'm saying is we are safer than five years ago"
Marge says, trying not to get into confrontation, "I can walk around the
village now at night and that's because of them"

"and five years of boredom and fear have taken over an interesting
place" Harvey replies, looking away from marge, "interesting maybe"

Pete cuts in, "but I will take safe over what this place used to be like" his comment making marge lift her glass in agreement, "what about you matt?" she asks, looking at the young man, "your staying quiet on the matter", "that's cause he craps himself anytime the vigilantes look at him" Harvey chuckles, watching matt take his second shot, potting his ball and hitting another, this time going wide, "I have no opinion on the matter Marge" Matt says, standing up and stepping away from the table, Harvey stepping up and lining another shot, "a safe way to be" she says politely, putting her glass down and taking a crisp, "so what times the party for todd?" she asks, "my little Kieran cant wait", "six" Harvey and matt say at the same time, "apparently stripper will be there too" Harvey adds, "well at least it will get the numbers up" she smiles, matt looking away slightly ashamedly, "such a shame my boy is yours only friend, really should encourage him to get out and play more" she says quite politely, "here, kierans going with some others to the cinema next Saturday, why not send todd? I can pick him up"

"I appreciate it marge but" matt says kindly, "I cant afford to send him to the films, " "oh" marge says, "well I'll pay, it'll be my present to him" she says, taking and crunching another crisp, "I insist" she says, seeing matt about to say no, "is a good present marge" Harvey says, taking his shot, the white ball striking true, his target going down the pocket, "nice shot" pete says, pulling a cigarette from his pocket, "give me a shout if anyone needs a drink" he says, going out the door for a smoke, "anyone else?" Harvey laughs, "there all down the sun by now" he says as he takes another shot, the ball going down the pocket,

"so with me and Kieran, you and kim and todd, Stripper and I suppose you Harv, that's seven" Marge counts, "so I'll make some pasta salad, enough for seven" she smiles, "looking forward to it" Matt says awkwardly, looking at a clock on the wall, "well I need to go" he says nervously, feeling Marges smile and gaze on him, "need to go relieve a babysitter" he says, downing the last of his pint, "but I'm winning" Harvey protests, "oh here" he replies walking to the table, hitting the white ball onto the black, sending the black ball down the pocket, four of each yellow and red balls still In play, "I lose" he shrugs, "goodnight" he says grabbing his coat from a peg, "goodnight dear, see you Monday" Marge smiles, "okay night" he says, leaving the pub, Harvey quickly following through the door, "come on mate, we still got half hour before you need to be back"

"no sorry harv" he says, throwing his coat on, "don't let that cow ruin your night" he says pointing towards the door of the pub, "its not marge mate, just feeling tired is all" Matt replies quickly, "okay fine" Harvey says holding his hands up defeated, "fine, here you free tomorrow?" he asks, "fancy a laugh? I got an interview you could come too" "on a

Saturday?" matt asks vaguely interested, "yeah at a garage, they work Saturdays" harvey says with a slight shrug , "could be fun"

"im good mate" Matt replies, looking at his friend, "besides got plans", "staying in all day and not seeing anybody?" Harvey asks bluntly, "come on matt you got the time to hang with a friend, here next Wednesday morning petes coming round mine, we going to watch some films and hang", "I'll see you Monday mate" Matt replies almost sternly, avoiding committing to anything, "see you later" he says walking away, Harvey watching him go, "alright…see you Monday I guess" he says softly, watching his friend cross the road, walking down a pavement passed the local church and cemetery, Matt fades to the darkness, Harvey turning round and going back in the pub.

"wasn't something I said I hope" Marge says, seeing Harvey come back in, munching on a mouthful of crisps, "dare say it was" Harvey says, looking at the remaining pool balls, stepping over and brushing them into the pockets, "he's lucky to have you, a waster if you ask me" Marge says taking a sip of her wine, "if you ask anyone actually," she says between sips, "but still…lucky to have a friend I guess", "he's alright marge" Harvey says, clearing the last of the balls, a small thud sounding as they hit the bottom of the tables pockets, "just run down" he adds,

"we all get run down deary" she says placing her glass gently on the bar, "but we don't earn what little for our kids and drink it away every Friday night" she says rather accusingly, "oh leave it out marge" Harvey says defensively, "he has one beer a week and makes it last a few hours", "well.." Marge says eating another crisp, "still a waster, never held down a job in his life," her comment causing Harvey to down what's left of his pint and put the empty glass on the bar, "not true, was a locksmith for a few years,..before….you know" he says slightly softly, trailing off, "yeah five years ago that happened, should be over it by now" Marge says sternly, "if it were just him id understand but he has a wife and kid"

"can we just…." Harvey says, seeing Pete come back through the door, "can we just change the subject please" he says, Marge looking at him and sighing slightly, "look I don't hate the fellow, im just saying what everyone else thinks, " "well your not in the company of the like minded" Harvey says firmly, Marge, "is that so?" she says looking at Pete.

****

The walk home from any pub can often be called many a thing, to some it is known playfully as the walk of shame, to others a mighty triumph of overcoming the ills of too much booze, but for the like of Matt Meadows, it was as simple a thing as any, and as such had no special occasion or merit to its achievement. For Matt never drank beyond a pint a week, not out of principal or ceremony, simply for the cost of drinking more than one, for he earned nothing and had little income to his name, save what the government and council provided, yes matt was poor, but even he had a spot of determination that such a situation would not prevent a slight luxury at least once a week. And so the walk was simple, so too was it short, for matt lived not far from the pub at all, in fact he often thought about the time it took, the shortest achievement being less than a minute from one door to the other, and so in the darkness, Matt came to his house, the second passed the grave he used to say to any asking where he lived, though seldom ever asked, for most knew where Matt lived. For a man from such simple a background with nothing to his name, owned a house that would say otherwise,

An eighties built red brick four bedroom house, with a large driveway and double garage at the side, a small front garden and a slightly larger back garden behind a fence and gate, oh yes, matt lived here, and if by size the dwellings would surprise to say such a man lived here, then the state of it would truly remind you it was certainly Matts house. For it had seen better days, in fact since its creation it could be safe to say its been down hill since. Water wearing the mortar to chip and crack between the bricks, ivy growing as high as the roof, weeds everywhere, even places no one would think a weed dare grow. Weeds coming out the cracked window frames, weeds and moss around the door frame, somewhere a small pavement existed leading from the front garden wall to the main door but for its encasement in moss you would swear such a thing didn't exist.

It was fair to say, the house was just as its owner, run down and in need of work, and for the most, in need of attention of time. Alas however, it bothered Matt far less than his neighbours, for it was home, and for him that was all it needed to be, so with a jingle of keys as he searches his pockets, pulling out his house key and sliding it into the lock, he opens his door, and if you thought the state of the outside was bad, then the inside was a shocker too.

A main hallway with a large staircase leading up as you step into the building, the carpet on each step stained and peeling from the wooden structure below it, the carpet of the hallway a dark grey where once it was cream, plugs and switches on walls gaffer taped into position as wires hang where they have done for the passed five years, a toilet on the ground floor with no flush and walking passed to a kitchen with a single cupboard and fridge and cooker in need of a good scrub and all the space for more fittings a family could need. Remnants of failed shelving on the floor and a sink and tap that would block daily, this was an advert for a makeover if ever a house needed one.

And yet, as matt enters his lounge, the living area was surprisingly comfy, although still in need of a good paint job, with flaking walls and dusty carpets, the sofas worn and the tv large and box like where nowadays you would think to see a thin and streamlined model. A dvd player loosely plugged in and dvds scattered around and flimsily piled upon each other, but still, the place felt comfy.

For though the sofas were old they were big and deep, with near a dozen big cushions of different colours on each of the two and a small captains chair in dark green leather angled for the right viewing of the television, a fireplace with a wood burning stove although old and rusty could give out some warming heat in the cold of winter, and the paintings on the wall made it feel even the cosier. Streaks of bright colours, dark silhouettes of otters and wild fowl, a heron too dancing among the bright orange and blue brush strokes of the art pieces, these grand and large paintings, made even this dingy place feel warm, even made Matt smile sometimes in fond memory, for they had been his fathers, as had the house.

"back early?" the babysitter, a young girl called Anne, sat in the deep of one of the sofas asks, seeing Matt step into the lounge, turning the tv off with a click of the remote control, "yeah," matt says softly, "how was todd?" he asks, "oh he was fine, went bed couple hours ago" the young lady says, stretching her arms and standing up" you alright if I go, think I'll join your kim for a swift one" she says smiling, Matt reaching into his pocket and finding ten pounds, handing it to the lady, "can you ask kim for the rest whilst you down there?" he asks, the babysitter looking frustrated and slightly embarrassed, "yeah sure darling" she says, taking the ten pounds and leaving the lounge, "same time next Friday" she asks, opening the front door, "yes..." matt replies as the door closes behind the babysitter, "please" he sighs.

"alone again" he says, sitting down on the sofa, slowly kicking his shoes off, finding the remote control and clicking the button to turn it on, a brief flash of pornographic content flaring up as he quickly hit's the button to change the channel, "gods sake anne" he groans, flicking through the channels quickly, "bit of respect" he sighs, flicking through, trying to find a decent channel, landing on an advert, "hey kids fancy some fun?" a large blue dolphin says, its eyes spinning and its mouth formed to a huge grin, "then have your wish fulfilled with my new channel..." he says with a loud cheer of background actors jumping up and down in fake joy, Matt quickly changing the channel again, "damn fish" he moans, flicking through and coming to another channel, with two men sat in chairs talking about what seems a serious subject, "so mike you play scrumpy the dolphin" the interviewer asks, "that's right" the man replies, using a silly and exaggerated voice to answer, making a few in the audience laugh, "and now you have decided to start your own channel and break from disn...." the interviewer asks, quickly cut off by the screen changing with an angry click of the remote, this time coming to stop on what seems to be a nature documentary.

Matt sighing and leaning back slightly, a nervous glance looking to the clock on the wall, the second hand seeming to thunder with every tick, the eye lids of the mans eyes growing heavy and heavier with each click and roar of the clocks mechanism, the sound of a lion hunting a buffalo and the smoothing tone of the narrator describing the events on the tv aiding in the fall of the eyelids. And with little ceremony or much time passing, Matt falls asleep.

****

 If time passes quick then it is hard to say how long it takes to pass, or at least if it feels slow it is easier to say it has been a long night but yet the calamity of keeping track of the hours when one sleeps is a disastrous undertaking, for either way it feels long or quick, the simple passage of time, long or short, was the length that had passed when Matt awoke. A quick glance to the clock told him it was morning and not an early time at that, in fact his next clue he had slept through a dawn was the tv loud and sounding with a child closely fixed near it, the kid staring wildly into the picture of some pigs jumping in holes and dancing in the mud, a young enthusiastic reporter with big glasses talking about the rolling motions of the swine, his voice jarring and instantly his manner with which he spoke marked him clearly as a children's tv presenter. And so that is how matt awoke, too a report on pigs in mud.

"todd turn that down" matt asks, sitting up and yawning as he looks at the clock again, almost surprised that it was nearer lunch than breakfast, "sorry dad" the kid replied, a young boy with short hair and wearing simple clothing, his eyes a dark brown and freckles upon his cheeks, a normal boy, nothing out the ordinary. With a quick fumble he finds the remote and hit's a few buttons, the mans voice now talking about how often pigs defecate becoming quieter and faded, todd looking round to his father.

"its news popper" he says, referring to the show he was watching, "I know what it is" Matt laughs gently, "you watch it enough times for it to haunt me" he smiles, his son looking at him with a mischievous look, "well if I had my own tv you wouldn't be so spooked" he says, his comment probing his dad for a desired response, "and I would spend more time alone" Matt replies quickly though kindly, sitting up in the sofa and straightening his back as he stands up, "and what father wishes there son shut away from him" he smiles, his son looking away and back to the tv, "well its my birthday soon" he says, almost upset, "and kierans got a tv in his room from his sixth birthday"

"well then feel sad for him" matt says, his son not turning round to

acknowledge his comment, "or I suppose feel happy…mother like that"
he says gently, trailing off as he sees his son not responding to him,
"todd" he says, his son biting his lip, paying hard attention to the pigs, the
volume rising as he hit's the button, "one day I will buy you everything a
good parent should" he says, "but for now I can give only me and time
together"

"rather scrumpys channel and a flat screen" Todd says, his tone slightly
jarring to his fathers ear yet none the less he grabs his shoulders, "you
don't need no dolphin to make you laugh" matt says playfully, "not when
your old mans the tickle monster" he says, tickling his son, the boy
laughing slightly as he flinches from the sensation of fingers tickling his
back, dropping the remote to throw his hands back and try to stop the
onslaught,. His laughter getting louder, "dad stop.." he laughs. Matt
continuing for a couple more seconds before kissing his son on the head,
"another round?" he says playfully dancing his fingers in the air, "no" his
son laughs, "no more rounds"

"then no more on this channel" Matt laughs, "makes the monster mad"
he says in a playful gruff voice, his son finding the remote and picking it
up, placing it into his lap, "no more for today" he says, seeing his dad
huff cheerily, "the only promise the monster gets" todd says quickly,
"well that will have to do" Matt nods, a large smile on his face, "you
hungry?" he asks, walking away towards the lounge door, "no mum
cooked a breakfast," todd says, "you slept through"

"could of woke me" he says gently, so gentle his son didn't hear, the
boys eyes and mind fixed on the show before him, the pigs now piling
into a butchers trailer as matt enters the hallway. A loud flushing sound
coming from upstairs as a door opens, and the stepping of feet down the
stairs sounds, matt looking as he walks into the kitchen, suddenly coming
to a stop as he realises he hasn't a clue who the socks or ankles on the
steps belong too, a strange pair of legs and a thin waist, a well formed
midrift and some long blonde hair atop a beautiful set of eyes and a bright
red set of lips, a woman he knew now he saw her, the babysitter from
before, anne.

"Anne?" he asks slightly taken back from seeing her so soon, the
young lady looking at him with a grin, "oh so up now hey?" she says,
looking up the stairs as another set of feet grace the steps, these socks and
ankles well known to Matt, "yeah" Matt replies, "spend the night did
you?" he asks, slightly awkwardly, "no silly" she laughs somewhat
mockingly, "we having a girls day out" she says, looking at Kim as she
gets to the bottom of the stairs, Anne grabbing her shoes and pulling them
on, Kim doing the same, barely acknowledging Matt standing in the
hallway, "kim?" he asks, looking at his wife,

A plain looking lady, many would say, yet striking with her eyes and faultless hairline, her shoulders petite and her brown hair barely falling to touch the top of her neck, a bow tie at the top and a whisp of hair standing upright, wearing tracksuit bottoms and a grey hoody some might call her a bit street-like, but that was often the misconception of her sort. For truly to any, no matter there judgment or prejudices, Kim was stunning. A fact which had often been a thorn in matts side, for beauty often seeks company of beauty, and in the case of matt, he was far from equal. Something many people often took great pride in reminding him.

"going out, look after todd" she says, not really looking at matt, pulling on her trainers, "see you later son" she shouts, "bye mum" comes the reply from the lounge, Matt looking puzzled at his wife, "where you going…" he asks, his voice ever so slightly sounding nervous to ask, his wife just looking at him as Anne opens the front door, "out" she says, a slight shrug, "be back for dinner" she says, walking out the door, "left over beans in the pan" she says, closing it behind her and her friend, leaving matt staring at the closed front door of his house "bye then" he says, his voice soft and his eyes looking to the floor.

A brief pause to think and he sighs, "you need the toilet?" he calls to his son, the answer "no" coming from the lounge, "I'm about to use the shower so go now if you need to" he says taking the steps up towards the top, "I'm fine" todd calls back, Matt ignoring the answer and continuing to the top, reaching the landing.

To his left a small room with a closed door, "todds own castle" written on a sign hanging from the door knob, to the right of that a larger room with no sign, the door ajar and showing a large double bed, with no evidence a man once cohabitated in it, lipsticks and perfumes and magazines cluttered the cupboards and tops of the drawers, the usual stuff, as well as a distinctively pink theme. Pink curtains, pink sheets, pink duvet covers, the colour was everywhere, which is more than can be said for matts stuff, for looking and turning to his right, he opens a third door, revealing a small room and a single bed, his room, his bed.

Now this was a mans room, as surely as pink bedding defines a ladies so too does the clutter of something so unkempt define a mans. With books piled in the corners upon each other and motorcycle magazines littered around the floor. Dark grey bedding and a simple blanket with a bat symbol embossed upon it, this was a mans room, or at least, that of an elderly child. Matt didn't much care for its state, as he enters and finds from a top drawer a set of clothes, a simple green top and a pair of trousers, with a step back out he walks to another door, opening it wide to reveal the bathroom

Not much of a sight, simple in its premise, a green bath basin with a shower above, a toilet of the same colour and three different tooth brushes on a sink of similar shade to that of the toilet. Towels strewn about the floor and bottle upon bottle of half used shampoos and soaps line the bath, but nothing out the ordinary here. Just like the rest of the house this place needed work, with grouting needing to be redone and few tiles still the same shade of white when first fitted, yet it was a comfort, just as the house was as a whole. And Matt looked forward to a shower most mornings, for truth be told he only had three simple pleasures, and this was one from his list.

Music and hot water, if you were to quiz him on there effects he would reply simply, "a simple pleasure, and so cheap a comfort too", as he turns on the shower radio, and turns on the tap, both the water as he flicks a lever to make it spring from the shower, and the ballad playing, made him feel an easy ease, the steam rising as he adjusts the temperature, his clothing falling from him as he puts the clean clothes aside, and strips from the ones he had slept in.

"nevr found me a woman" the blues voice hollers, "that can keep me at bay", with a quick tug on the collar he removes his shirt and jumper from over his head, the clothing falling to the floor, "never heard no sweet words, no there aint nothing they can say" he sings with the music, the sound of the water and blues filling his ears, "im a gambling man, I got me some debts" the two voices call out, as the trousers fall, a thin body and ill formed muscle reflecting in the mirror of the bathroom, slowly steaming up from the temperature rising in the room, "oh im a rambling man, yet I havent come across…a sweet one yet" the voices sing in unison, as matt removes his boxer shorts, and steps into the shower, the water striking him with a silent pleasure and calm, his hand finding a shampoo bottle, as he rinses his hair, his curls falling around to hang below his shoulders, "and yet I would borrow every coin ever struck" the voices sing, "to find me a woman who knows how to fu.." the harmonica cutting in before the word comes out , causing Matt to smile broadly as he runs his fingers through his hair, "oh lord, im a gambling man, with no love to keep me true to who I am…I aint no mean guy, nor this shallow sight you see…"

The shampoo squirting onto his hand as he rubs it into his hair, "its just a case of…." the voices holding the tune, the word drawn out as the song comes to a close, "a case of mistaken identity" "man I love that song" Matt smiles, as the radio presenter laughs and begins to talk about a phone in, matt rinsing his hair as his finger finds a button on the radio, with a click it shuts off, matt going silent, his eyes closed as the water and shampoo runs down his hair, down to the plug hole below.

Now it has to be said the short silence that followed was not unlike many that had happened before, indeed it would often happen, play a song then reflect in the shower, this was a part of the routine he enjoyed, but this morning was like no other, this time, the shower had tears to join them. This time one of the three things on the list to keep the darkness at bay, had failed.

It was a strange feeling, this emotion Matt felt. Not being able to put a finger on the cause or find specific reason for the outburst, made it the much worse, and could this man cry. If the shower were off you would think it still running, and the redness of the eyes would make you think shampoo got too them, but alas, no soap nor product touched them. This was grief. And it was abundant as the steam around him, as legs shake and water falls, his lips bitten shut as he thinks on a time far better than now. And as a knock comes to the bathroom door with a child's voices saying, "dad I need a wee", so the shower turns off, and the day conitues as normal.

****

So often a day dawns for one and so to another, such is true for our young friend Harvey, who for the effort he is putting in, seems sweaty and out of breath. His feet planted firmly on the pedals of his black mountain bike, the road behind him long and a horrid reminder to him that he will again have to travel it on the journey home. The road before him becoming shorter with each sprint of speed on the pedals, his bike racing along the road, passing tractors in large open fields, potatoes falling from the harvesters into awaiting lorries, a few farmhands giving a cheeky wave, the prhase "rather you than me" becoming a contsatnt saying on the journey. Each one saying it believing they were saying something clever, though to Harvey having heard it fro the third time it had become a retched reminder of his undertaking, for he was not best pleased with his cycle ride.

For the road stretched about three miles and was straight and surrounded by fields, which on a nice day makes for a pretty sight, however this day, was not such a time. A strong wind and spurts of downpours had racked his body, his form shivering as he pedals all the quicker to escape the torrents, his body constantly reminded of his twenty a day smoking habit, his coughs reminding him he was in fact incredibly unfit. His body aching as he nears his destination, a small village just next to his own, which is why he had ventured here, for it held the garage he was going to be interviewing in.

With a cough and a huff and a sigh the last bout of rain had subsided he enters the village, cycling fast to a crossroads, waiting as a landrover passes then pulling out to the road, a quick cyle and spurt of speed and he takes himself towards the garage. A large place, with fuel pumsps and a small shop at the front, mechainics and machinery to its side. Pulling in and hitting his brakes, with a squeek he finds a place to lay his bike, his eyes taking in one of the mechanics as he pulls up.

"Harvey Flint?" the man asks, looking at the rain soaked man before him, "that's me" Harvey replies, "friends call me harv" he says, stepping towards the man, "Bruce" the man says, holding out a hand and shaking Harveys, seeming to be disappointed at the weakness of Harveys grip,

"this way" Bruce says, walking through a small door and into the reception of the garage, a small fish tank in the corner alongside a coffee machine and a couple of chairs, a large desk taking centre place, bruce opening a fold of the desk and allowing Harvey through, gesturing to a small back room, "in there" he says, pointing to a small sofa chair sitting near a smaller desk, "with you in a second" Bruce says, walking out the reception through a small door leading to the main workshop, cars up on jacks as mechanics work below, a motorbike sitting ready at the mot bay, "just gotta finish up here" he says matter of fact, walking over to the motorbike, Harvey entering the small room at the back, taking a seat on the small sofa chair.

The room wasn't much, Harvey thought to himself as he waited, a few calenders and folders but nothing of any great artwork or distinguishing features, "a working mans room", he thought to himself, "such a foreign sight". the sound of a motorcyle starting up and revving sounded for a few moments, the noise travelling to harveys ears, making him shudder.

For a few minutes he was on his own, sitting alone with his thoughts, and to be fair where most would be nervous, Harveys most definitely were not. For most would be nervous if an interviewee wanted the role and was desperate for it, however the young man was far from inclined to think such a thing, to be blunt, he didn't want the job at all. Not that he didn't like engines nor did he lack any respect for those who worked on them, for Harvey he just didn't want to work, anywhere or doing anything. If a job was offered where he could sit and play games on his phone all day he would still resent having to travel to and from the office, and even if the job entailed working from home he would resent having to get up from bed. In short, he didn't much care for working, and it was that simple.

"sorry to keep you" Bruce says, emerging through the door, his face seeming a bit more flustered than previously, the man sitting down behind the desk, grabbing a bit of paer and a pen, with a click the point emrging and ready to scribble down the notes of the interview.

"so" he says, looking up at Harvey, "worked on engines at all, cars, motrbikes, tractors maybe?" he says, seeing Harvey shrug, "nope" he replies, "never had an interest in them" he says quite candidly, Bruce writing something down on his paper, "up til now you mean?" he asks hopefully, Harvey smiling, as he answers, "nope" he says, "don't get me wrong I enjoy a good car show, couldn't care less about bikes but certainly no interest in fixing or maintaing cars either" he explains,

"so the reason your interviewing for trainnee technician is?" Bruce asks, his voice slightly jarred and his face showing he wasn't best amused by the answers, "got to attend interviews every now and then" Harvey shrugs, "mother moaning at you is it?" Bruce asks, putting down his pen and looking accusingly at the young man, Harvey smiling at him, the facial expression probably not the best choice for the situation, "dole office mate" he admits,

"ah" Bruce sighs, looking at the door of the office, "I don't mean any direspect, but I got work to do" he says, standing up, ushering Harvey to do the same, "no disrespect taken," Harvey says happily, standing up and holding out a hand, Bruce shaking it somewhat annoyed, "how old are you?" he asks, not letting go of the young mans hand, "twenty six" Harvey says, "I hope by your next birthday you grow up" Bruce says, letting go of the hand and letting Harvey go, the young man walking through the door, Bruce going to open the fold of the desk for him,

"your not the first to say it" Harvey says, his eyes catching the sight of a VigilanteS member walking through the door, his tag on his front chest naming him Ratchet, the tall and well built man sporting a large beard and black haired dreadlocks, the man placing his motorbike helmet on an empty seat, Harvey quickly wanting to leave,

"you cycled from Isleham to get here didn't you?" Bruce asks, Harvey looking at him as he answers, "yeah" he says, "three miles in a storm just to keep your handouts" Bruce says, looking the young boy up and down, "six if you count the journey home" he adds, shaking his head in disspointment, "if only such energy was applied with more meaning" he says. Looking at Ratchet as he steps to the desk, his hand not moving to open the fold of the desk, Harvey awkwardly stuck behind him,

"how'd the ol thumper do?" the biker asks, a thick Scottish accent to his voice, his demeanour seeming friendly as he leans on the wood of the desk, "failed the m.o.t I'm afraid" Bruce says, his tone blunt and straight to the point, "what?" Ratchet asks, "a mistake surely" he asks quite honestly, "ol thumper been roaring sound for last five years" he says defensively, "faulty brakes, poor tread on the tyres and a hole in your exhaust big enough to fit an apple" Bruce says, pulling out a bit of paper from under the desk, "get them fixed and bring it back within the week and I'll retest for free" he says, finding a set of keys and handing them to the biker,

"you know what I think" Ratchet says softly, his hand going to his front pocket of his waistcoat, his smile broadening, as Bruce doesn't even flinch, "think theres been a mistake mate" he says, slowly pulling something out, Harvey feeling nervous and shaking as he looks for another exit, the door to the main workshop closed and the owners hand

still on the fold of the desk, Bruce just watching Ratchet without even a
flinch, as a wallet slides from the pocket, fingers finding notes and laying
them on the table, nearly two hundred pounds by Harveys quick count,
"m.o.t cost forty friend" Bruce says plainly, "then a hundred and sixty
might change the result of it" Ratchet says smiling, "how about you go to
the printer and correct those spelling mistakes there", he says, pointing at
the paper on the desk, his finger firmly pointing to the word "fail"

"or I can phone every mother in the country" Bruce says, his voice calm
and collected, the bikers smile fading, "and apologise for one of there
loved ones killed in a traffic accident I could have prevented" Bruce says,
"or maybe the police" he says pushing the money on the desk towards
ratchet, "and use this as evdience of a bribe"

"woah" Ratchet says, stepping back and picking the money up, keeping
forty pounds on the desk, "worth a go man" he says, forcing a fake laugh,
"come on got to give it a go havent you?" he says, looking at Harvey, the
young man looking away, his face showing fear and disgust, "well then
heres your reciept" Bruce says, sliding the paper towards Ratchet, "and
the bike is out front" he says sternly, "so no harm done" he says, his
voice filled with authority,

"no harm done man" Ratchet smiles, picking up the paper and folding it
into his waistcoat, "will get it fixed and be seeing you in seven days man"
he says, walking over to the seat and picking up his helmet, "cheers" he
says, leaving the garage reception, the door slamming behind him.

"how do you live with them?" Bruce sighs, lifting the fold of the desk,
letting Harvey out, "we don't " he replies, his voice squeeeking and
fearful, "safe journey Harvey" bruce says quite nicely, "I'll make sure the
job centre know you attended the interview",

"thanks" Harvey says, walking to the reception door, "that was…" he
says looking at Bruce, his voice trailing away, "that was brave" he says.
Bruce just looking straight back at him, no emotion showing, "no it was
legal" he says sternly, "grow some balls and work out what you want
from life mate" he says, Harvey looking away from him, "do that..and
maybe one day you'll be doing something you love.." Bruce says bluntly,
"just like me"

"see…see you then" Harvey says, opening the door, bruce saying "see
you" back at him as he leaves, the cold rain pouring down again, Ratchets
bike roaring to life as the biker starts it on the forecourt, Harvey watching
him pull away, as he looks at his own bike laying on the ground. The seat
soaking wet, another journey ahead of him.

****

The rain was falling outside this evening, the rain falling with a mighty
force, splattering over the gazeebo of Matts back garden, where huddled

underneath, sat Kim and her friend anne, a bottle of wine and a couple glasses each, both smoking away and laughing, there giggles and jokes carrying through the open door leading to the kitchen, where matt stood, a bunch of vegtables and fake mince before him. A large cutting knife and large board resting on the kitchen worktop, a frying pan and sauce pan behind him, sitting ready to be used on the hobs of the oven.

It wasn't real meat, this recipe didn't need it and for matt neither did he, for through choice he long ago decided to go the route of militant vegetarian. Not for any great reason, it certainly was an ethically based decision, more a pricing concern and a need to experiment more with his meals. For truth be told, cooking was second on Matts list, of things that calmed him. It wasn't a great expensive venture or search for self longing, it was simply cooking, that brought him the most joy he had yet discovered, in fact he had once been a chef, only for a day before being fired for not turning up the next but still, he had enjoyed it.

Looking at the ingredients before him, he had decided to make a chilli, using imitation mince in place of the real thing, and the decision as it often did had annoyed his wife into ordering a kebab with her friend, for she did not share his love of vegetarianism, and often reminded him of her point of view on the matter. And so as the words of kim and anne rang in his ears, "god put some meat in it", he began to chop away.

First slicing up an onion, the sting hitting his eyes and forcing a few tears, but as soon as they had come, so too had they left, as with quick motion and some degree of skill, it was quickly sliced and put to one side. Next the mushrooms and celery, falling to the same fate as the onion, quickly sliced to adequate lengths, as he picks up all the ingredients from the chopping board and throws them in the pan, a click on the oven and the hob comes to life, a big red circle forming under the pan, the onions starting to sizzle, as the doorbell rings, Kim walking passed him, barely acknowledging him at all, the sound of the door opening and the sound of money being handed over as the door shuts,

"todd, your burgers here!" Kims voice shouts, the sound of a young boy running through the hallway, feet quickly disappearing back to the lounge, the sound of the tv sounding as the volume seems to go up. Kim walking with two foam packages, rumbling through the cutlery drawer, taking out a couple of forks and disappearing outside again, the sound of Anne coming through the doorway, "bout time, bloomin starving" "here you go, chilli and mayo" Kims voice says, "he still cooking>"
"yeah..leave him to it"

Matts face tightening slightly at the comment, his eyes turning back to his onions, giving them a stir til they brown off, then grabbing a tin of toamtoes, pulling the ring pull with a slight pop he dumps the lot into the pan, quickly stiring, then lowering the heat, walking back to where his vegetables lay. Grabbing the knife and picking out a small chilli pepper, cuting it into strips, then placing it into the chilli mix, stiring and then returning his left overs to the fridge, then finally, adding the fake mince to the pot.

A quick stir and then the lid goes on the pan, a low heat and left to simmer for a while, Matt smiles, as the smells start to form in the kitchen, the joy taking him far from the building, to somewhere far beyond.

****

"where'd you get it!?" a gruff voice says, in the dark of an alleyway, the slight form of a road in the distance at its end. Overhanging trees making large branches and large hedges providing some relief from the rain for the three men, Crusher and Ripper clad in there colours, the other man held by the scruff of his shirt, his thin body shaking as Crusher gives him a good shake, the body rattling in the air, "where'd you get it?" Crusher asks again, the young man, Paul, in a fit of tears, his voice squeaky and begging, his eyes red, though that could have been from what he just been caught smoking, the smouldering stub of what looked to be a ciggarette end on the alleyway floor, wet brown leaves surrounding it, along with Pauls tears.

"stop crying" Ripper says, his voice menacing and harsh, "tell us where you got it from", "I'm sorry, I don't usually smoke, I promise it was a one off" paul cries, his hands trying to gently wrap around Crushers wrists, hoping the motion would loosen the grip upon him, the plan failing as Crusher shakes him again, "im not interested in excuses" ripper says, "I want to know where you got it from"

"I grew it myself" he says, Crusher dropping him to the floor, "so if we go to your house we'll find a plant?" the large man asks plainly, "no…I ...." Paul tries to speak, his words failing him, "come on then, lets go see your mother have a cup of tea and straighten this out" Ripper says, "maybe she knows about your plants" he says, gesturing to Crusher, the large man pushing paul along the alleyway, "no..please…my mother doesn't know" paul tries to explain, his plea met with a shove as the men walk along the alleyway, "well she's about too" Crusher says plainly, "your near the old post office arent you Paul? Number fifteen is it?"

"please…we don't need to tell my mother..please" he begs, still pushed along by the large biker behind him, "just a cuppa and look at some plants" Ripper shrugs, "sure your mother wont mind" he adds, Paul shaking as they leave the alleyway, the lights in the nearby houses making him shiver more as he sees evidence his mum is currently in, the light at fiteen being on where it had not when he had left, "please im begging you" he cries, "please…I didn't grow it myself" he says quickly, the two bikers stopping and staring at him, Ripper smiling, "so you lied to us?" he asks, his voice sinister as he looks at Crusher, the two men sharing a knowing smile, "I wouldn't know how too" Paul says, defeated and cold, "had a spider plant once, thing lasted two days" he says, his voice trembling, "please don't tell my mum" he pleads, "just a one off is all"

"one offs like this happen elsewhere" Crusher says gruffly, leaning to speak directly in the mans ear, "but not here where VigilanteS patrol" he says, his voice echoing fearfully in Pauls head, "so where did you get it from?" Ripper asks, "and no more lies"

****

The chilli was done, in fact it had been for a while, the remnants of it remaining in Matts bowl as he ate the last of it on the sofa, his legs crossed as he watches some rubbish Todd was watching, something about sunny beaches and overpaid morons, he really wasn't paying attention, enjoying and focusing mainly on each mouthful of his creation, the spice and sizzle of his craft bringing him the joy he had long waited for since putting it on the hob. His son having finished whatever burger he bought, the remants of any leftovers now resing in the bin, along with the wine bottle and the two foam packages both kim and Anne had consumed, thy young lady having said goodbye to todd and more a grunt too Matt. Kim now in the bathroom, apparently having the worlds longest shower, or at least to matt that is what it seemed, for the boiler had been sounding for the last half hour, the growl of it acknowledging the running of hot water, a noise that often jarred him in its persistence most evenings.

With a clank the spoon sitis in the bowl, the last eveidence anything had once resided in it long gone, Todd yawning as his programme finishes, "night dad" he says, standing up and stretching, kissing his dad on the forehead, "night son" matt replies, returning the kiss, "chilli smelt good" Todd says with a smile, stepping out of the lounge, "not as good as a burger though right?" Matt asks playfully, "never as good " todd jokes, walking away, the sound of small feet running upsatirs followed by a loud shout, "night mum!"

And so matt got up, finding the remote and turning off the tv, placing it on the sofa and walking through to the kitchen, where at the sink, he began to run the hot water, placing the plug in the hole and squirting washing liquid into the pool, a brief "ahhhh" sounding from upstairs in a histerical female voice, Matt quickly realisng what he had done, shutting the hot water off quickly, "well I guess im done showering then!" an agitated voice calls, down, "sorry kim…" Matt tries to shout back up, a door firmly slamming shut before he can offer an apology. His eyes returning to the task at hand, the hot water tap turned on again. "going to feel that one shortly" he moans to himself, his hands feeling the bubbles rise, the saucepan and bowl being dunked under the water, a sponge undoing the mess on there surfaces.

With a dunk and a final rinse, the bowl and the saucepan are placed on the drying rack, the lid and the chopping board and knife next, the two of them cleaned with a quick scrub, matts eyes trying to focus on nothing but the task, his mind indulging in the warmth of the water, a distant song long since heard, playing in his mind as he places the cleaned things on the draining board. The sound of a door opening pulling matts attention away, as footsteps sound on the staircase.

"are you trying to kill me!" Kim says, walking through the kitchen door, an unlit cigarette in her mouth, "trying to give me a heart attack" she says, her wet hair hanging to just belwo her shoulders, a dark pink dressing gown covering her form, with matching slippers on her feet, her eyes full of disappointment. "I'm sorry" Matt says, watching as kim huffs and exit's the kitchen, going out the back door and pulling a lighter from her dressing gown pocket, a click sounding as she lights the thing, a small red smoulder coming from the tip.

"your always sorry" she says, "always the same thing…" she says with a disgruntled sigh, Matt walking outside and joining her, "I didn't think" he shrugs apologetically, "my mind was elsewhere"
"elsewhere" she laughs, "your never here to be elsewhere"

"I know…" he says, trying not too create an argument, "you know" Kim mocks, "that's all I hear too" she says, taking a long drag on her cigarette, her eyes barely looking at him, "you know what else you can apologise for?" she says, her voice getting angrier and angrier, Matt not answering quick enough as she sneers at him, "my best friend in front of everyone asking me for money because my husband couldn't afford to pay her" she says savagely, Matt looking away from her, he knew the look she was showing, all too well

"no answer?" she says, frantically drawing a breath on her cigarette, smoke coming furiously from her clenched teeth, "you had fifteen quid, only gave her ten" she says, her voice almost shouting, "no" Matt says defensively, "I said I had fifteen quid on me, I needed five pounds for.." he says, "for what?!" she shouts, her cool demeanour if ever she had one disintegrating in front of her husband, "what do you need five pounds for? For a pint? A well earned pint after doing nothing all week!" she yells at him, "you knew kim!" Matt shouts back defensively, instantly regretting it as her fists begin to clench, "you knew.." he says softer, his legs beginning to shake, "you knew I only had fifteen pounds on me"

"so its my fault!" she says, her voice a torrent, "you went out with fifteen pounds knowing Anne charges fifteen pounds" she yells, "so you knew your pint would leave you short and its my fault!?" she screams at him, "I doint think" Matt says, "I thought you would give her a fiver before you left" he says, his voice a bag of nerves,

"oh you are just something else" she says, her voice turning from torrent to sand, her look making him feel ashamed, "something else" she says, her eyes filled with disgust, "no wonder you drink alone" she says scornfully, "well we used to drink together" Matt says, his voice breaking and his eyes filling, "and now I hear your drinking down the sun?" his voice loosing any weight or meaning, a desperate squeek taking its place,

"don't you dare!, don't you dare" she says, throwing her smoke to the floor and holding a firm finger on Matts face, her other hand balled to a fist, "you drove me there, you drove me there, don't you dare" she says trying hard to calm herself, trying hard to fight a growing temptation fed by frustration and fury, "everywhere I go, everywhere I hear there laughter, there questions, everywhere Matt! Only to return after the years of defending to find again a slob that has made no effort!" she sneers, "whilst I work to bring a hundred pounds a week to this pitiful household you do nothing and bring more!" she spits on the floor, "you drove me away from whatever this is" she says, poking hard at Matt, "and I am looking forward to Monday!" she says, going to slap and punch him, holding herself in mid air, her hands making no contact, Matt falling to the floor, scared to be hit.

"Monday?" he cries, "Monday…?" he sobs, "our sons birthday" she says, stepping over him, her voice fillled with scorn, "finally I can have a real man in my house"

****

Chapter 2

There was an explosion, that much was clear. The remains of what could be reasonably guessed as the missing front porch of a lodge on the marina, and the charred body parts to go with it. Plus the smouldering fire still seen lightly burning away at the widely dispersed splinters, and the plants that once stood upright and tall now hanging broken and burning, all leaning and torn in the same direction as each other. Coupled with witness reports, that in fact, there had been a explosion. Detective inspector Bruce had a good lead, and a good feeling, that in fact, he was looking at the aftermath of an explosion. Although, as he looked at the remains of a burning harley Davidson, the bike easily identified by the metal badge being lodged in the woodwork of a neighbours house, a forensic man taking it and matching it to the twisted form of the bike, the detective was still unsure, as to what had caused such a thing.

The marina itself was not known for faulty gas works, in fact the place was a jewel, setting Isleham village far apart from many neighbouring villages, boasting such a large marina was impressive for a settlement so small, but above all else what set it apart was its beauty. With near forty narrow boats ranging from holiday boats to liveabords and a mash of cruisers and river craft the marina was large, not to metion the near hundred odd lodges upon its grounds. Each being the size of a small bungalow and many of them used for full time occupation, with a few summer homes for the wealthy and retired, and as such, it was unusual to hear of a gas explosion there. The odd flooding, maybe a small electric shock from time to time, but this was a first, and the detective knew, it was as serious as it could be. For this incident had not just woke the whole marina, it had claimed a life too.

The body of which the detective found interesting, the charred lettering of VigilanteS clearly on his back, the name Titan on his chest. His head, half burned and far removed from the body, the explosion seeming to have removed it, having knocked out a heron as it hit the riverbank the other side of the river. Which whilst the rspca saw to the bird, the forensics had seen to the head, and now, in the midst of a flaming wreck of what was once a porch, the detective looks around him.

A gathering had amassed, which was good. A chance for witnesses to come forth without having to track them down, all were eager to give there account of what they thought had happened, a rare few explaining that they just heard the bang, nothing more. Ladies screaming in there nightwear of a loud bang, men in ther boxers and rugby and footbaall shirts telling the officers they knew nothing and just wanted to see the scene in peace, the detective smiling as he hears a large lad say "finally god reigns in his saviours", a comment out of all them, that finally made the detective speak, turning to see the large man, dressed in black and white striped pyjamas, "why do you say that?" he asks the man, the large lad looking at him, "thought you all loved your local police force" the detective says, a dry smile on his face, the large lad not answering, taking his gaze away from Bruce.

The crowd give way, to sirens on mighty trucks, as at last the fire service leave the scene, having secured and made safe the area, leaving a fire investigator to help conclude the cause, they leave the marina, the crowd parting to let the three fire engines go, then quickly reurnting to stand at the makeshift barriers and police blue and white tape. the detective watching them all, looking for something he wasn't sure about.

It had seemed to the detective, at least on arrival, to be a closed case, though a notably messy one, it was not often half a wooden lodge went up in an explosion of fire and splinters, nor was it often for a body to be involved, in fact such a thing hadnt happened locally for a good five or so years, but for all its meaning and weight, the incident had appeared a closed case. for it looked to him, on first glance, a biker had tinkered on his bike late at night, and somehow it had exploded. and yet, as he watched the crowds clamour and excited chatter, as he saw what seemed to be some scared and some midly happy faces, something pulled him from his first conclusion.

"know that look" the fire inspector says, walking over to the detective, a man in his fifties and muscle on his top half of his body would put any body builder to shame, a grey beard and short hair, an aged looked to his eye, "Thomas Checker" he says, shaking the detectives hand, "cambridgeshire fire service, lead investiagator on this," he says in a friendly voice, Bruce feeling the strength in the handshake,"Checker?" he muses lightly, "I know" the fireman sighs, looking at the wreckage of the motorcycle,

"any theories?" Bruce asks, the fireman laughing, though not horribly, more of a surprised chuckle if anything, "yep" he says nodding, "see that?" he says, pointing at the ground of the driveway of the half a lodge, a large blackness of soot and ash forming distinctly in a certain area, a small crater no bigger than a mans foot, "the residue and debris goes towards the house from that crater" Thomas says, tracing with his finger the clumps of driveway towards the half a lodge, "the motorcycle is behind that crater, and witnesses said he would park close to the wall of the porch" Bruce adds, seeing where the fireman was going, Thomas giving him a gloomy look of understanding,

"we found debris of a gas tank, which would sit under the porch" the fireman says, "like pretty much every lodge, the marina isn't plugged into a mains gas supply" he says, "which accounts for the porch" he says, gesturing to the wreckage around him, "but if the primary explosion was here" bruce asks, pointing to the crater, some feet away from where the fireman was implying the gas bottle had exploded, "well that's where theory comes in", Thomas says, almost apollogetically, although his voice is filled with conviciton.

"the bike is behind your biker friend" he says, pointing at the remains of the charred bike, "an explosion erupts infront of him, the fire of which forces him backwards, the embers and fallout catching the bike, igniting the fuel tank, the tank combusting and the flames and pressure so close to the gas tank of the lodge, igniting it, your friends body having fallen back against the wall from the initial explosion, the gas bottle he is likely close too sending his head flying" he says, pointing at each variable as he speaks,

"you think three seprate explosions?" Bruce asks, "in quick susccession," Thomas explains, "barely a second apart from eachother", "is this theory or…?" the detective politely tries to ask, " look at the remains of the body" the fireman replies, "the legs near the crater" he says, pointing to the rather gruesome sight of legs near the crater, a bunch of forensics in masks taking pictures. The fireman explaining his theory, "if there was an explosion, small and localised and quite low to the ground, it would be strong enough to rip the legs from the body, the torso and rest of it falling backwards from the blast, we know this because of the size and scale of the blast by the crater left" he says, "the body falls back as the pressure and fire of the explosion engulf the motorcycle, the pressure and force ripping the tank open and the fuel igniting, the combustion and following explosion enough to rip through the small gate that stands half a height of the motorcycle that houses the lodges gas bottle" he says, pointing at the next doors driveway, the small gate below the lodgings main footings visible for all to see, "the gas bottle explodes as the body falls on the bike against the wall and the resulting pressure as I said, " he says, his hands open and his tone finalising, his voice still friendly,

"sends the head flying" Bruce sighs, "a good theory" he nods, looking around him, seeing the crowd start to disperse, white tents starting to be put up around the crime scene, a full cordon going on as the the remaining torso and body parts are lifted into a waiting ambulance, "so whats the source?" he asks, "the intitial explosion?"

"look in the crater" the fireman sighs, the detective stepping over to the small hole, looking down into it, the shallow depth and width showing to hold nothing his eyes could discern, "I see dirt" he shrugs, the fireman coming over to him and stooping down, "metal frgaments there and there" he says, his finger pointing, showing a well formed chunk of metal, and another beside it, a thick black soot at the craters bottom too, "and have a good sniff" the fireman says, inhaling loudly, the detective doing the same, "smells..." the detective pauses, "spoke to one of your sergeants" Thomas says, "says a man walking his dog thought he saw a bright flash, like flames, from the riverbank, exactly at the moment the lodge went boom"

"a flash from over there?" Bruce looks, his eyes taking in the far riverbank, "what flashes flames from fifty yards away to explode on impact?" he says, the question more a way for his mind to process the scene than an actual inquiry, "spent some time with explosives" Thomas says, "twenty years bomb disposal and royal auxillary fire service" he says gently, "I know an rpg site when I see one"

****

Sunday had come, and for most it was a relaxing time, for it was a very brittish thing, to do nothing too strenous on the seventh day. many chose to praise there lord and crowd the churches and sing there songs of praise and worship, some saw it a chance for long walks with hounds and children, the entusiastic parents willing them on to try and keep up. oh yes, sundays were a relaxing time, and in the village of isleham, there was much that could be done, for if we divided it into four, we would get a clearer picture.

the first part of the four pieces was the marina, which as discussed was truly the jewel, a large river flowing into it and encompassing in a large circle the land on which the moorings and lodges sat. a single way in and a single way out if travelling by vehicle, a single bridge crossing the river that led to a road. this road leading to the lower quarter of Isleham. allotments to the left as you pass and countelss walking paths for the parents to drag there children around. houses too to the right, some offering fresh eggs and veg, one even offering a fine haircut.

the second of the four pieces was mainly buildings, some new and some old, some run down and some looking just fine, a bowling club and a graveyard too, one of two graveyards in fact, the viallge had to offer, and a pub, one in three. this one was called the rising sun, and it was more modern than its rival the griffin, yet no less grand. depending on who you asked of course, for it was the clubhouse of the VigilanteS, a fact no one really knew, whether the landlord had agreed to or not.

the third of course was the griffin and the next graveyard, a long road leading out towards a city called Ely near ten miles away, following at is start is an old church, older than the griffin it was believed, and so on a sunday many would congregate to it, a relaxing time for all, most would agree. but of course it wasn't the only chcurch, in fact it had often been a boon of contention for it was felt there should never be more churches than pubs in a place, yet in isleham this was true, for there were three churches, a fourth being built.

the last piece would be where another road divides, where one route would take you towards other villages and towns, such as Mildenhall where only Mildenhall folk would describe it as decent, or Worlington or Newmarket. the other road leading to places such as Fordham, which in turn could lead to various routes. these roads in isleham were sided by houses of every scale, large, small, old, modern, all surrounded the roads, a large green park with football fields running alongside the route to Fordham. at the roads base where one could turn right, a road lead passed the local shop and the third pub could be found, the merry monk. though this was used for mainly eating and so the locals who mainly wanted to drink left it alone. its trade often booming with passers by, its reputation for a good meal its resounding feature.

Anyway, the point is, on a sunday, indeed any day, in Isleham, if one were so inclined, there was much that could be done. for it was a sunny day, and the foul winds had subsided later the previous evening, so had he decided, Matt could have gone for a walk around the miles of footpaths, ducking and twisitng around the allotments, greeting people who cheerfully work hard growing there veg and tending there chcikens.

meeting dog walkers and seeing new and friendly faces, in fact Matt
could have gone to the pubs, any in fact, and gotten a beer or just a half if
that was all he could afford and sit and chat and learn new names and
people. perhaps he could have gone to the marina, walked around and
adored the wildlife, maybe find a friendly rower and go on a voyage.

yet as people have there routines, in which they proudly stick too, so
too does Matt, and that was why he was fast asleep in his bed, his snores
loud as he dreams of happier places, his houehold below him brustling
with life.

in the lounge todd and a young boy named kieran play, the two boys
holding a deck of cards with mythical beasts on them, each taking a turn
to damage the other ones health, each taking time to look at the
opponenents cards on the field, chatting about a dolphin as they do, "and
then, Scrumpy brought on his friend whisky the weasel" Kieran says
playfully, laying down another card in face of him, this one showing a
horrid looking vampire creature, Todd biting his lip as he looks at his
own hand, "I attack for two damage" the young Kieran says, tapping on a
rat card and spinning it to its side, todd writing on a bit of paper his
current health, the numbers clearly showing Todd was due to loose,
"who's whisky?" he asks excitedly, "he's this clown, well he's a
weasel…but hes a clown" the young boy explains, his voice quick and
rushed as he watches Todd take his turn.

laying down what seems to be a dragon and tapping two elves, "I
attack for eight with these" he says, Kieran laughing "I got death touch"
he says, "so they die too" he says, picking up and removing his slain
cards, Todd whimpering slightly as he writes the current score "oh and
theres mixy" Kieran adds, "but hes just a chef…hes not my favourite,
scrumpy says hes the best chef ever but his programme is boring", he
says, drawing two cards from his deck, laying down another vampire and
tapping the previous one and rat card, "I attack your dragon for six" he
says, Todd smiling, "hes down to cight health then" he says, satisified his
best card had not been destroyed. Kieran playfully tapping his own cards,
"death touch" he says, Todd sighing as he removes his dragon, his
mother hearing his groan, "you winning son?" kim shouts playfully, from
the kitchen, a glass of wine in hand and two others as she picks them up,
a playfull "no" answering her as she steps out into the garden.

Anne and marge sat on deck chairs, smoking and nattering away as
Kim brings out the glasses, "well strippers up in arms!" Anne says,
"reckons an old VendettaS killed him", "oh please" Marge laughs, "they
moved up north years ago" she says, taking a glass from kim, sipping on
it with a deep gulp, her leopard skin coat sitting loosely over a thin black
top, "well that's what he reckons", Anne says, taking the other glass from
kim, the young lady sitting down with her own and joining the

conversation, "why was Titan there?" she asks, "I mean it was Strippers home", "Titan would always go round and feed the cats for him" Anne says, "Stripper reckons they got the wrong man, probably thought it was him"

"well I have to say" Marge smiles, "its all very exciting", her comment met with a scoff from Kim, "a man has been killed" she says, "yes" Marge says, "with a grenade launcher too" she chuckles, "in a village meant to be kept safe", "well the VigilanteS all been dragged in for questioning" Anne says, her voice filled with warning, "and they are angry as hell"

"so be carefull what I say?" Marge shrugs playfully, "come on, nothing ever happens around here anymore", "a fact I thought you appreciate" Kim adds, Marge smiling at ther, "well of course its nice to feel safe, but…"she trails off lightly, " I used to have such fun back in the day"

"well strippers been in all day, some detective was giving him a right thorough going over" Anne says, "he says they'll find the culprit" her voice still filled with warning. "wouldn't like to be him when they find him"

"so wheres stripper staying?" kim asks, her voice sounding very curious, "round crushers I think, his ol lady made a room up for him" Anne says, "oh jillian, " marge says fondly, "been meaning to visit her, has she got her kitchen fitted yet?"

"yeah, nice one too," Anne says, taking a sip of her wine,"whens yours being done then kim?" marge asks innocently, knowing too well it was a bone of contention, Kim sighing and looking through the door behind her, the wreck of a kitchen ever plaguing her sight, "whenever he gets round to it suppose…"

"well I think you need a medal" Marge says, Anne nodding her head in agreement, "living in such condition…with such a man.." "can we not?" kim says, "a mans been exploded and still we fall to talking of my nightmare life…" she pauses, "suppose monday wont see stripper then" she sighs slightly, "doubt he'll come to todds birthday with all this going on"

"he'll be here," anne says, the comment making the two ladies look at her quizically, "he says things need to carry on as normal, thinks something like this can unravell things" she says with a shrug, "and with the police involved they gotta be seen doing nothing out the ordinary", "there you go" marge says, poking Kim, "your dream man will come to your party" she chuckles,

"if only I were single" Kim smiles, "you are" Anne says, "if its just a bit of fun your after, your single" she says with a wink, "especially when your married to Matt", "im surprised you two never met before" Marge says, "he's been around five years", "we stayed away from them" Kim says dryly, "my husband didn't want to associate with them"

"well given his father I cant say I blame him" Anne admits, "but it been a long time kim" she says fondly, "time to branch away…" she pauses, "from all this" she says, her eyes taking in the house and garden, "although meeting him at at your kids birthday party in front of your husband…is well…bold" Marge says, taking another sip of wine,

"he asked what I was up to monday" kim shrugs, "I told him,…look I don't know if anything would happen, but I certainly wont be at my sons biirthday party" she says sternly, "I just…just want to spend time and see"

"well you'll have plenty of that" Anne says, "sure his attention will be elsewhere at the moment", "just be careful" Marge says, her voice actually sounding surprisingly sincere, "man like that will wreck a marriage, not hold one down for himself" she says almost lovingly, "but if its just a bit of fun your after…"she pauses, looking at the house, "who can blame you"

"not to mention someone tried to kill him" Anne adds, kim looking at her as she smiles, "but then does the danger make the longing stronger?" she laughs, "certainly doesn't hurt" kim admits, the three women laughing.

✳✳✳✳✳✳✳✳✳✳✳✳✳✳✳✳✳✳✳✳✳

and so, where sun fades and bustle comes to a still, the evening comes, and with it a silence across the village. the streets lit by lamplight, the roads quiet. Yet each household was not. Behind the doors everyone spoke excitedly, some scared, some confused, but all spoke of it, all spoke of the man killed at the marina. There wasn't a household not speaking of it, and as the silence of each street echoed as loudly as the concern for what had happened, the patrols started afresh, a new avengeance felt with the roar of the motorbikes,

Where once six bikes would happily cover the area, taking there time and the club members taking it in turns, tonight was different, tonight they had orders from the president. Tonight every bike was out on the roads, all fourteen of them.

Each taking a separate road and riding slowly up and down it, pausing for great lengths to stare into peoples homes, hoping to see something that could explain the events of last night, each member adamant to try maintain some order, and they were not alone. For the police had decided a patrol car would help ease the growing tensions, the vehicle sitting at a driveway or layby for an hour or so, and slowly move onto another spot, the officers keeping close watch, seeming to take great interest in the VigilanteS.

Stripper hadn't cared, he knew the police would be watching, for that was to be expected, and for the most part, he had felt they were on the same side. And so his order for a hightened patrol had been a balanced one, for if he tried to show strength at a time of grieving it could ignite the tensions, but so too to do nothing more than the normal would be to show they didn't take the matter seriously, perhaps emboldening there attacker to strike again. Stripper had thought about it hard, and he had decided on the patrols to be constant, with every member completing them.

His name had become mud, in only a night. Or at least that is how he had felt, that someone would so openly try and kill him or attack his club had made him feel the bitter taste of disrespect. Having sat at the police station facing the hundreds of questions thrown at him, he had felt his vision take a serious blow, and that was a hard pill to swallow, and so the bikers were out in force. The roar of the bikes thundering down small country lanes and main roads alike, Stripper himself slowly passing the griffin pub, his throttle easing as he slows to a few miles per hour, his eyes taking in only a few in the public house, his motor thundering as he accelerates away, determined to see something somewhere that would help him discover an answer.

"out in force tonight" Harvey says, turning his gaze from the griffin window, having watched Stripper ride passed the pub. His friend Pete working behind the bar, an elderly man, near sixty years old sat beside him with a pint, a man called Gus, "can you blame them?" Pete asks, Gus nodding his head and grunting his agreement,

"another one harv?" Gus says, pointing at Harveys empty glass, "very kind" Harvey smiles, Gus nodding to Pete, the young man picking up the glass and filling it with an ale, "least I can do, after my daughter…" he pauses, his voice slurred and his mind not really thinking before it speaks,

"its alright gus" Harvey smiles at him, though his tone was slightly awkward, for drinking with your ex's father had its perils, "call it even" he says, the filled pint coming to him, pete popping it on the bar, "you want one" gus asks, Pete taking the ten pounds from him from the bar, "thanks" Pete smiles, oeping the till and taking out the change, "think I could use one" he says, closing the till with a gentle slide and click, walking back and popping the coins on the bar in front of gus, his hand going for a lager glass, filling it from a tap,

"you know she's devastated" Gus says after a brief pause, his voicee sincere, "absolutely mortified at whats she's done" he says, looking at Harvey, "we were long going to break up before…" Harvey says, trying to be polite with his words, sudden emotion taking over him, "anyway, its fine" he smiles, his eyes trying not to catch Gus's. "Stippers fault" Gus says, his tone matter of fact, his slight drunken state not noticing the rising awkwardness of the conversation, "took adavatage whilst she was drunk"

"might be enough there Gus" Pete says friendly, taking a sip of his lager and resting the glass on the bar, his eyes trying to connect to Gus, "just saying" he replies, looking at Harvey "she isn't half sorry, cant stop crying about it"

"and im sorry too" Harvey says to him, "but its done" he says with finality, "so please…" he says gently, letting the comment hang in the air, "so who you think blew up Titan?" Pete asks, the question coming from nowhere but a good diversion none the less, "news is saying a suspected rpg as well" he says slightly overhelmed by the comment, "can you imagine?"

"well it wasn't me" Harvey smiles, his friend sharing the same innoccent look, "wouldn't know where to get one anyway" he jokes, "bloody Arabs" Gus grunts, the comment making the two look at him somewhat confused, both trying hard not to laugh, "Arabs?"

"they used them all the time, back in the days I was fighting them" he grunts, "Kuwait and Iraqis, thousands of rpgs between them", "whats a war in the middle east decades old got to do with a biker being blown up in Isleham?" Harvey asks slightly bewilderd by Gus mumblings, "just saying, that's where you get the rpgs, Arabs" he says, taking a large swig of his pint,

"you were there?" Pete asks intrigued, "Kuwait?", "Iraq" Gus says with a smile, "didn't know you were a veteran" Harvey says, surprise in his voice, "photographer" Gus says, "civilain" he adds, "wrong place wrong time, couldn't get out the country for a few months, got some good pictures of it all though" he says, taking another swig, "earned me a pretty penny when I got back" he adds, smiling at the fondness of the memory, "every paper wanted my pictures,"

"what?…." Pete pauses, almost nervous to ask, "what was it like? War?", the question making gus look up quiet seriously at him, "don't matter your hatred for Arabs ," he says, the racist comment actualy said with an odd fondness, "you wouldn't wish it on any breathing" he says sadly, "was a horrid thing, poor souls, on both sides of it"

"you mangaed to get out?" Harvey asks, actually intrigued by the conversation, "yep..brought back some pictures and some souveneers, bought a house and settled down" he shrugs, "customs were much more laxed back then" he says, looking to the bottom of his glass, "and I enjoyed collecting weird and wonderful things" he says softly, downing the last of his drink, "anyway" he says, "another if you will"

"right you are gus" Pete says, taking the coins from the bar and opening the till, taking the glass and refilling it, "question still remains though" Harvey says, watching his friend fill up the glass, "have you travelled to Iraq? And where were you last night", "I went down the sun after shift

mate" Pete says laughing, "about thirty or so witnesses" he shrugs
playfully, "besides must be other places you can buy an rpg other than
from the Arabs"

"life imprisonment just to own one" Harvey guesses, thinking on the
matter, "no parol and a short trial" Gus adds, seeming to know a bit about
it, pete returning with the old mans pint and placing it in front of him,
"same with any weapon I'd imagine" Pete muses, "instant hearing, instant
sentence", "why an rpg though?" Harvey asks, "I mean if you wanted to
try to kill someone,…just stab them or get a gun or
something…something other than an rpg"

"maybe they struggled getting hold of a gun" pete suggests, "right but
finding an rpg was a doddle" Harvey mocks, the two friends sharing a
laugh, "Strippers a large lad too" Pete adds, "I mean the killer got the
wrong man but still, there not the kind you try and stab" he says, his
voice sounding respectful as he says it

"so I guess the question is…" Pete suggests, "why?, why kill stripper?"
he asks, the question lingering, "blokes a twat" Gus says, the comment
making the two men smile at each other, though Harvey seems to smile
more than Pete, "marriage breaker and self imposed policeman" he adds
scornfully, "no disagreement here" Harvey says, taking a long gulp of his
beer, "is it only people who drink here that hate the club?" Pete asks
slightly defensively,

"must be why your always quiet" Harvey says, seeing his friends
reaction and knowing the speech about to come, one that often came
when talking of the VigilanteS, "people love them" Pete says, "you go to
the sun and see them all flock to try and drink with them", "yourself
included" Harvey says, Gus surprisingly grunting his support at the
comment. "myself included" Pete admits, "but they are a good bunch" he
says defensively, "and you are the minority whilst stripper holds the
majority"

"well rehearsed, this speech good friend" Harvey laughs gently, "four
years you have tried to get there attention, yet no rockers or patch" he
smiles, Pete sighing as he takes a sip of his pint, "maybe im not strong
enough" he confesses, "have to eat a thousand eggs a day to catch up with
them lot", "you havent got it in you" Gus says to pete, "thanks a lot" Pete
groans, Harvey still smiling, "your not like them Pete" Gus says kindly,
"you couldn't turn on your own"

"shaking kids and telling them to behave, putting down on there luck
souls in accident and emergency for making a mistake on there patch"
Gus says, "stay clear son" he says warmly, "people like that get
overthrown eventually", "by bazookas mainly"Harvey adds, his friend
smiling, "maybe…" he trails off, "I think the real reason" Harvey says
playfully, looking at Gus, "pete goes to that pub so often is a certain lady

he likes…" he says, laughing as Petes skin reddens a bit, "leave it alone" Pete says, almost laughing,

"oh really?" Gus asks intrigued, "and who might that be?", "a certain friend of our friends wife maybe?" Harvey aks, his tone playfull, "stalking for the last four years perhaps" he adds, his friend laughing, "she's nice" he shrugs, "but I don't know whether I would" he says happily, "think shes more into the bikers", "well if your talking about Anne I think the bikers have all been into her" Gus says, the comment making the three of them laugh,

"if you like someone tell them" Gus says, "don't waste time pretending your something your not" he says, standing up and downing the rest of his pint, "a bit of fatherly wisdom for ya both eh?" he smiles, tapping Harvey on the shoulder, "had hoped to add you to the family one day" he says sincerely, "but despite marys actions I hope we can still be cordial"

"of course mate" Harvey smiles, "have a good night" he says, watching Gus walk out the front door, "good night lads" he smiles, closing the door behind him, "see ya Gus" Pete shouts after him, "coming for a smoke?" Harvey asks, picking out a smoke from his pocket, "yeah" he says, finding one of his own, both pausing and watching as another bike goes slowly passed the window, the rider taking his time to stare through the glass, a roar and twist of the throttle and quickly it passes, the two men rolling there eyes, "anyway" Pete says, the two going towards the back door of the pub, "how'd your interview go?"

****

The morning had arrived, and for Matt Meadows, it had posed the usual hardship, for even though he didn't work, Monday mornings still held great effort for him. Firstly the bustle of getting his son ready for school, making sure the uniform was clean and on straight, making sure a packed lunch box went with him, making sure his wife got up and ready for her job, which she did independently anyway but still worth mentioning. The point is, the Monday mornings were always hectic, in fact they were the most hectic of all the days of the week.

Once kissing his son goodbye and watching him depart on the schoolbus he had to awkwardly watch his wife ignore him and get into her small silver Nissan micra car and dirve off to work, a job in which they barely spoke about, for it was not the most pleasant of subjects for either party.

Then came the greatest effort, for his wife would travel along the Fordham road to get to her job on the outskirts of soham, but never once in the last few years had she offered to give Matt a lift. For his first destination was a bus stop in Fordahm, Isleham having no bus service, a fact that had caused a lot of complaints over the years.

So the effort came from simply getting to where he needed to be, and much like his friend Harvey, this required cycling, an endeavour Matt had become quite good at, so much so it had become the third thing on his list of things he really enjoyed, so long as the conditions were correct of course. There needed to be no strong wind and no rain, for an enjoyable cycle he needed a nice sun and a gentle breeze. For Matt, the feeling of cycling set him free, the open road and the wind through his hair, and although only a three mile ride, it was enough to keep him happy.

And so Matt had again made the journey, cycling passed the fields he had done so many times before, tractors out and harvesters collecting potatoes, the same humour following him as happy hands waved at him "rather you than me", Matt happily replying with his years old comeback, "no! rather you than me".

The bus stop wasn't often busy, depending on which direction you wished to go, on one side of the road a bus would take you to the large city of Cambridge, this one was always packed, with students and young minds alike, and the other side, would take you to the smaller city of Ely, the bus stop not always having anyone standing at it, but every Monday at nine o'clock, it would have Matt.

Putting his pushbike in the local beer garden of a large pub called the crown and padlocking it to a bench, Matt always waited, for at least a few minutes before the bus would arrive. Costing just a pound and half the bus would take you to ely and return to Fordham, and matt once again sat on the seats, watching the world go by, his thoughts filled as his sense of freedom is dwarfed by his mind.

"A failing marriage? A failed marriage?" He thinks sadly, "and no job or purpose to save it" he says, to himself, looking through the windows of the bus. His thoughts plagued with answers and questions, riddles and thoughts of darkness, his eyes trying not to well up, as often they did on this journey. The time to pass was relatively short, less than an hour counting for the plenty of stops and pick ups the bus would make, and so as before on countless occasion. Matt arrived at Ely.

Dozens of shops and pubs, an array of bus stops and an impressive catherdral,Ely was large, not as large as Cambridge in any sense, more a large town than anything, city status owing to the mammoth of ely cathedral. A large and time aged buidling, with sweeping scenes set into its stone and an array of beauty covering every inch of it. Matt had visited it many times, as a family with kim and todd, he remembers, looking at rising spire as he steps off the bus, the memory bringing a pain to him as he looks away, determined to get to his purpose.

Having disembarked near a large pub called the hereward he walks along the pavement, passing kebab shops and a bric and brac store called thing me bobs, the place busrting with trade, the whole street filled with eager shoppers, all making there way to the main centre, Matt looking left and right, and crossing the main road to the shops the other side, coming to a pet and garden shop he loved very much. Stepping in for a quick visit, a young lady at the till smiling at him "havent sold her yet" she says happily, Matt nodding his greeting, walking passed an isle of dog treats to a set of cages near the end.

Finches and canaries, chirping away, little zig zag patterns on the feathers and liitle orange feet and little red beaks as the zebra finches dart from one perch to the next, making little shrill but very loud "beeps" and "meeps", the canaries singing a beautiful song as they dance around with the finches, Matt smiling as he watches there little hops and bursts of speed as they jump from one end of there cages to the next. There neighbours, a selection of hamsters and gerbils, tucked away in there bedding and little grey tails poking out of little holes of burrows and wooden homes, matt looking at them briefly, his eyes quickly resting on his favourite, a large canary, all alone in its cage, removed from the others for being picked on, feathers missing from multiple fights, an eye absent too,

"hello destiny" he says fondly, the name of the bird written in big black ink on a white tag attached to the cage, a price tag of four pounds and a polite note asking for a good home only, "how are you?" he smiles, watching the bird chirp and dance from perch to perch, her flight slightly awkward and chaotic,"still free for you matt" the young lady calls from the till, "just got to get a bird cage" she says fondly, Matt looking at the bird, "maybe one day girl" he says to the canary, "maybe one day" he says,, addressing the lady at the till, "maybe" the girl smiles, Matt walking out of the store, "see you next week" the girl says fondly as he leaves, "see you" matt replies kindly,

Walking left from the pet shop door matt walks along the street, passing a dozen or so people, all eagerly walking to get there shopping done, large bags in there hands, Matt coming to a driveway, where at it's base, sit's a jobcentre. A building with bright green wording so none could miss it if they were to look, and for maybe the two hundred and fiftieth time, matt walked towards it. The large automatic doors opening as he enters, the place packed with people.

To quote a rather nice liquorice based brand, allsorts were here. Young and elderly, seeking advice from advisors and frantic fingers poking at screens with the latest listings of jobs, young girls with young children in there arms, young men with sons running amok, whilst others simply sat, as matt did, on a line of comfy chairs, awaiting there call into an advisors office.

Looking around him, Matt saw familiar faces, a young lady with her son looking through the screen before her, her glasses reflecting the words of prospective employers. Looking at the door of the office now opened, a middle aged man walking out and leaving the building, an older man holding the door open, his eyes seeing Matt, where he had always sat at the exact same time each week, "mr Meadows" he says, his voice niether fond nor coarse. Matt standing up, and walking into the small office, taking a seat at the mans desk, the man closing the door and sitting before his computer, his name badge naming him Dean.

"thank you for coming" Dean says, clicking the computer on, "always" Matt replies, his voice slightly sullen, "so…" Dean says, reading through an email on his computer, "fired from retail…again" he says, reading from the email, "failed to turn up for a couple of shifts without notice so was let go"

"I just couldn't…" Matt tries to explain, "yes" dean says, clicking the computer and closing the screen, turning his full attention on Matt, "a recurring theme" he says, his voice not accusing but none the less feeling very much like acusation, "it comes and goes" Matt says, "much like your work ethic" Dean says, his voice slightly stern, Matt not responding

"five years and nearly twenty different jobs Matt" dean says, relaxing his tone slightly, "when does it end?" he asks honestly, his eyes filled with kindness and some degree of sympathy to his voice, "you come here every Monday without fail" he says, carrying on without letting matt speak, "same time and same routine, why cant you apply it to a work life?" he asks, Matt not answering, "look im not going to berate you, I tried that before and still we're in the same situation" he says with a slight sigh, "what do you need matt? What do you need to get back on your feet and working?"

"we've had this chat a hundred times" Matt says, "always the same answer", "maybe its time then" Dean suggests, "to talk to someone, a proffessional", the words falling like coal at a feather party, "we've been through this" Matt groans, "yes and still you are sat in front of me" Dean says sternly, "because your mental health is keeping you on benefits"

"I don't want to talk to anyone" Matt says stubbornly, "I don't need to". "they can help matt, "dean says kindly, "you've got some stuff going on you need to address, find out the matter help find ways of dealing with it", "I know the matter" Matt says, his voice actually sounding angry, "don't need no shrink telling me that"

"well" Dean says, hands open as he turns back to his computer, switching the screen back on "I will put it in my recommendations none the less" he says, typing away on his keyboard, "for the fiftieth time" he adds, the slight attempt at humour not causing a smile, "so…what job do you want to try next, got a garge near you still looking, apparently the last applicant was deemed not suited"

"cant I?" matt pauses, taking a breath, "cant I just not try another, just for a while…" he asks, his voice slightly pleading, "got things at home I need sorting, a few weeks and…" he trails off, Dean sighing, "I suppose this marina business is hitting your village hard?" Dean asks, Matt just shrugging, "its not that, just my marriage is going through the blender" he says, "I can put a stay for a week" Dean says, typing on his keyboard and looking away from the screen, "but if you want your benefits to keep being paid your going to have to at least start looking for work again come next Monday" he says, "I'll put in your case you get a weeks exemption from looking for work, on mental health grounds" he says, the last words emphasised.

"thank you" Matt says softly, his mind racing with thoughts of shame, "however" Dean says, "you will meet one requirement, call it a favour" he says, leaning forward, his demeanour friendly and caring, "you talk to someone, even if its just your G.P or a nurse" he says, Matt looking at him and thinking of an argument, "then at least the file will show you tried to adress the reasons for your work absences" Dean adds, Matt not answering, feeling a slight veiled threat underlying the statement, for many a poor mans benefits had been taken or penalised for far less than what Dean was asking. "fine" he sighs, "one time though" he submits, his heart feeling heavy,

"I will book it now" Dean says, "nearest gp surgery soham?" he asks, matt nodding reluctantly, "there you go, Wednesday eight thirty, I'll put a chat with a nurse as requested by your case officer" he says, tapping away at the keys of his computer, "anything else we need to discuss?" Matt asks, "if you would like to" Dean says with a warm smile, "then I'll be off" Matt says standing up, "need to get to the bank and buy some things for a barbeque" he says, "kids birthday today, hoping to catch the box office too…"

"well have a good one" Dean says, standing up and shaking Matts hand, "go to this appointment and just talk", "I will" matt replies, shaking the mans hand, "see you next week" he says, Dean opening the door for him and Matt walking out, his eyes cast to the floor as he walks out the main door of the building, "see you next week" dean says, watching the man leave, his eyes taking in the seating area, a man in dark green and a hat on his head, a big brown beard and aged look about him, "Fidel" Dean says, gesturing for the man to enter. The door closing behind him as he does.

****

With a thudd the door closed, the meeting room filled with uniformed police sat at there tables, a large white board with pictures of the parts of the biker blown to hell upon its surface, various scribblings and large words and red circles upon it. The room filled with eleven officers, there black and white uniforms worn proudly and there conversations coming to a pause as Detective inspector Bruce walks in, the fire inspector Thomas following behind, both in plain clothing, with the muscled fireman going for a grey polo shirt and dark blue jeans, the inspector wearing his usual black top and black trousers. The two men walking to the front of the room, the police officers watching intently as Bruce holds out a newspaper for them all to see,

"Bazooka boy" he says, his voice slightly mocking, "is the name the local press in all there wisdom have deemed to give our assasin" he says, the policemen and policewomen laughing at the name, "says the man, odd thought they called him a boy" he grunts, reading the paper aloud, "shot a rocket launcher or what is believed to be a rocket propelled grenade at the home of the leader of a bike club, killing one man and wounding a heron" he sighs, throwing the paper onto the table before him,

"so it is fair to say the world awaits us to wrap this case up" he says, "and as no rpg or device for firing a grenade has been recovered from the scene, the rivers apparently holding everything else other than what we are looking for, it is safe to assume the killer still has the weaponry, and is as such a very great threat" Bruce says, the officers nodding, "so due to the nature of the arsenal involved I have brought fire inspector Thomas Checker aboard as a consultant on this case", "hello Thomas" the officers say in friendly unison, Thomas saying hello back with a friendly smile

"now add to this the mix of the intended target, and I think you will agree this is a delicate situation we are in," Bruce says, the officers agreeing. "so" Bruce says, "did anyone get anything from the VigialnteS?" he asks, his voice not sounding hopeful, a young blonde lady with an offciers cap on sighing, "all thirteen" she says, "where were you satarday night around eleven and twelve, no comment" she says, the officers nodding there agreement, "didn't matter the question sir" she continues, "all was met with 'no comment'"

"can you think of anyone wanting to harm the club?" one officer says, a young man at the back of the room, "no comment" he says, imitating his interviewe, "can you think of anyone with access to that kind of weaponry?" the lady continues, "no comment" the entire police room says in unison, the officers rolling there eyes and sharing knowing looks,

"so nothing from the club then?" Thomas asks, not the least bit surprised, "was one thing sir?" a young lady ventures, all eyes turning to her, "got an email from the club asking for the waistcoat of Titan to be returned to them, says it's club property", the comment met with a loud sigh,

"well Heath or 'Stripper' as hes known, was about the same use too, six hours of no comment and not enough coffee for me to keep hearing it"

Bruce says, his voice slightly jarred. "so think its safe to say the VigilanteS wont be helping us in this matter"

"but it definitely involves them" Thomas says, "no matter there co-operation", "indeed" Bruce says , "we have a patrol car keeping an eye on Isleham, if they do something we'll know about it" he says plainly, "so what of the village? Any luck with the locals?"

"to scared or proud to speak out about the club sir" the blonde policewoman says, "some said they saw someone in black leather walking along the road to the marina as they drove passed, a large suitcase in hand, a black motorcycle helmet on there head" "well that's a good lead" Bruce says, "were they seen walking back from the marina?", "one said they saw the same figure running at about midnight, a lady having a smoke outside her house said they were holding a suitcase, disappeared out of sight, thought to have gone right at the roads end"

"height?" bruce asks, scribbling the description on the white board, "varies sir" the lady says, "six foot or five and a half" she shrugs, "we asked around if anyone else had seen him but no luck..." she pauses, as the detective writes between five and a half and six foot on the board, "any traffic coming through any of the roads at midnight?" Thomas asks,

"just us responding sir, didn't see any vehicles or anyone in black on the way", a young officer replies, "I came from the Fordham road" Thomas says, "didn't pass anyone either", "phoned the coroners and forensics sir, they came from the mildenhall road, said they didn't recall seeing anything en route" the blonde policewoman adds

"so for assumptions sake" Bruce says, "lets fancy our suspect found lodgings or returned to a dwelling in Isleham," he ventures, "assuming of course they didn't mange to slip out, and that our person in black is the one we are looking for"

"so question everyone, ask about black leather jackets and black helmets, who outside the club uses them, has a motorbike or used to" he says, the officers taking notes, "talk to the lady again, get her to show you the route she described when she saw the suspect running, talk to the marina too, speak with the lodge and boat owners, see if they saw anything, find out if any of them have a black leather jacket and black helmet...you know what to do...you know what to ask" he says, writing on the board 'chief suspect' and circling it around the description of the person in black.

"so now we have a suspect, we have a victim" he says, "but was he the intended one or not?" he asks aloud, "was 'Titan' the target, he was known to go to 'Strippers' house to feed his cats, or was it wrong place wrong time for our biker friend here", he says pointing at the picture of the severed head, "so what do we know about Titan?" he asks,

"club member for two years sir" the young officer says, "moved from

Wales to Ely four years ago then moved to Isleham three years ago, no wife no children, parents in Scarborough, no siblings" "well liked?" Bruce asks the room, "yes sir" the officer says plainly, "locals loved him, siad he was fair and helped keep the streets safe, didn't sleep around much and was very approachable" the officer says, reading from his notebook the description he had taken over the last few hours, "but then?" he sighs, the officers looking at him with a knowing smile, "he was a VigilanteS member...so"

"could be an attack against the club itself" Thomas ventures, "were they well liked?" he asks, the officers all nodding, "oh yes" Bruce replies, "and with it the hatred for us ever blossom" he says slightly mockingly, "but not without enemies" Bruce admits, "they had good reason to have a few of them"

"most outlaw clubs do" Thomas says, "a good lead to follow perhaps", "sorry sir" the young officer says, Thomas looking at him with a smile, "there not an outlaw club sir, not one percenters or affiliated with anything like that" the remark making Thomas look rather surprised " VigilanteS Thomas" bruce explains, a dry smile on his face, "the only crimes they committ they would have you believe are to stop more serious ones",

"and as such" bruce continues, "has made them an enemy or two, the chief suspect of whom is this group" he says, pointing at a bunch of photos on the white board in the far corner, the name VendettaS above them, "a club previously with a clubhouse in Isleham" he sighs, "nasty bunch they were, never got to murder but there list was a dark story" he says, Thomas taking in the pictures of large and scrawny men alike, twenty two at a count, "I heard of these" he admits, "moved up north I heard"

"it's a close kept secret within their ranks" bruce says, pointing at the VigialanteS board, photos of all fourteen menbers on it, "but a body went missing and half a dozen were put in intensive care, a month or so of brawls, the VendettaS the losers...the VigilanteS the winners" he says, "a final massacre would send them on there way"

"Pattersons pass" the young blonde officer says, "near the old shop now a house, on the corner of the new one" she says, Thomas looking at her, "ah yes," he sighs, "heard of that," "you and the whole world my friend" Bruce sighs, "a VendettaS member killed and two VigilanteS injured, one of us too, died of his wounds four days after, stabbed when trying to break up the brawl"

"the club used it as a way to wipe everything clear" an officer says from the middle row, "two of there members went to prison for there part in the killings and they drove out there rivals," "Stripper stepped up and declared the lawlessness would end" Bruce says, "the dealers the

VendettaS had used, the rival gangs the muggers and the thiefs all at war
with each other, wiped away" he says, doing a wiping motion with his
hands, "all were brought to tow, through fear and a lot of people going to
Accident and emergency, the villagers seeing the VigilanteS as saviours"
he shrugs,

"by all the villagers?" Thomas asks, "well that's the question isn't it?"
Bruce admits, "and with the answer perhaps our motive, so supsects…"
he says pointing at the board of the twenty two photos, "a rival club
driven out, a disgruntled viallger perhaps?" he says, looking at the police
force before him, "get out there," he says, "get some answers"

****

Stripper had taken to driving for today, it was not often such a sight
would be seen of a president of a motorcycle club, yet sometimes it was
necessary. And today it was, for he knew that the roar of a Harley
Davidson could come across as intimidating, the looks of passers by
usually confirming they were wary of the sound. A large built man in full
motorcycle club colours upon a loud and noisy stead, well, he had to
agree it could come across as slightly aggressive.

It had its uses though, a good purpose at that, for it would also shake the
nerve of anyone trying to do something they shouldn't on his patch of
turf, and moreover help keep the fear of him and his club on hearing the
bikes loud thunder. It was useful, but not for todays occasion, today
required something a bit more subtle, and though a tiumph spitfire might
not come across as a practical car for the modern working man, it
certainly had a purpose all its own.

Firstly the rarety and look of the vehicle would be a good conversation
starter, often prompting strangers to approach and talk about engines and
motors and there love of old brittish cars and bikes alike. A handy thing
to gain peoples trust, and to help the image of being approachable.

Secondly it could sit another person alongside him, without the jarring
effect of having a pillion as sometimes he did on his bike, not that it was
a problem doing so, but because just like a loud engine intimidating
people, seeing two club members on said beast could only add to the
tension. And so, in need of a subtle approach, Stripper had driven. The
Fordham gargae before him as he pulls up, Crusher in the car beside him,

"wait here" he says, turning off the engine and climbing out the car,
"aye pres" the man replies, watching as his brother walks towards the
main garage door, his eyes catching the sight of the large wrapped present
tucked behind the seats, the bulk almost blocking out the view of the rear
window, a glimpse of a police car pulling in to the side of the road, a
hundred yards away. "my taxes at work" Crusher groans, looking away
from the car and back to the main door of the garage, as stripper enters.

The sound of drills and machines whirring filled the small room, the workshop beside it filled with all manner of cars and mechanics, removing wheels and replacing tyres, one mans legs hanging above him as he leans far over into the engine compartment of a van. The reception desk empty, as Stripper hit's the bell, the ring making a young man walk out from the workshop, barely out of his teens he looks at Stripper, a slight nervous shake to his step as he approaches, "yes Sir?" he asks shakily, "Bruce about?" Stripper asks, the man nodding, "I'll go get him" he says walking back through the workshop, "thanks" Stripper smiles, a few moments later thinking he could hear the words "sounds like trouble" followed by the form of Bruce the garage owner walking through the door,

"help you sir?" he says politely, "fine garage you got here mate" Stripper says genuinely, "thank you" says Bruce, "understand my brother gave you some grief" the biker says, coming straight to the point, "your Brother?" Bruce asks, Stripper looking the man in the eyes, "yeah Ratchet told me what happened" he explains, "no bother there sir" Bruce says sternly, "put him straight about the matter", he says, not breaking eye contact, "well…" Stripper says, letting the word hang there, "just wanted to apologise" he says,

"accepted" Bruce says, "not what we're about" stripper continues, "new members take a while to learn that" he smiles, "like I said" Bruce says, "the situation was sorted", "well I had hoped we could start a discussion…" stripper smiles, "unless you got a motor in need of service or repairs" the owner says plainly, "could benefit us both" stripper says firmly, "what would benefit me is getting through my backlog of oil changes and brake servicing" bruce says without any anger or bluntness, his face giving the expression the conversation was over, "well…" stripper pauses, "another time perhaps" he says, trying not let his frustration show, "wont take anymore of your time then," "thanks for dropping by" Bruce says, "and tell your brother to get that bike looked at, have an accident on that thing if he isn't careful"

"oh I will" Stripper says, waving a hand in goodbye, walking out the door of the garage, Bruce watching as he goes, "you think that's the matter settled" a nervous voice asks, the young man leaning on the door of the workshop, "well a president just said it was" Bruce scoffs, "so I doubt it" he sighs, "why they started coming here?" the voice asks, "there garage closed on them" Bruce groans, "apparently no outsiders wanted to use it," he says shaking his head, "a violent history will do that to a business in its area", he says, looking at the young man, "right, time to learn why fuel injection is better than carburettors" he says, changing the subject, the young man walking back through the workshop door, Bruce following him, "count yourself lucky you're the only one who got the job, still an opening for another if you know anyone" he says playfully, "might need all the staff I can get"

And so outside, Stripper walks back to his car, the light beginning to fade as the evening draws in. looking at the police car with a sigh he enters the triumph, putting the keys into the igniton and starting it up, "sorted?" Crusher asks, "should be" he responds, "gonna need him compliant if we gonna start using him", "can always help him understand the way of things, ol priory didn't complain to the odd bribe" Crusher grunts, "too much heat at the moment" Stripper says, looking in his mirrors, seeing the police car sitting patiently, "mind you Ratchet screwed this one up" he sighs, "give him chance to resolve it", Crusher smiling slightly, "police wont know, make sure he shakes him good enough so he sees our way of thinking"

"business as usual I suppose" Stripper smiles, "not much of a biker outfit if we cant keep them on the road", "I'll arrange it" Crusher says, "any news from up north?" the president asks, his brother shaking his head, "VendettaS disbanded month or so ago, problems with Angels or something" Crusher says, "doesn't mean one of them isn't after some revenge though", he adds, Stripper pushing in the clutch and selecting gear, pulling out onto the road, "keep asking round" he says, turning the car in the road, accelerating and changing through the gears, passing the police car that just so happens to pull out seconds after passing,

"what about this weed problem?" Stripper asks, "thought we had more pressing concerns pres" Crusher shrugs, "but if you want business as usual I'll sort it, I know the lad selling it, he wont do it again after a visit from mc" he smiles, "I want him scared not beaten" Stripper says, "bodies in hospitals arent going to help relieve any pressure" he says, watching the police car follow him from behind, "leave it with me" Crusher promises, "I'll sort it"

"just hope we can get all this sorted by next week" stripper sighs, "our party needs to go off without a hitch, remind people we still mean and keeping the streets clean", "it will, got the caterers sorted, barbeques, cakes for the pudding" Crusher shrugs, "plenty of booze being bought in at the sun", "gonna be our fifth anniversary" Stripper says firmly, "a landmark that needs to be celebrated, not just by us" he says, slight warning to his voice, "they love us" Crusher says happily, "the party will be a hit" he says, looking behind him, "talking of which, don't you think this is a bit much", he says pointing to the large wrapped present behind him,

"what anne says the boy really wanted" Stripper says, "bit expensive though for a boy you don't even know, do this too often whole village be inviting you round to there kids parties" Crusher says, "was just going to get him a train or a book or something" Stripper says, pulling left onto the crossroads just outside the Crown pub, the car roaring with accelaration, "so why this?" Crusher asks, slightly amused at it all,

"pretty sure someone just tried to kill me," Stripper says, "and news I'm a kind man doesn't hurt," he says, watching the police car turn the same corner, "plus the mother is smoking" he says, Crusher laughing, "an expensive way to get your shaft oiled", "think of it Crusher, the village thinks someone can kill one of ours and fear we act like monsters, there respect turning to fear and too soon its not enough to keep the past at bay" he explains calmly, "giving a ten year old his heart desire isn't going to stop an assasin, but it will keep those who like us on our side when we catch him, and hopefully a five year celebration will one day be a twenty"

"you think to deeply sometimes" Crusher laughs, "anyway wrecking another marriage isn't going to win you any favours" he adds, "when it comes to Matt Meadows I doubt anyone would care" Stripper scoffs slightly, "besides, I've had pretty much every woman now, Kim is the mssing piece of my collection"

"all this sleeping about mate" Crusher laughs, "gonna get you in trouble, disgruntled husband, spurned lover..." he ventures playfully, "I'm the pres mate" Stripper says with a playfull tone, "not much they can do about it", "unless one of them has a bazooka" Crusher laughs, "poor Titan" he sighs, realisng his humour had struck a bit deep, "deserved better", "funerals Wednesday, bodies released tomorrow, we'll give him a good send off" Stripper says, his foot hitting the pedal hard as he passes out of Fordham, a long and clear road ahead of him, the car thundering to life with a spit and a thump as the engine roars, accelerating quickly to sixty miles per hour, the police car behind trying to keep up, "not breaking no speed limits" Stripper laughs, seeing the distant frustration in the officers faces as there car fails to accelrate at the same rate,

"you gonna bone her at the kids party then?" Crusher asks, "not with the hsuband there" Stripper laughs, "I'll set the groundwork then have her ready for our celebration" he smiles, his brother beside him chuckling. The car storming acorss the road, with amighty cackle of the engine the tyres taking the slight rise of a bridge just above an old railway line, the car steaming down the other side, a short moment later the car pulling into Isleham, passing the park on the left and turning left at the junction, "don't do nothing tonight" Stripper says, "make the garage look like a break in tomorrow night" he says, the car passing the old pattersons building, both men looking at it with mixed expressions, the car continuing to pass the local shop, coming to a halt with a sudden push of the brakes. Pulling outside the large church and graveyard, just opposite the Griffin pub, "same with the weed dealer" Stripper says, climbing out the car, "I'll be back at yours about nine I reckon" he says climbing out the car, Crusher sliding over to the drivers side as Stripper pulls out the large present from behind the seats. "pint after?" Crusher asks, as Stripper closes the car door, "yeah pint" Stripper agrees, walking away as Crusher drives off, the police car catching up, pausing as it sees the president walking with a large present in his hands.

"off to a kids party" he yells, a large smile on his face, "just down there if you want to join" he says mockingly, the officers deciding to turn in the road and pull up opposite the graveyard, Stripper walking down the street, named pound lane of all things, which made Stripper chuckle, for he had heard Matt Meadows was as borke as it came, the bikers feet carrying him passed the first house, his eyes coming to look at the dilapidated red building before him, "christ.." he sighs, walking up to the door and ringing the bell, which oddly didn't seem to work, resolved with a few heavy knocks to the door.

****

The knock came as a surprise, for Marge was about ready to leave, her son trying to find a lost shoe and the present for Todd wrapped in her hallway, ready to be picked up at there departure. They were determined not to run late, and the time was telling them in ten minutes they probably would be. The house itself wasn't much, but beautiful none the less, bright cream sofas in the lounge with leopard skin throws and a wonderous ktichen, filled with all sorts of herbs and spices in special jars, a fine gas oven and light wodden table at tis centre, a small staircase, with a small door underneath leading to a basement, leading upstairs to two seprate rooms and a well fitted bathroom, complete with a jacqousi bathtub. Marge lived well and comfortable, and part of that was her charm.

She always said life was about meeting people and letting yourself go once in a while, and she loved a good party, especially hosting one herself, that is what she loved the most, though it tended to be very rare and a much smaller, intimate affair. And so in her charming way she had dressed for the evening, her choice of clothing a gorgeous cream set of trousers and a tiger stripe top, with of course, her leopard skin coat thrown over it, and so having put on her boots and awaiting her son to discover his lost shoe, she had been surprised to hear the door being knocked on, so walking passed the present for Todd, she opens her door. Two men, one holding up a badge that marked him as constabulary, the other looking somewhat like a fireman,

"sorry to disturb madam?" detective inspector bruce says kindly, "just trying to get some statements from thos we missed yesterday" he smiles, Marge looking the fireman up and down, her eyes happily undressing him, "quite alright" she says, "off out?" Bruce asks, seeing Thomas roll his eyes slightly at the womans gaze upon him, "friends kids party" she replies, "this about the other night?" she asks, her voice sensual as he asks it, "want to search me for an rpg" she asks, "want to know if I'm bazooka boy?"

"think that'll be okay" Thomas says hopefully, his eyes pleading to Bruce, "don't need your whereabouts madam," Bruce coughs, "just trying to get any background we can on anyone you might feel would want to harm the club member known as Titan, or Stripper even?" he asks, sensing his colleague beside him would want the questiononing ended as quickly as possible,

"well no one here in my household" Marge replies, "lovely fellas, proper men" she says, her comment hanging in the air for a moment, "did you see anyone in black leather and a black helmet carrying a suitcase saturday night? Between eleven and twelve?" Bruce asks, "oh yes…" Marge says, the two men looking at her hopefully, the large lady turning to shout indoors, "have you checked the bog!?" she shouts, her son calling back a second later, "found it",

"please madam?" Bruce asks, "any insights, any feelings you can offer", "no…none" she says almost disappointedly, "but strippers going to be at the party im going to, I could ask him if you want" she says with a slight, cheeky smile, "if you could" Thomas says, almost mockingly, "that everything?" marge asks, "or do you want to come in" she asks slowly, the two men suddenly slightly fearful, "nope," Bruce says, "been most…helpful" he says, gesturing to Thomas it was time to leave, Kieran running up to join his mother, present in hand,

"hey little one" Thomas says kindly, "I lost my shoe" Kieran says playfully, "did you" Thomas smiles, "where did you loose it?" he asks, marge smiling at the encounter, "well it thought it might have slipped under mums personal door to the basement" Kieran says excitedly, "but mum wont let me down there, im not allowed down there" "that's mums little hobby hut isn't it" Marge says playfully yet sternly, "do all my artwork down there" she says to the detective, "so where was it?" Thomas asks, "in the bog" Kierean says, mimicking his mother, Thomas laughing at the joke, "well…have a good party" the two men smile, stepping away from the front door, "thank you, good luck with your searching" Marge smiles , pulling the door closed behind her and Kieran, walking out onto the pavement, the mother taking the childs hand,

"just one thing" Thomas says, pausing before his colleagiue knocks on the neighbours door, the fireman noticing something unusal on the side of Marges house, "three extractor fans" he says pointing, "one for the oven two for the hobby" Marge says honestly, "paint fumes bring my skin a rash " she winks, "need a good cream rubbed on me for days without them fans" she says, her eyes looking the fireman up and down, "well…make sure there wired properly" he says looking away, going slightly quieter, "number one cause of house fires…fualty wiring" he sighs, feeling the womans eyes leave his attention, "don't worry, had proffessionals see to it" she winks, "come on Kieran" she says, her son happily walking beside her, a birthday party to get too, as the two men knock on the neighbours house

****

"hey hey!" Harvey smiles, the door opening as matt pulls it, his friend standing on the front garden path, the moss and grime crunching under his feet, "hows the party?" Harvey asks, seeing no sign of happiness on his friends face, "better now you're here" Matt replies, stepping aside to let Harvey in, the young man entering and lowering his voice as the door closes, "whats up" Harvey asks, handing a small wrapped present to Matt, "I'll show you", he replies, gesturing for him to follow, leading him to the lounge.

Empty but decked out, a small table with cakes upon it and banners saying happy birthday, lots of colours and crisps and sweets in bowls, the presents piled on the table, as matt puts Harveys with the others, his friend looking at the rather large one taking up most of the table, "who brought that?" he asks, Matt just shaking his head, "our saviour" he says, his voice sounding bitter

"stripper?" Harvey asks, his eyes looking at the bulk, "what do you reckon it is?", "don't know" matt replies, "but its going to be better than what I got him" he says, "weighs a tonne too", he adds, "didn't think he knew Todd that well" Harvey muses, his voice as bitter as Matts, "he doesn't" Matt says, "doesn't stop him eating my food though" he says, lowering his voice, "Todds playing cards upstairs, Stripper and marge and kim are out there" he says, gesturing towards the garden, "can I go play with the children?" Harvey jokes sourly, "trust me it would be better than this" Matt sighs, walking out of the lounge, his friend following him through to the kitchen, a small ensemble of drinks on the kitchen counters, small lager bottles and bottles of fizzy pop,

"think I'll need one of these" Harvey says, twisting the cap off a small green lager, "whens the food?" he asks, taking a quick gulp, "ask Stripper" matt says, pointing to the back door, Harvey looking quizzical as he steps out, the answer becoming instantly obvious,

Now it should be said, that there is certain protocol to a barbeque, doesn't matter the culture, all races and creeds could probably agree, that at its core, one rule exists above all others, you don't tell the host how to barbeque. Such a thing was rudeness, such a thing was not accepted, and in some parts of the world, certain people might consider it a good cause for murder. And yet, standing at the large half a drum barbeque, Stripper stood, with Matts apron upon him. His spatula flipping the burgers, his tongs rolling the sausages, and for Harvey, he instantly felt as violated as his friend,

"ah whos this then?" Stripper asks, seeing the young man step out into the garden, "is that Harvey I see?" he asks in a friendly voice, "hey stripper" he replies, "cooking up a feast hey?" he asks, seeing kim and Marge sitting under the gazeebo, both with a glass of rose wine and chatting away, "thought id be a good guest" he responds playfully, "ol matt here was burning the sides" he says playfully, "be ready in five"

"hey harv" Marge says, winking at him, a big smile on her lips as she watches the man come sit beside her, matt joining, Kim not looking at either of the two, "isn't he good?" she chuckles, "such a nice man" "yeah" matt agrees falsely, "such a good man"

"well im sorry guys" Marge continues, "left my pasta on the side at home" she says, tutting to herself, "damn police made me forget about it, will have to try my delights another time" she says, the comment making Harveys ears prick slightly, "police?" he asks, pulling out a smoke, and lighting it,

"asking if anyone wanted to hurt me" Stripper scoffs, "could you believe the implication, me?" he laughs, "everyone loves me", "sure do" Kim replies, her voice quite light and teasing, in which much the same could be said for her dress. Something that had annoyed Matt, for she had never worn a dress before today. "reckon they were after you then?" Harvey asks as innocently as he can, hoping not to stir the biker the wrong way, "undoubtedly" Stripper says, flipping another burger, "so what you tell them?" Harvey asks, "only that I knew one person" Marge smiles, "and his name was Harv" she jokes,

"that true?" stripper chides playfully, "do you want to shoot me with a bazooka" he smiles, Harvey becoming nervous at the question, "no…course not" he says, taking a quick drag on his smoke,"surprised you found the time to come tonight" Matt says a bit bluntly, "with everything going on" he adds, Stripper looking back to his burgers, "yeah well, show must go on and all that"

"wheres Anne?" Harvey asks, trying to change the conversation, "oh her and scooter are…well they doing a job for me, be back in the morning" Stripper says, cutting in before Marge could answer, "a job?" Matt asks, Kim giving him a disgusted look, "got a bike I bought near London, they're picking it up, and Anne well…" he laughs, "she wanted to keep the boy company"

"wouldn't we all darling" Marge chuckles, "that boy got some muscles developing" she jokes, "id give him a hand getting a few of them stronger", the joke making Kim chuckle, the two lads rolling there eyes beside them, as Matt rolls himself a smoke, lighting it and joining the rest in the habit, that is all, except Stripper. The man focused on the task at hand, "how long your nut burgers need Matt?" he asks, picking up a pack of vegetarian burgers, "couple minutes each side" Matt ventures, the large biker taking them out and throwing them on the barbeque, the flames flickering with a cackle as the moisture drops onto them.

"so tell me" Stirpper asks, turning to look at the small group under the Gazeebo, "how come I barely met any of you? Not you Marge obviously" he says, the question making both Matt and Harvey search for the right words, "well we were social recluses" says kim, "but not me" she winks, "not anymore", the comment making Stripper laugh, "ah good to hear" he smiles, "and you Matt? don't drink down the sun much, see you every now and then in the griffin"

"thought that was your pub" Matt says, instantly feeling a weight drop on him, like a boulder falling on his tongue he felt the wrong words had just been uttered, "not my pub" Stripper says, showing no sign of anger at the comment, "always more than welcome" he says, "do love a good bit of company" he says, his eyes looking kim up and down, though whether he knew he wasn't being subtle about it was any bodies guess, "foods done" Stripper says, looking at the meat and the half cooked veggie burgers, "grab the rolls would you Harv" he says, the young man getting up and bringing over a plate of flat and long rolls, burgers in the flat, hotdogs in the long.

"Todd! Kieran!" Marge shouts, the sudden noise and depth to which her tone could go making Matt jump slightly, "food!" she yells again, the sudden patter of excited feet racing down the stairs, the two children, both with faces painted, todd as a superhero and Kieran as a giraffe, "Harvey!" Todd says, hugging the man, Harvey laughing "hey little un" he says fondly, "been painting each others faces?" he asks, "hasn't Kieran got a nack for it?" Marge says proudly, "gonna be an artist one day, just like his mum" she giggles,

"forgot you're a painter" Stripper says, "done anything recently?" he asks, Marge smiling, "not for a few years, just need to recapture my flare" she says playfully, Harvey letting go of Todd, "well your sons got the nack" Harvey adds, "you look good Todd", "thank you" the boy replies, taking a burger and hotdog and putting it on his plate, Kieran doing the same, "having a good birthday?" he asks, the kid nodding, "I have to wait til after food to open my presents though" he moans happily, "well im sure it will be worth the wait" Harvey says, the two children racing back upstairs,

"ah to be that age again" Kim smiles, standing up and grabbing a plate for herself, a few sausages and burgers going into buns, "still got your youth though" Stripper smiles, "better than what I got, forty years and wrinkles" he jokes, Kim looking fondly at him, Matt standing up and grabbing a plate too, "you got any kids Stripper?" he asks, trying to steer the conversation away from his blushing wife, "no" Stripper says bluntly, his tone seeming to change somewhat, "not anymore" he says, kim slapping her husbands arm, "don't be so horrible" she says coldly, "sorry…" matt says, suddenly embarrassed and ashamed, "Stripper sorry mate…I..I forgot" he says, his tone apollogetic and sincere, Harvey grabbing a plateful of food and sitting down

"no harm mate" Stripper smiles, taking his gaze from the two and picking up his own plate, "not a subject for a party any rate" he says, picking up some burgers and sititng down under the gazeebo, Harvey feeling awkward at the home wrecker sitting so close beside him, "heard from Mary?" he almost wanted to ask, the tension growing in his bones as Stripper munches on a sausage, "you know Harv, been feeling a bit down since losing Titan" the biker says, a mouthful of meat as he says it, "guess you could say I lost a loved one" he continues, his eyes connecting with the young mans, "guess im just saying I know what I did to you" he says, his tone sounding honest, "so…"he pasues, "I am sorry about mary"

The comment making all four brace from the surprise of it, Marge almost smiling at the thoughtfulness of it, Kim almost fluttering herself to mid air with her overwhelming appreciation of the mans candour, Matt guessing a more sinister route to the words, and Harvey, well Harvey was almost in tears. "I know I apologised before mate" Stripper says, "but it isn't until your almost killed you realise the crap you done to others" he pauses, "so, I am sorry" he says, his voice quite soft, his hand lifted up in a meaningful way, Harvey grabbing it and clasping it, "and I thought this party would be awkward" Harvey chuckles, his voice strained with emotion, "you can do better than her" the biker says, releasing his grip, "come down the sun some time I'll show you a whole wealth of em" he smiles, Harvey taking his hand back,

"ah bless" marge says, "nice of you Stripper, good for you Harv" she says, her voice quite taken aback, "appreciate the apology mate" Harvey nods, his mind seeing the knife used to butter the rolls, his hand grabbing it quickly and stuffing it into the mans jugular, blood everywhere, his mind overwhelmed by the thought, his friend matt coming to sit beside him, "so is there a funeral date?" he asks, changing the subject quickly, "for Titan?"

"be on Wednesday, gonna have him cremated then have his ashes brought down Fordham road to the marina, scatter them there, his mum and dad will be there" Stripper says, his voice slightly sad, "he always loved the water" he shrugs, "just feels fitting",

"well we'll be there" Kim says, "showing our support", "so will the whole village I iamgine" Stripper smiles, his mouth continuing to much on the suasage, "well if you and your boys need anything" Marge says kindly, "you just come give me a knock", "thanks" Stripper smiles, Matt looking at his friend Harvey, his eyes fixed on the butter knife, "any closer to working out who did it?" matt asks, Stripper looking at him sternly, "I'll know soon enough" he says, his voice filling back with authority, "don't you worry about that" he says, finishing his sausage, the sound of hurried feet racing down the stairs, "finished!" Todd shouts happily, "well that must mean time for presents then" Kim laughs, the adults all putting there plates aside, standing up one by one, "to the lounge then" Matt sighs, his friend looking at him cautiously. The children racing through the kitchen, coming to sit on the sofas of the living room, the adults following suit, "here" Harvey says, handing Kieran a bowl filled with sweets, "finish these up, save me from my sugar addiction" he jokes, the young boy grabbing a handful, Todd quickly doing the same.

"so…" Matt says, awkwardly, picking up a small present from the side, "this one is from Harvey" he says, handing the present to Todd, the blue wrapping paper with dinosaurs on it quickly being torn open by hungry fingers, the paper falling away as a deck box of new monster playing cards is revealed, "cool!" todd says, Kieran looking at them, leaning on todd for a better look, "it's the hydra deck" he says excitedly, "thank you" the young boy says, giving Harvey a good old hug,

"hydra deck?" Stripper asks intrigued, todd holding it up for the biker to see, "you battle monsters and lay out mana and try to kill each other" he explains excitedly, "I got a dragon and a forest elf one" he says, "now I got a hydra one too", "sounds pretty fantastic" Stripper nods playfully, "good gift Harv" he says fondly, the young man smiling a dry smile back at him,

"well now ours" Marge says, prompting Matt to grab a slightly larger present, green with what looks like leaves as its wrapping, again quickly destroyed as the boy tears through it, "im going to take you out on Saturday to see that new super hero film you really wanted to see" Marge says, "going to go with Kieran and a couple of his friends, have pizza and some ice cream" she smiles, "so just a little something to say happy birthday" she smiles, as Todd pulls out a jumper, a simple plain blue jumper, "hope it fits" she winks, "thanks Marge" Todd says, the lady leaning over to get a big hug from the little man, "we'll have a lovely time Sunday" she says, kissing his forehead, "my treat" she smiles, "thanks auntie marge" he smiles,

"this one is from Anne" kim says, grabbing a present from the pile, "who is very sorry she is missing her special friends birthday", "apparently the power of boners is stronger than friendship" Harvey says under his breath, no one seeming to hear him, as they all watch todd pull out a snow globe from a bag, his face slightly puzzled, "ah bless" Marge sighs, giving Todd a playful squeese on the shoulder, "she's not much good at getting presents" she jokes, kim chuckling and Stripper smiling, Matt looking to the next present, "from nan and grandad" Kim says, "and mum and dad say sorry they cant see there grandson, just a bit of a long way to come from Canada" she smiles, placing a kiss on her sons head,

Bright red wrapping paper and quickly dissolved to nothing, as the boy rips it open again, revealing a massive knitted coat, "oh wow" Todd says, holding it up to look at it, "ahhh" Marge says, "your mum must have made that herself kim" she says fondly, "try it on" kim says, the boy standing up and putting it on, it fitting absolutely perfectly, as all nans crafts often do. "you can ring her in the morning, say thank you" Kim says softly,

"hell of a coat boy" Stripper says, "you look the part now", "two more left" Matt sighs, "Stripper you mind which one first?" he asks, the question feeling awkward, "mine last" he winks, "promise you its worth it" he says happily, Matt sharing a troubled look with his friend, then kneeling down to give him his present, "from your mum and me" he smiles, Todd smiling as opens the gold wrapper, a bar of chocolate inside, the boys face looking to force a smile, "look under it" his dad whispers, Todd turning the bar in his hands, "what....?" the boy stammers, "what is it?" Kim asks, her voice grating to Matts ear, "you had one job" she groans, Todd crying. Holding up two tickets in his hands,

"Scrumpys live show" Matt says softly, "they are going to be in Cambridge on Sunday night" he says, "so I got you and me a ticket", his son jumping form the sofa and grabbing his dad hard around the neck, "thank you" he cries, "I know its not a T.V" matt says, "not fair!" Kieran moans at his mum, "why cant I go to Cambridge", "well they…" Marge stammers slightly, "they only announced it this morning, I mean the tickets were…how did you afford that?" she asks shocked,

"old man still got some surprises in him" Matt chuckles, "good for you mate" Harvey says happily, his face lighting up, "good for you", kim looking shocked, "we cant afford.." she tries, Matt holding up a hand to silence her, his son still embraced around his neck, savouring every moment, "not now" he whispers, looking her firm in the eye, "not now"

"well," stripper says nervously, "kinda feel I should have gone first now" he chuckles, "that's the show ender that is" he says, almost kind of surprised at the affection before him, "um…" he says, not knowing what to say, "open Strippers present Todd" Matt whispers in the boys ear, "I love you daddy" Todd says, tears rolling down his cheeks as he pulls away, "I love you too" he says, standing up and slowly picking up Strippers present, placing it down in front of him, Todd opening the wrapping slightly slower than the last times,

"oh my god" Kim says, a box with a flat screen tv inside showing as the wrapping paper falls away, "its one of them smart ones" Stripper says, "bought you a years subscription to that channel you wanted too" he adds, Todd looking at him, "for…for me?" he asks, the room looking surprised at him, his tempearture suddenly raising, feeling his plan had taken a bit of a nose dive, although kim was blushing a bit still, "thank you" she says, giving the man a large hug, "happy birthday Todd" he says, the boy looking overwhelmed, "I get to see a live show and watch the channel too!" he screams, jumping up and down, "thank you" he shouts, joining his mother in a hug, the biker embracing the two of them. Matt smiling, though he knew he hadn't been entirely embarrassed, he still felt strange at the stranger buying such an expensive gift. "thanks mate" he says, his eyes filled with anger.

⁂⁂⁂⁂⁂⁂⁂⁂⁂⁂⁂⁂⁂⁂⁂⁂⁂

Chapter 3

The night hadn't gone well, or at least that is what most passers by would have thought, had they heard the commotion coming from the dilapidated red house on pound lane, the arguing going into the early hours of the morning. The guests having left and offered the usual farewells, and the happy child put to bed, the young boy agreeing the flat screen would sit in the main living room in place of the old one, his father concerned he would miss out on family time if he were to have a tv in his room, which surprisingly, Todd had agreed to quite happily. Seemingly overwhelmed by the sheer quality of his gifts, his excitement of seeing a film and a live show over the next weekend all he could talk about.

It had taken a while for him to fall asleep, perhaps from the excitement keeping him awake or the tears of happiness keeping him from drifting off. Nonetheless, sleep had eventually taken him, his eyes closing as the last of the guests had left, Harvey smiling and hugging his friend before leaving, "where did you get that money from?" he had asked, Matt smiling awkwardly, avoiding the answer, "I couldn't live with letting my son down another time" he had said, "so I did what any parent would do"

He had left it there, his friend not getting any more out of him, the door closing and Harvey going his own way, still with questions in his head. Matts wife Kim however, was not so easily side stepped, her fury after clearing away the rmenants of the leftovers, spilled out as she slammed the bin shut, the leftover burgers sinking to the bottom with a thudd. "where did you get the money?" she had snarled, "they were four hundred quid a ticket when I looked!" she had explained, holding her phone up to show the tickets on sale online, "eight hundred pounds!" she snarled, "where did you get that from?"

"Dad had left some money" he had shrugged, his found strength from hugging his son and seeing hm so happy had quickly dwindled, the nerves coming to his tone, "I was saving it for…" he tried to explain, Kim stepping into him, her snarling face coming close to press against his, "all this time!" she spat, "all this time you had that kind of money", "it wasn't eight hundred" he says defensively, "that's the scalpers price" he had tried to point out, Kim not budging an inch, "you had that kind of money! Do you know how many times we needed that" she says, tears actually falling down her cheeks, "I know…" Matt says, "but it was dads money" he says shaking, "I promised to only spend it on something Todd really wanted"

"Todd wanted his mother and father to be able to feed him food not in a bloddy tin can!" Kim had yelled, "todd wanted to go to more school trips, more cinema to see more films, Todd wanted his bathroom not to look like a trash heap!" she had shouted, "Todd wanted his mother home during the school holidays instead of pulling extra shifts, because todds dead beat dad can't hold down a bloody job!"

"kim…" Matt had said, "kim please…it was dads money" he had said, tears falling down his cheeks too, "it had to be saved for something special", "special!" Kim had roared, her finger violently pushing into Matts temple, "was it not special enough when our electric was shut off during winter? Was it not special enough when I was off sick and surviving on sick pay for the three of us!?" she shouts, her anger boiling to a level Matt had seen only a few times before, and matt was scared. "sixteen Matt" she had cried, "we were sixteen and one night" she huffs, "all this came to be because of our youth, because of our stupidity" she cried, "I know" Matt had said, his tone trying to calm the argument, his voice trembling as she had dug deeper with her finger on his temple, "ten years," she said, her head shaking, "five were fine maybe but…" she had stammered.

"my dad died Kim!" Matt had cried, trying to appeal to her, "im sorry my tragedy got in the way of your youth" he had said, "im sorry my dads death has robbed me my life and you yours" he had shouted, kim stepping away and looking away from her husband, "im sorry I have done nothing" he had said, his finger pointing upstairs, "but fail my son, each and every year" he had sobbed, "it was his tenth kim,..his tenth and that stupid show means so much…"

"look at me" kim says, her hands going up and down her body frantically, "look at me!" she had screamed, "do I look like a monster! Is that what I am to you, you think im angry you brought Todd so much joy" her voice breaking, "is that the image before you, a fiend or demon?"

"kim…" matt had pleaded, "it was my dads money, it was a promise kim…" he had sobbed, "its not today" she had said, "not today at all, all of them, all the days, all my horrors for being married to a man such as you"

"and what of my shame!" he had roared, sudden anger coming from within, "what of my torment that you go out and talk and laugh with your friends about me!, that you invite the man you want to fuck and ruin our marriage with to my sons tenth birthday party! A man who wanted to shame me in front of my son and a man that robbed me of my…"

"don't you dare!" Kim had roared back, her hand turning to a fist, the blow coming hard and fast, catching Matts jaw and sending him tumbling to the floor, "so I want some fun!" she had spat, "can you blame me? After years of this" she said, pointing at Matts lower half, the man crawling along the floor backwards, coming to rest shakingly against the kitchen cooker, "I just wanted" she had cried, unballing her fists and frustratingly running her fingers through her hair, "I just wanted to feel affection again" she explained, her voice dry and croaking, broken and soar, her eyes cascading, red and bloodshot, "and I…I just cant do this" she had finally said, "this" her hands pointing at her and him, "this is done",

"then go!" Matt had spat, "just go!," "like some tramp" kim had said, "you think im going to live on the street like some tramp!" "I don't care!" Matt screamed back, "you want to go then go!", "oh im going to go!" she said pointing at Matt, "I got a real man now that wants to look after me" "stripper!?" Matt had laughed darkly, "your delusional!" he had spat, "call me that again!" she had threatened, jumping forward towards him, a fist raised up ready to strike him, "look at you," she had spat on him, "stay down here" she had said kicking him, "I'll be gone by the time you wake up, you stay in your crappy dads house" she had said, walking away

"kim" he had pleaded, his side hurting where he had been kicked, "kim…." he had cried, the sound of footsteps and a slamming door of the bedroom sounding to the kitchen below, and so, Matts marriage was over.

****

The news was on, and the police meeting room was very silent, the faces fixed to the television, as the screen shows the form of a heron, a large sling about its wings, a splint on one of its legs. A news reporter talking quite fondly to the rspca member holding the bird, his hands lovingly stroke the creatures neck, the birds beak playfully darting up and down, the man swerving his head evey now and then to avoid being skewered,

"so misty here has had four oeprations so far", the rspca man explains, "one on the wing, setting the bone back in place, two setting the leg and one to remove a tooth from its kidney" he says, pointing to each bandage as he speaks, the reporter smiling as she pulls the microphone back to her mouth, "so misty is due a swift recovery?" she asks, the rspca man answering slightly conservatively, "well she is doing well, but she has a long road ahead before full recovery," he says, the heron almost impaling him again, as his head ducks from a cheeky peck, "well she seems to have plenty of life left in her" the reporter smiles, looking back at the camera, "as for the hunt for the so called Bazooka boy, local police constabulary and fire services are still on the search…"

"turn that off" detective inspector Bruce says sternly, holding the door open as Thomas follows in behind him, the young blonde policewoman with the remote control hitting the red button, the screen going a sudden black. "misty looks like she'll make it sir" she says to the detective,

"misty?" Bruce asks, looking confused at the officer, "the heron sir, said shes on the road to recovery", "oh god" bruce says, rolling hie eyes, "they named it" he sighs, his colleague Thomas coming to stand beside him, "well if the bird is getting the brunt of the attention then you can bet we will be for it next" Bruce says firmly, "so…what have we got?"

"two accounts confirm the man in black and with the suitcase, they confirm he is of slim build and definitely no taller than six feet, he was seen cutting across towards the rising sun pub sir, he was later seen going down pound lane toward the griffin and then the last sighting was down a place called little London, a street near the shop sir " the blonde says, reading from her notes, "so we questioned everyone down there?" Bruce asks, "everyone sir" the young man from the third row says, "none had motorbikes or owned one recently, one guy had had one in the sixties but swore he never wore leathers, another was an old photographer that wouldn't stop talking about Kuwait and Iraq" he shrugs, "nothing though,
"

"we watched the houses too" the blonde policewoman adds, "nothing out the ordinary", "what about our motives?" Bruce asks, "anyone enlighten us on Titan or Stripper?", "an elderly man had said he worked at the priory garage before it was shut about a month ago sir" another police officer reports, "had nothing but bad things to say about it"

"what about the garage?" Thomas asks,"the VigilanteS used to use it for there work sir" he says, looking at his notes, "buying, selling repairing motors, the usual," "so they owned it?" Thomas asks, "no sir, just like the sun they just use places, keeps the business looking a legitimate venture whilst they avoid paying taxes I would guess" he shrugs, "at least to this mans mind sir, the VigilanteS were deling in stolen vehicles, said they would grind engine numbers away and replace license plates," he says, Bruce smiling at the officer, "something we have never been able to proove" he adds

"so why did it close down?" Bruce asks, "economy sir, according to this gentleman that is, people heard the rumours of what was going on and refused to bring there trade to them, the company faced financial ruin and the club just walked away, no trace of any wrong doing to tie them there" he says, his voice quite matter of fact, "didn't you say Stripper was at the Fordham garage yesterday?" Bruce asks, his eyes taking in the two officers he had sent to tail him, "yes sir"

"and the reason for the visit?" he asks, "unknown sir" one of them replies, "well we can drive there and find out for ourselves then" he says, looking at Thomas, "you think he's trying to establish another foothold? With everyone watching him?"

"I think financially he's going to be suffering, the clubs main source of income just closed on them, he could be desperate" he shrugs, "what happened to the old garage?" he asks, "bought for land for new homes sir" the young officer replies, "no bid from stripper or the club?", "no sir, sold for a few million" he says, "too pricy for our club then" Bruce nods, "okay, so motive…you think maybe someone unhappy with the garage closing? Maybe someone who found out they had a vehicle stolen? Disgruntled former employee of the priory garage?" he asks, the young officer nodding slightly, "well that narrows down the search then" he groans, "right, get to interviewing all former employees, find anyone who reported a bike or car stolen and see if they fit our suspects discription"

"what about Stripper and Titan?" he asks, "any news on anything recent they could have done?", the young blonde office responding, "nothing on Titan sir, but stripper had recently slept with another mans girlfriend" she says, "well find the boyfriend and question him then" Bruce says, the officer agreeing with a nod and a scribble in her notebook.

****

The book fell from his hands, the childrens story dropping to the floor of the empty boys room, the bed removed of sheets, the shelves bare and the clothes gone. And that wasn't all, everything was gone, his son and wife, his life, gone. His eyes had cried all night and the late morning air had awoken him from the ktichen floor, his head and side seeming to no longer ache, yet his heart, his heart was. For the house was silent and bare, and todds room was the worst, for little trace he had ever lived there remained, though todd had little stuff and few belongings, they had once filled this barren room.

Kims room was much the same, save the curtains still hanging and the bedding still there, everything else had been packed and ,matt supposed, it had all been stuffed into the back of a Nissan micra, though the bathroom was exactly how he had left it the night before, save the odd towel and toothbrushes, he was genuinely surprised she hadn't taken the sink too.

There had been a note, placed in a ball next to him, which he guessed had most likely been thrown, uncrumpling it on its discovery, the words scribbled and rushed in an angry form of calligraphy, its message pretty simple, "I am not taking your son from you, you can take him Sunday for the show and then we can go from there, don't call me or try to see us, have gone to stay with Stripper whilst I get my feet back on the ground" , it hadn't received the greatest response, the paper falling fowl of being flushed down the toilet, an angry foot kicking it in the basin, swear words of every language helping it along the piping.

And so it was, standing alone in a house once made for a family, Matt was finally alone. This time it felt final, this time it felt real, and so the tears had poured and screams and flung things resounded for a good few hours, till at last he came to todds room, somehow hoping to find him still asleep, somehow hoping he had just dreamt it all. But he hadn't, all that remained was the childrens story book, and that had been dropped, he had guessed, his mind racing and then coming to a constant numbness, as he leaves the room, slowly walking down the stairs, he finds the lounge, and slumps down onto the sofa. His head burying into the fabric, a muffled scream coming from him, seeming to last a good while, his hand frustratingly grabbing a cushion, throwing it hard, the motion bringing some degree of comfort, his hand finding another and another, his rage building as he stands up and feels the underside of the furniture, with a grunt flipping it over and screaming, his body falling to the floor as he goes quiet, his eyes trying hard to bring more tears, to no avail, his eyes deciding they were a perfect shade of red for the occasion. An image catching the corner of his sight, a large flat screen tv, glinting in the morning light shining through the windows.

"so you take my son but you wont take the tv!" he yells, going to strike the thing, finding the remote and smahing it against the tv stand, the motion snapping the thin thing in half, the remote coming apart in his hand, the tv shooting to life all of a sudden, a dolphin singing a song, "shut up!" Matt yellls, pressing the red button on the broken half of the remote, the clicks doing nothing as he frantically presses over and over, the dolphin singing, "I like to sing, I am a dolphin, this is my favourite thing…" he sings, Matt searching the tv, finding no off button on the sides, "ah!" he yells, going to strike the screen, something suddenly holding him back, his son.

Thoughts of his face, if ever he returned, seeing the destruction his dad had done to his precious gift, the fist fell to the side, "todd…" he whimpers, "I cant…" he says, crawling over to the upturned sofa, slumping against it . Looking at the singing dolphin, "I sing about fish and dream of the sea, so come if you wish and sing with me…" the dolhpin says, his googly eyes moving in a fun and silly spiral motion, "I hate you" Matt spits, "your not even a good singer" he sighs, his eyes

taking in the destruction he had wrought, the cushions having dislodged
his piles of dvds, the cases scattered across the floor.

"and now kids, a special welcome to my good friend.." the dolphin says
ecstatically, "mixy!" he says, a show suddenly starting up, the picture of a
chef, seemingly meant to represent a pixie with small wings at his back,
as his whisk stirs into a pot, the theme tune for his show playing, matts
eyes drawn to it, more out of exhaustion than anything, "oh what new hell
haunts me now?" he sighs,

"add some eggs and some flour, tis the time for mixies hour, chocolate
chips and coconut, time to see what the chef is cooking up" the young
voices sing, a live audience of children cheering as the camera zooms in
on the chef, a silly and overly large chefs hat on him, a large moustache
and a big smile, "well high little cooks" he yells, the audience cheering,
"hey mixy!", "I'm out" Matt sighs, lifting himself up,walking out the
lounge, the door slamming shut behind him

****

The truck door slammed, as scooter climbed out, his feet coming to
rest on the car park of the rising sun, Anne climbing out the other side,
the door closing behind her too. The truck holding in its back the bike
they had collected, a greeves motorcycle, Scottish and old, perhaps fifties,
worth a small fortune, exactly what had been paid for it. Scotter looking
at the bike, checking the strapping and making sure it was secure.

The sun was out, that's not a pun, the actual sun in the sky was shining,
and the early afternoon had seen the VigilanteS motorcycle club gather at
there favourite drinking hole, there bikes, a collection of different models
of Harley Davidsons were standing proudly in the car park, the parking
directly in front of the building, the pub itself a large yellow and cream
structure, with green doors and a proud sign above it,

"missed call" anne says, pulling her phone from her pocket, "twenty of
them" she says, slightly shocked, "fancy a pint?" scooter asks,
"no…should ring back kim" she says, tapping away on her phone, "well
see you later leanne" he says, walking to the front door, the young lady
staring at him, "Anne!" she says, correcting him, "sorry…names…. you
know"? he says with a shrug, "whatever" she says, walking away, turning
left and disappearing from scooters sight, the man having a quick
chuckle as he sees her go, opening the front door and walking in

****

Crusher had rang as soon as he discovered her, sat on his chair at his
dining table, sharing a cup of tea with his wife, the young lady explaining
she had dropped her son off at school, and for the reasons she stated, "her

friends not having a spare room" and "I didn't know where else to turn"
she had come to find stripper. Crushers hand instinctively picked up his
mobile, his conversation pretty brief, "get to mine, now" he had said,
hanging up as soon as he had said it.

It was fair he wasn't in the best mood, having gone to the coroners and
then a crematorium, getting his friend ready for his send off tomorrow,
Strippers car coming in handy, as the task took far longer than he had
expected, not to mention picking up Titans mother and father from the
train station, making sure they were comfortable in a spare lodge on the
marina. It was fair to say, he had had a rough day, and wanted nothing
more than to meet his brothers for a pint. The thought seeming a far off
possibility, taking in kim sobbing at his kitchen table, his soft hearted
wife seemingly letting anyone in for a cup of tea, the thought reinforced
when anne arrived, just walking through the front door and letting herself
in, brushing passed Crusher and racing to sit by her friends side, .

"I've left him" kim sobbed, "ive..." she stammers, "oh kim" anne says
giving a big hug to her friend, Crushers wife Jillian patting her shoulder
reassuringly, "take all the time you need" she says softly, "how? I mean
what happened?" Anne asks quickly, Crusher sighing and walking out the
house, no one seeming to notice.

walking to his garage and pulling open the door, it raises with a well
oiled slickness, "there you go buddy" he says, putting a small cardboard
box containing a small urn onto one of the shelves, his motrcycle sitting
centre piece with his presidents beside it. "plenty of room for you in here"
he sighs, patting the box kindly, "think my house is getting s bit full
lately" he groans,

"the hell is going on?" Strippers voice says, the man stepping through
the garage door, "you got a problem" Crusher says, "no..we got a
problem" he adds, Stripper walking into the garage, "whats up?" "your
bit of skirt just split up with her husband" Crusher says, "what? Kim?"
stripper asks, "she's having tea inside" Crusher says mockingly,

"well what the hell is she doing here?" Stripper asks, his voice
thoroughly confused, "probably seeking the comfort of her saviour"
Crusher laughs slightly, "well..." Stripper says, lost for words, "she
wants to stay here for a while...with you" his brother jokes, though his
laughter is dark and his tone sounding pissed off, "well..." Stripper
stammers, "she cant!" he says forcefully, "well you go tell her then I'm
not doing it pres" crusher says, "your mess" he smiles, "so you'll kill for
me but you wont chuck out a harlot?" Stripper scoffs, the situation
overwhelming him, more than slightly, "you went to that party, you laid
the groundwork" Crusher laughs, a shrug falling from his shoulders, "oh
for god sake" Stripper moans, walking out the gargae, "I'll sort this
myself"

He moved quickly, his feet taking him through the open front door and to the kitchen table, where the three women sat, kim crying and anne and jillian listening intently, "Kim?" Stripper asks, his voice awkward and unsure what to say, "oh thank you!" Kim shouts, standing up and rushing to embrace Stripper, "im sorry, im so sorry.." she cries, "I didn't know where else to go"

"okay" he says, his arms hanging at his side, jillian and anne staring at him, "I left him…I left him I had to" she cries, her tears flooding his shoulders, "its good you came here" Stripper sighs, "VigilanteS always help there neighbours" he says awkwardly, "we'll make sure your alright" he adds, Kim sobbing, "so I can stay here, todd too" she gasps, taking his comments as a given she had got what she wanted, "I mean…Anne?" he asks, looking at the young girl, "one bed bungalow shared with my mother" she says shaking her head, "sorry kim, if I could I would…" she says sincerely,

"marge maybe?" Stripper ventures, "please" Jillian laughs, "you wouldn't survive a day in that house, o.c.d doesn't describe that ladies housekeeping, not to mention she only has two rooms, both of which are occupied" she says, her eyes resting on Strippers, "we got a spare room" she says, "todd and her can stay til they are sorted"

"thank you" kim cries, letting go of Stripper, looking at Jillian with genuine eyes, Crusher walking in behind Stripper, "you don't mind darling? If kim stays with us for a bit?" Crusher looking at his brother, his eyes trying not to pop, "what about her house?" he asks, jillian giving a tutting sound at the comment, "it was Matts fathers" Anne says stubbornly, "he got the right to it" she admits, reluctantly, "can soon get him to sign something saying otherwise" Crusher says, "no!" Kim says, "don't you harm my sons father" she says, her tears forming in her eye to a sudden look of fear, "pres?" crusher asks, Stripper looking at kim, "alright, stay here a while," he concedes, "we'll sort something more permanent for you when we can", "thank you" kim cries, "go get your stuff deary" jillian says, standing up, "I'll show you your room" she says,, the two ladies looking the two men in the eyes as they pass, jillian giving her husband a loving squeeze on the shoulder as she walks passed.

"well at least she wont be here forever" Crusher says, Stripper looking at him, "well your lodge will be fixed soon, she can move in with you when its done", "shut up" stripper says sternly, the large man losing his smile, "you got work to do" he says, ignoring anne, "scooters at the sun, Ractchet too" he says, "go see to it"

∗∗∗∗∗∗∗∗∗∗∗∗∗∗∗∗∗∗∗∗∗∗∗∗∗∗∗∗∗∗∗∗

His garage door flew open, at least, not the main door of the double garage, but the side one, a normal door, only accessible from the garden, the brown wood chipped and the handle and bolts of the locking mechanism rusty and squeeking, the hinges echoing as he threw it open, the wood thundering on the brick as it hit, Matt walking inside and throwing on the light switch. The hum of old bulbs coming to a cackle and a spark, as the flourescent tubes lit up, revealing the garge within. And it was a tip.

Piles of old books and old motors and machines long since forgotten, bags of clothes and reels of electrical cables, this was once a working mans garage, which you would never have guessed, for the five years of dust built up on all the surfaces.

Matt had never been in here, well, he had, but not since, not since five eyars ago, the sight of the place a strange land to him, his feet stepping carefully towards where he knew a certain tool used to be stored, if memory served him, he hoped it would still be there. Walking passed a large and dust covered harley, his eyes not taking it in, his purpose for being here taking front and centre, a shelf with a collection of electric tools, the one he wants, exactly where he remembered it.

Picking the large thing up, he inspects it carefully, pulling a sliding mechanism and seeing a large nail in the magazine, he looks at the plug, dark black and covered in grime, whiping the filth from it he looks for a socket, plugging it in and flicking the switch on the wall. He pauses, looking at the nail gun, holding it closer to the light of the bulbs, his arm coming to outstretch towards the far wall, his hand steadying as he pulls the red trigger of the device, closing his eyes and flinching as the trigger clicks, nothing happening.

With a slam he puts it down on the side, unplugging it and cursing, wiping away the rest of the grime and looking through a small set of drawers, finding a small scrwdriver that matches the screws on the plug, with frantic movement he swears and starts to undo the plug, placing the screws to the side as he removes them, prying off the plastic and revealing the circuitry inside. Using the screwdriver he removes the fuse, holding it up to the light, the inside of it showing the metal strand inside long since disintegrated, "fuse" he mutters, looking around him, looking at all the small trays and pots on the worktops, pulling open each one desperately, "fuses!" he shouts, getting angrier and angrier, throwing the shelves from there fittings and the trays to the floor, some of them bouncing off the mtorbike behind him, the noise not ceasing his efforts, more trays flying until finally, he holds three up to the light, one too big, one the wrong ampere rating, the two getting tossed aside against the wall, the third just right.

With a quick motion he pushes the new fuse into the plugs bracketing, the fuse getting caught in a weird angle, "oh come on " he shouts, picking up the screwdriver and using it to pry the thing in, the metal slipping and catching the tip of his finger, the accident not drawing blood, but painful none the less, "oh for god…" he yells, dropping the tool and shaking his hand., the pain making him step back, his behind rubbing against the rear of the mtorcycle, a quick blow and a shake of the the finger and matt picks the tool up again, finding the screws and slipping the fuse into place, tightening the plug back up, he once more plugs it into the socket in the wall.

   With a hand outstretched he aims at the wall again, his finger clicking the red button, this time an almighty sound of heavy pressure releasing onto metal rings out, the nail digigng deep into the mortar between the bricks, Matt looking at the nail gun, a horrifc smile on his face.

   His elbow bending, as he brings the barrel to his forehead, his eyes closing as his fingers feel the trigger, his mind at peace, his body ready for whatever awaits, a click and a thud as pressure being released sounds, the sound of metal absent, Matt looking, his hands shaking as he pulls open the slider to see inside the magazine, the nail gun empty, "for fuc.."he groans, throwing the thing at the wall, a heavy clatter and a smash sounding. His hands grabbing his face "such a simple thing…"he moans, tears filling his palms, "I cant even…" he breathes deeply, "I cant..", he says, his eyes catching something through his fingers, a smudge where the dust had been wiped away on the rear of his fathers old motorcylce, a sticker in black and white. "when you care you are chained, when you don't you are free", Matt looking hard at the sticker, his phone suddenly sounding in his pocket, the vibrations making him jump,

   "yeah" he says reluctantly, "hey matt Meadows?" the familiar voice asks, "yeah I guess" he says with a sigh, looking at the shattered remains of the nail gun in the far corner, "still here" he says, his tears still falling as he wipes his eyes, his vision staring at the bikes sticker, "dean Marshall here, just a friendly reminder for your visit to the gp tomorrow, thought id just check your still up for a chat"

＊＊＊＊＊＊＊＊＊＊＊＊＊＊＊＊＊＊＊＊＊＊

Detective inspector Bruce hung up his phone, his coleague was driving, the fire inspector insisting it was his turn, to which there had been little argument. His boss, to whom he had just concluded his conversation, was for a better term, pissed off. Which considering the circumsatnces, was understandable, for sometime between them climbing in the car, and the journey towards Fordham garage, the herons conditon had deteriorated, another tooth having been found in a lung, the world apparently in uproar, animal rights activists now joining the ranks of people demanding justice, they wanted answers, they wanted bazzooka boy, and detective bruce had no real new evidence to present to his boss, at least, not any that he felt would soon lead to the capture of the suspect. And so with a huff, he hand hung up his phone, the car passing through soham, taking the main route from Ely to Fordham,

"bad news?" the fire inspector asks, seeing the look on the detectives face, "world seems more concerned about a bird than an assasin" Bruce groans, "people like birds" Thomas agrees with a smile, slowing the car with a slight depress of the accelorator, passing a large pub called the fountain, the car driving along the main street of Soham, passing a church and then a whole collection of shops, kebab houses and fried chicken outlets, a tattoists and another pub, and then another again, "is any of this making sense yet?" Bruce asks, the question hanging in the air,

"we got someone in black with a suitcase with an rpg in it" Thomas says, slowing down aagain as he passes the soham school, the young teenagers apparently breaking for lunch, dozens of them flocking the streets and the roads in there uniforms, red and black ties around there necks, "makes sense to me" Thomas says, waiting as some kids cross the road in front of him, waiting a second and making sure the road was clear, accelerating again, the car passing a mix of houses, a small vetinary centre too, "why an rpg though?" Bruce sighs, watching as they pass another pub, this one large with a large forecourt and garden, the car coming to a petrol garage as it approaches a large roundabout, "makes a statement" Thomas says, "someone saying enough is enough…" he ventures, flicking on the indicators of the vehicle as he pulls onto the roundabout, leaving soham he takes the second exit, a brief burst of speed down a straight road, and they enter Fordham,

"well its life in prison" Bruce says, "just for having the damn thing, let alone firing it", he sighs, "so you wouldn't go telling anyone you had it, not anyone you didn't trust anyway" he says, watching through the window as the car comes to a small roundabout, a garden centre straight ahead and the road leading to Newmarket or turning off towards Cambridge if you were to take a right at a separate tunring, the two men taking the first left, heading down the main road, passing houses as they drove, "and getting one?" Bruce says, "where do you even…" he shakes his head, "that is an answer that has eluded me too much" he says, "black market" Thomas suggests, "sure there are gun dealers able to get hold of whatever a would be assasin needs"

"well…" Bruce says, "sounds like something an organised outfit would have a hand in," he says., tapping on his phone, "rather than a disgruntled employee,", putting the phone to his ear as it rings, "its me, I want a check on the VendettaS movements in the last six months, everyone of them, also…try and find out where someone could purchase a rocket propelled grenade" he says, hanging up the phone, "find the source" he ventures, Thomas nodding his agreement, the car pulling passed an old converted fire station, passed another pub and a shop, coming to pull into the forecourt of Fordham garage

Thomas turning off the igintion, both undoing there seat belts, "if your looking at outfits that can access that kind of arsenal" the fireman says, getting out the car and closing the door, the detective doing the same, "then the VigilanteS?" he asks, "an inside hit" Bruce nods, "not uncommon" he agrees, as the two men cross the forecourt "had crossed my mind, a member who isn't so keen on the leadership" he ventures, "well?" Thomas asks, " its possible" Bruce admits, "but considering all other possibilities I would put it as unlikely" he pauses, reaching the front door of the garages reception, "they don't use weapons" he says, "at least potentially, not until recently" he admits, "explains why they're so well built then" Thomas says, the two men walking through the main doror,

"good afternoon sirs" a young lad greets them from behind the reception desk, detective bruce holding up his identification badge for the young man to see, "any chance I can speak with the owner?" he asks politely, "sure" the young man says, his voice sounding nervous as he disappears into the workshop a rushed voice seeming to say, "sounds like trouble to me", all manner of clangs and rattles sound from the area, cars on jacks and a pair of legs dangling down from an elevated van, Thomas taking a good look with a smile as Bruce the garage owner walks in,

"afternoon officers" Bruce says, to which the detective smiles, "detective inspector Bruce Turnpike and this is fire inspector Thomas checker" he introduces them, "Bruce Jaggard" the garagre owner nods, "I own this garage, not the fuel side of it mind, the mechanic bit" he says, a soft joking tone to him, "two bruces" Thomas smiles, "well this wont get confusing" he jokes, "just call me di turnpike" the detective says, sharing the smile, "so how can I help you?" Bruce asks,

"we understand a man known locally as stripper came to see you" the detective asks, "a president of a bike club called the VigilanteS,?" he adds, the garage owners face giving nothing away, "he did" he shrugs, "what of it?", "what was the visit about?" Thomas asks politely, "one of his lads had failed there bikes m.o.t" he shrugs, "wanted to know what needed to be done to get it through"

"well didn't you explain that to the lad who's bike failed?" the detctive asks, "what was his name?" he adds, "ratchet" Bruce says, "and yes, I explained it to him of course" he smiles, "Stripper wanted to make sure there was no bad feeling about failing the bike" he says, "well why would there be?" Thomas asks, "it's a legal requirement"

"exactly what I explained to Stripper sir" Bruce nods, "and he accepted this?" the detective asks, the garage owner nodding, "accpeted it, then left" he shrugs, "nothing out the ordinary", "did he say anything?

Threaten in anyway?" the detective asks, "no" Bruce says, "you know the priory is closed now" Thomas asks, "yeah sad, nice guy who owned that" Bruce says, "well that means your there local garage now", "I know, " bruce nods, "these guys have there own warped sense of law" the detective says, his voice filled with warning, "we think they used the priory for its workshops," he adds,

"to sell stolen bikes and cars" Bruce says, looking at the two questioning him, "I know the rumours" he sighs, "whether there true or not" he shrugs, "never been proved", "if you are being threatened or pressured...." Thomas says softly, "I'm not, just a misunderstanding over an m.o.t" the garage owner says, "okay" the detective nods, "come across anything suspicious lately, anything out the ordinary, heard of any fights, any brawls, any comments you thought stood out?" he asks, Bruce shaking his head, "nothing out the ordinary, just been business as usual"

"well," the detective pauses, "sorry, last name Jaggard?" he asks, "a brother in Ilseham?" he adds, pulling out a notepad in his pocket, "come across this name before" he murmers, flickering through the pages, "a niece?", he asks, "Mary?, father is Gus Jaggard" "yeah that's him," bruce smiles, "whats the bugger been up to now?" "talking about Iraq and Kuwait mainly, officers said it was all he would talk about" Thomas says politely, "sounds like him" Bruce agrees,

"your niece" the detective says quickly, "she just broke from a long term relationship?" he asks, "so im told" Bruce says slightly flatly, "guy was a waste of space, came here for an interview the other day, didn't recognise the name til after he had left", "not close with your niece then? Not close enough to meet the boyfriend?"

"family differences" the garage owner smiles, "doors always open for them, they never want to walk through it" he sighs, "know the feeling" the detective agrees, "its believed the reason for the break up was Stripper, an affair perhaps" he says, seing the Garage owner give nothing away, "sounds like mary, havent seen her for years, but sounds like her, sounds like him to...any way, I got a heap of oil changes to do" he says, the two men before him nodding and smiling, "okay then" the detective says, putting his notebook away, "if you need us, call us" he says kindly, "will do" bruce agrees, "good meeting you" Thomas says, the two men walking out the main door of the reception. "trouble?" the young man from the reception asks, standing at the doorway of the workshop, Bruce letting out a sigh, "back to work" he says, walking back into the main workshop.

"think he was telling the truth?" Thomas asks his colleague, the two men walking back to the car, "I wouldn't doubt it" Bruce shrugs, getting in the car, the fireman doing the same, bruce grabbing his phone and dialing a number, putting it to his ear as the car fires up, putting seat belts on then pulling out of the garage, "its me, I need a warrant to search Gus jaggards property, yes sir, no sir, just a feeling…" he says to the voice on the phone, "well put whatever reason you want sir, call it a drugs search or something, yes sir, thank you sir" he says, hanging up, "Gus?" Thomas asks, the car pulling onto the main road, "something doesn't add up," he says, "have to wait for the morning for the warrant, but I bet you we will find something there", "just a feeling?" Thomas asks, "just a feeling" the detective agrees.

As the car pulls from sight of the garage, a small white car sat a few yards away sits in wait, the young scooter and the large Ratchet sat on the seats, the large Scottish man reaching for his phone, dialing and putting it to his ear, "think our friends been talking pres" Ratchet says darkly, " think we just seen a couple of coppers leave the place, do you want us to…?" he pauses, as the voice down the phone speaks quickly to him, "okay pres" he says, hanging up the phone, looking at scooter beside him, "your gonna earn your patch another way" he smiles, "leave this bugger alone for now" he says, starting up the car, "pres says you can help Crusher instead"

****

The evening had drawn in, in fact it had become quite late, when Harvey had at last managed to show the two young police officers out of his home, the door finally opening for them as he played the good host, saying a farewell and a thank you for coming. The two officers just nodding as they exited his home, piling into there police car and driving off. The door of the bungalow closing as there car started.

Harvey didn't live a life of luxury, though sometimes he felt he did. For the place he lived was small, but very warming. The front door leading into the lounge, small dark grey sofas opposite a big tv, a fish tank on the wall with multiple sorts of exotic varieties. Dvds alphabetically organised to run along multipe shelves above the tank, a small solid oak coffe table too, the lounge area felt quaint, with a gas fire place at one end and a fresh and new looking green rug covering a nice shade of silver carpet. Two doors on the far wall.

One would lead to a small kitchen, well maintained and fitted with aging appliances, a microwave and an electric cooker, a silver kettle, a sink, a washing machine, the usual. A small garden outside, a single apple tree growing within it, a black mountain bike propped against it. A tortoise too, in a large run made of chicken wire and a wooden box to help protect from the elements.

The second door of the lounge, lead to the bedroom with a bathroom to its side, both well cleaned, both well maintained, the bedroom having a dark blue as its theme, dark blue bedding, dark blue curtains, everything dark blue, the bathroom going for a lighter and sea side feel to it, using white for the bottom of the walls, a lighter sea blue for the tops. Despite a small number of cannabis plants growing in the bath tub with some heating lamps propped above, nothing was particulary out the ordinary.

It had been hard for Harvey, convincing one of the officers his toilet was out of order, the lie determined to keep the young lady from seeing his bath tub, her colleague smiling and telling her to just hold it a while. To which luckily the officer had, much to Harveys relief, if you pardon the pun. The questions had been quite simple really, the three sitting on a sofa and talking quite casually, the usual being thrown at him, "do you own any means to fire a rocket propelled grenade?", they had asked, "did you take the break up with mary hard?", "did she?"

If Harvey was being honest, it had felt good to talk about it. His voice quite emotional at times as he had explained firstly, he most definitely didn't have any way of obtaining or firing an rpg, getting the obvious answer out the way first, then talking about things he didn't realise he really wanted to talk about. Whether it had been the comfort of the police officers being near him or having perfect strangers who didn't know him he felt a freedom come from him, as he had talked as openly as he could about everything that had gone on, feeling a weight drain from him with every word, his voice finally expressing his hidden sadness at his relationship coming to an end,

The conversation had taken a few hours, the officers being as kind and receptive as they could, there notebooks filled with information and genuine smiles on there faces as they had shaken the young mans hand, the young policewoman ending the conversation by saying, "well my darling, sorry to say I really need a wee, time to go i think", the statement holding a friendly finality to it, Harvey smiling as he had felt his woes taken from him, his thoughts of Mary now carried by others. And so the door had opened, as he said a fond farewell, watching the two get in there car, the door closing as he sighs, and sits on his sofa with a slight smile.

"you think we should still go?" the voice of scooter said, sat in a small white car, the large figure of crusher beside him, there two expressions looking puzzled as the police car passes where they were waiting at the roadside, "people getting too familiar talking with police" Crusher grunts, "should be coming to speak to us instead, we're the ones keeping em safe" he groans, picking up his phone and dialling it, "its me, cops just left here too" he says, the voice quickly responding to him, "leave it with me" he says, hanging up the phone and looking at Scooter, "you want to be one of us?" he smiles at the prospect, "want to earn your colours?" he asks dryly, Scooter nodding, "then you gotta learn how to shake people, keep em in line", "so we doing it?" Scooter asks, "you lead" Crusher says, getting out the car, "I'll support" he grunts, the car door closing behind him. The young prospect doing the same, "shock and awe" Crusher says, the two men quickly walking to the door of the bungalow, a quick look around them to make sure no one was watching, the dark of the night revealing no one peeking through any lit windows from the neighbours homes.

It started with a mighty kick, Crushers boot hitting the handle and lock of the front door, the thing flying open with an almighty force, the two men piling in, Scooter taking the lead, a young Harvey shooting up from where he had sat, his face a mask of absolute terror, the form of scooter coming to bare on him, the mans fist landing clean on Harveys right eye, the blow taking him down to the floor as Crusher quickly slams the door closed behind them,

"been doing some dealing" Scooter shouted, lifting the man up, his arms flailing, "come along Michael not nice to lounge about when you got guests" Scooter sneers, "who the hell is micha.." Harvey had tried to ask, his voice cracked and broken, a fist coming into his gut form the young prospect, "oh I don't care your name" he had jested, hitting him again, the man screaming from the pain, "I can smell the weed" Scooter says, looking at Crusher, the large man stepping passed the two, looking through the door of the kitchen, following his nose stepping to the other door, opening the bathroom with a grunt, "time for a bath" Crusher says menacingly, pulling the small heating lamp hanging above the bathroom off with a clatter, the bulbs breaking on the floor, his hands quickly turning the taps and putting the plug in, the sound of running water filling the small lounge, "scooter please.." Harvey gasped, the young mans hands holding him upright, his head throbbing and his guts in twisted agony, "it was only a few quids worth…"

"someone takes a shot at our club!" he says coldly, "and now we find someone thinks they can sell on our patch too.." he says, looking toward the door leading to the bathroom ,"bath time" Scooter says, dragging him screaming to the bathroom, the plants having been torn and tilted to float in the bathtub, the hot water filling the basin a third full, the green of the leaves and black of the soil making for a horrible sight, Crusher stepping to the side as Scooter drags the man to the bath tub, holding his head just over the basin, "you don't do that here!" Scooter says, "not on our turf!" he yells, dunking the mans head below the water, holding it there as the arms thrash and legs try to kick out, holding him there for half a minute, lifting his head up just slightly out the water, wet soil and pieces of green leaves hanging to the mans face, black water vomiting from his mouth as he gasps for air, "you going to deal?" Scooter asks, "you going to sell this crap again?" he says, shaking the mans head violently, "no!" Harvey splutters, "no.." he screams, his head shoved under the water again, Scooter counting to thirty seconds, "well you wont mid if I make sure you remember what happens if you do" Crusher sneers, his voice echoing through the water to harveys terrified ears, the young man trying to thrash free as the prospect holds him in place. The large crusher walking out of the bathroom, loud smashes and clashes thundering through to the bathroom, as the tv screen shatters from a heavy boot, the dvds thrown everywhere and the kitchen appliances thrown to shatter on the kitchen floor. The bathroom filled with the sound of destruction, Scooters hands turning off the taps to stop the water overflowing, releasing his grip from Harvey, the man gasping for air, as he coughs and splutters, his face awash with leaves and soil,

"what you tell the cops?" Crusher asks, walking back in and landing a punch on the mans face, the blow sending him crashing into the side of the toilet, Scooter standing to one side to let the big man have his turn, "nothing.." Harvey coughed, his head spinning, "long time to talk about nothing" Crusher sneers, landing another punch, this one going for the gut, the wind leaving with a force from the young mans throat, "mary" Harvey cries, "they wanted to know about Mary"

"who?" Scooter ssked, looking at his large friend, Crusher shaking his head, "what she got to do with all of this?" he says, looking at the trembling man before him, ignoring the prospects question, "I don't know…" Harvey cries, his hands clutching at his gut, "well if you talk to them again" Crusher says, staring into the mans eyes, "we'll be back", he says, his voice filled with threat, "come on" he says, looking at the prospect, "no more dealing" the prospect warned, kicking Harvey in the side, the blow making a loud whimper come from the man.

And so the two left, Harvey crawling along the floor, hearing the front door close, picking himself up with great effort, his hands placed on the side of the bath, "you bastards!" he screams, raising himself up, his hand feeling frantically at his chest, a building knot growing and growing to the side of his heart, water still falling from his hair and lips, "you…bast…"he groans, a shooting pain coming from all directions across his chest, a frantic hand finding a phone in his pocket, his vision going blurry as he feels a fire burning at his blood, his head spinning and an unending tightness clamp at his lungs, his fingers poking at the number nine on his phone, the thing dialling, an answer coming quickly, "ambulance.." he sputters, his knees and legs shaking as he tries to hold the phone to his ear, "I need an ambul…" he stops, his world going dark as his body spasms and then goes limp, his head falling to hit against the bathtub, the phone scattering across the floor.

****

Warrants often took time in there execution, a search of a property being no easy thing, with every cupboard capable of concealing the smallest of clues and every bit of fabric and furniture able to conceal a whole host of evidence. It was not an easy or a quick thing to do, searching a house, especially one such as Gus jaggards house, for from the outside as the group of officers stared, it was a mighty beast, about to have every hair and bristle examined. The twenty men in blue and white coats, with masks of the same colour and white gloves, standing behind in an orderly queue of Detective Bruce and fire inspector Thomas, as the two mens fists knock politely on the door. The elderly and slightly grumpy form of gus opening up, seemingly uspet, to be awoken so early in the morning,

"what the hell?" he had said, his eyes widening as the cigarette clutched in his lips fell to the ground, the door swinging open further and further as his shocked face took in the dozens before him, "kuwait and Iraq?" Bruce smiles politely, "I'm sorry...?" Gus asked, looking bewildered, "you told one of my officers you were involved in the struggle over there," Bruce smiles, "and your daughter mary, is a person of great interest"

"who the hell...?" Gus had asked, "I have a warrant to search your property" detective bruce had said, as he held up the document for the man to see, "my officers will be respectful I promise you, everything will be put back exactly where it was" he had added, Gus taking the paper and looking at it, "well..." he stammers, "I best put the kettle on then" he sighs, stepping away from the front door and leaving the space vacant, "Mary in?" Thomas had shouted through, the two men stepping through and following gus to the kitchen, "no she went out early..." he pauses, "well, earlier"

"its half passed five" Thomas asked, watching the man sit down at his kitchen table and light another smoke, his eyes still peering over the warrant, "must have an early start at...work?" Bruce ventures, "no, she's off a few days from it" Gus sighed, his hand placing the warrnat on the table, "so where has she gone, so early?" Bruce asked, "think kids tell there fathers things" he chuckles slightly, "probably gone for a walk again, she likes the darkness for it"

"didn't happen to take a suitcase with her and a set of black leathers and helmet?" Thomas asks, his voice sounding slightly sarcastic, his friend giving him a knowing smile, "like I told your officers, only leathers in this house i got were from the eightis in Iraq" Gus sighs, "was a military unit of bike messengers, caught up in an ambush one of them was, helped one get to safety, gave me his uniform and helemt in thanks I guess" he shrugs, the detective actually not believing what he was hearing, "you told my officers you didn't own a motorbike and never had," he says harshly,

"help a man from death and he gives you a token" Gus shrugs, "don't mean you have to wear them or use em, just brought em back with me for some reason, along with some other things I had collected" he said, not really answering the detective, seeing the mans stern look, "never ridden a bike in my life, didn't tell no lie about that"

"but you were asked if you had black leathers and a helmet" Thomas counters, even his steady tone becoming slightly irritated, "no lie there neither, they were Iraqi military leathers weren't they" he says with a shake of his head, "so they were…" Bruce pauses, "christ, dark green," he sighs, "they were dark green, I brought twenty men with me to help unravel this and all I needed was to ask you some questions myself" he sighs, shaking his head, "and an Rpg Gus" he says sternly, "you pick up a few of them as well", Gus looking away from the officer, a slight shrug to him, "was loads of em after the war, just laying about"

"souevenirs?" Thomas almost chokes, "you brought back an rpg as a Souevenir?", "was the nineties, I been gone from home for years, would have looked a stranger and not a pretty one at that" Gus shrugged, "wanted something to impress the girls with back home, other than tall stories" he smiles, seeing the two men looking incredibly worried, "and mary knew you had them?" bruce asks, Gus looking at the two, "of course…" he pauses, Bruce quickly picking out his phone and pulling it to his ear, "and you know whre she likes to take her walks?" Thomas asks quickly, "marina mainly" Gus says, his tired manner suddenly becoming concerned and aware of what was being said, "no" he says, his voice suddenly stern, "not my Mary" he says,

"its me, I want all officers you have to help search Isleham, sir I found him, " Bruce pauses, "I know who bazooka boy is", he says, the voice at the end of the phone suddenly becoming high pitched and frantic, "every officer sir, thank you sir" Bruce says, hanging up the phone, "Gus you are under arrest I will get an officer to read you your rights" he says quickly, "Thomas we need to get down the marina" he says quickly, "right all of you!" he shouts, stepping outside the house the twenty men still waiting for perimission to enter, "five stay and arrest Gus and search the home, the others are coming with me, we have support coming in to meet and spread out, our suspects name is Mary Jagard and she is believed to be bazooka boy!" the statement causing a few murmours from the group, "now there is a funreal procession about to take place!"

"nine o'clock the bike club known as the VigilanteS will start from the wreck to end outside Strippers lodge," he says, the warning to his voice clear as day to everyone, "tensions are high, so I doubt we can stop the countless hundreds who are going to attend so even more doubtful is stopping the funeral itself" he says, his eyes taking in each and every officer, "now mary could strike anywhere along that route, she could be laying in wait at the marina or waiting in someones house" he says, an exaggerated extension of his hands showing the officers the weight of what he was saying, "I think she knows!" he shouts to them, "I think she knows she was soon to be caught, I think she is afraid and upset, I think she is unstable and I believe she is armed!" he says, "so start knocking on doors and do it fast, our bosses are sending the bomb squad and fifty more officers from across the area" he says, "even so.." he pauses, "that gives us three hours!" he shouts, "three hours to find someone in a village of thousands"

"if you come across the weapon do not approach!" Thomas shouts, helping his colleague, "we believe it as an old model from the late eighties to early nineties but it still has plenty of kick despite its age" he warns, pretending to aim something at the group, his hands imitating pulling a trigger, "of the twenty of you here with a single shot to the centre of your grouping six wouldn't know what hit them, the rest of you barely having a limb to show your families" his words hanging in the air, the officers eyes all becoming serious, "you see her, phone me!" Bruce shouts, "do not approach, is that clear?" he asks, the officers all saying "yes sir",

****

He had requested a phone call he drowsily recalled, rather than a face to face, and the time was nearing the eight thirty mark,his body still laying where it had many hours before, slooped behind the rear of a dusty Harley Davidson, the sticker still echoing in his thoughts, his eyes still red and blood shot, the phone clutched in his hand. His breaths short and his chest rising and falling as he barely moves, his head hanging slightly to the side as he rested, his mind far from the garage he was sat in, his mind remembering a terrible time, five years ago.

The rain had fallen, he remembered that, soaked and shaking as he had run to get out of the rain, his wife laughing beside him and there son shivering in there arms, the distance from there car to the house door having enough of a length for the happy family to get drenched by the force of the downpour. Matt hadn't had a beard, nor long curly hair back then, in fact he had been well kempt, well dressed in designer clothing and well groomed. A loving wife on one arm and a growing and happy boy on the other, the content family having walked into the house, as often they did, after returning from a fun family night out,

The phone had rung, his pocket vibrating as often it had a thousand times before, for he was a popular man back then, many a friend and many a kind word said about him, and so he had answered it, thinking it be another fun conversation to be had. But he had been wrong, and the sirens suddenly coming to blare down the streets as often they had before, held all new meaning to shake his life to the bone. A call an hour later, confirming his father had been stabbed.

Matt remembered it all in a blur, as he sat on the floor of the garage, he recalled the night, the ambulances had been numerous, the police cars and there lights and sirens filling the roadway ourside pattersons old shop, Matt crying as others did, for another had been stabbed too, there families piling into the back of an ambulance, determined as matt was, that there father would survive, but alas, neither did, the biker and the policeman, so far removed from each other, sharing the same fate.

"you did love them" Matt sighs, his mind back to the present, his eyes still beholding his fathers bike, "wasn't a second you weren't free spent on them" he smiles slightly, his voice cold, "used to say was the bike first and family second" he recalls, the comment making him look the whole thing over, "a joke as covered in the same dust", he sighs, suddenly realisng the thing was in a still and lifeless state, the dust covering the bike making it look ancient and unused, the phone in Matts hand suddenly vibrating, the movement making him take his eyes off the painful memory.

"Matthew meadows?" the voice asked, a young male by the sounds of it, soft yet firm, "yeah" matt says, holding the phone to his ear, "I understand you requested a phone conference, rather than a face to face, my name is Malcolm but you can call me Malc if you wish" the voice says in a friendly tone, "I am a nurse for.." he says, "I know who you are" Matt cuts in, his voice sounding disinterested, "okay" Malc says, "well may I ask why you didn't feel up to a face to face?" he asks,

"currently" matt says, looking at his legs then around him at the garage he was sat in, the place feeling empty and hollow, yet the nagging of fond memories gave some form of comfort, his eyes taking in all around him "unable to move" he sighs, "literally or figuratively?" the voice asks, Matt huffing, "both I guess", "so whats been going on, what has caused this sudden fualt in your motor function?" malc asks, his voice sounding sincere, "well wifes left me, im skint my son isn't living with me anymore, everyone hates me and my father was murdered five years ago" Matt says, his voice dry and sounding unapproachable, "well that would do it I guess" Malc says, his voice sounding unmoved , "so what do you need to do?" Malc asks, "to get yourself moving and heading to where you want to be?"

"where I want to be?" Matt asks, "I don't want to be anywhere" he says, "happy just here", "and where is here?" the voice asks, "in my garage, looking at my fathers bike" he smiles, "father was a biker?" malc asks, "yeah, yeah he loved his bikes" matt says, the fond memory of seeing his father work on the motor every weekend causing a quick glimpse of happineess to him, "and you? You share the passion?" Malc asks, "hate the bloody things" Matt sighs, "nothing but grief"

"so what do you like?" Malc asks, the conversation quickly beeing steered, "I'm into pottery myself" he says playfully, "still no good at it mind, made a pint jug that will leak a third before you can take your first sip" he jokes, Matt listening but not really caring, "I don't know" he sighs, "like music, cooking" "cooking?" Malc asks, "what kind of cooking?"

"vegetarian stuff mainly" Matt huffs, "chillis, pasta dishes, anything cheap to make" he says, "baking?" Malc asks, "people say its good for the soul" he jokes, Matt not smiling but titling his head so the phone presses between his ear and his shoulder, his tired hand dropping to his side, "I made scones a couple of times" matt concedes, "not much of a baker though" he admits,

"well maybe something new to try" Malc says, "something to help the day keep moving for you", "yeah maybe" Matt syas, his voice sounding disinterested, "when did the wife leave?" malc asks, the question quite honest, "yesterday morning" matt sighs, "sorry to hear that mate" malc says sincerely, "never easy, two divorces myself" he admits, "give it a while" he says softly, "let the son settle to the situation then try to reach acceptable terms" he reccomends, matt not really paying attention, his eyes staring at the sticker on his dads motorcycle, "yep" he says, his voice sounding far away,

"so why do you feel as though nobody likes you? You sound an okay guy to me" Malc asks, sensing he needed to change the subject, "thanks" matt says, not really meaning it, "suppose…suppose I just stopped being fun when dad died" he says softly, "well that's understandable" Malc says, "grief isn't fun" he says plainly, "wasn't the grieving" matt says, "was the descent that came from it" matt says, shaking his head, "ah, the downward spiral" Mal agrees, "know to well about that my friend, drinking, smoking " he lists,

"none of that" matt interupts, "I already smoked and I barely drank, still don't" he sighs, "stopped thinking clearly though, stopped caring about money and my work" he says coldly, "stopped caring how best to provide for my son" he says, his voice filled with shame, "and people hated me for it," he says, "and they are right to do so"

"you had lost a father Matt" the voice says reassuringly, "you are allowedd to grieve and act up every once in a while, sometimes our behaviours might cause some degree of harm to those close to us but that is the nature of the process sometimes" he says quickly, "everyone understands that" ,

"oh they understand it for a while" matt sighs, "until there love is superceded by judgement" he says, "there eyes once caring now searching through the wreckage you create", "your quite the philosopher there matt" malc says quickly, "I can tell already you have the habit of over thinking things…" the voice probes, Matt giving a short huff as he thinks on it, "maybe…" he admits, "maybe the years of doing nothing have given me time to think"

"people care indefinetly matt" Malc says kindly, "maybe not the same person about the same thing but the subject will always find an ear ready to listen, no matter how old the subject" Malc says quite firmly, "so some friends might have lost there temper or people might have walked way" he continues, "but that doesn't mean your feelings to what has happened to you are any less relevant"

"you think my friends lost there temper?" matt laughs, "do you know the vigialnte state I live in?" he smiles, his voice still cold and his tone barely interested in the conversation, "I wasn't allowed to mourn, those who did quickly told to stop, new order" he says mockingly, "new order had come and grief for the passing of the old was frowned on" he mocks, "people cared for a few weeks, then they would stop there questions and support, there minds racing with the dreams and ideals the new order would bring" he laughs, "of sixty people who knew my name only two could I now call friend" he sighs, "and they arent exactly the best of men either" he jokes darkly,

"do you feel hatred then?" malc asks honestly, "do you hate the people around you? For abandoning you to your grief?", "no" matt admits, the word hanging for a long moment, as he thinks on what to say, "not hate" he sighs, "I never hated anyone, still don't" he says, his sadness at his words gripping him, "not even the man who killed.." he pauses,

"your father? " Malc asks softly, "was he caught, the one who…" he lingers, "two were imprisoned for it" matt huffs, "but the man who caused it walks free" he says, his voice filled with no hatred, "I suppose its strange" he ventures slightly, "to think I cant hate him"

"and why is that do you wonder?" Malc asks, his voice gentle as he asks, " nobody was safe before he arrived" Matt says, "gangs and thieves" he sighs, "he changed all that by the time I had buried my father" he scoffs slightly, "my father just, a causalty of a war I had done nothing to help fight, how could I hate him? He didn't want my father dead…at least I don't believe he wanted any to die, not the sort you know?" he says, "but now…" he pauses, "now he takes my wife too"

"this man is the cause of your break up?" Malcs voice asks, his tone actually sounding slightly surprised by the revelation, "small world in Isleham" Matt laughs, his awkward chuckle, echoing down the phone to the nurse, "where else but here?"

"so now you hate him?" the nurse asks cautiously, "this man who has taken so much from you?", "no" Matt says again, "I miss the days when my father patrolled the streets" he says, his voice starting to sound like a cry, "when I had a family and we weren't safe for fear of what lurked around a corner, when I was a man able to protect his loved ones, my father making sure we were safe" he sobs slightly, "I don't hate him, I hate what I have become, this hollow form of a shell, which once had balls and purpose"

"so what now?" Malc asks, "now you admit to yourself how you feel, with everything that has gone on how do you get yourself moving?" "I let go" matt says, "and try to bring back what was lost", he says, feeling a small vibration in his pocket, the sensation growing more and more, the garage seeming to darken as the voice of Malc fades, "then time to get to it...." it says, as suddenly with a blink darkness surrounds matt, a sudden blink again and his eyes open.

His bedroom lit by the small amount of sunshine coming through the curtains, his phone sounding in his pocket as he huffs and rolls, clutching his head in confusion to his dream, feeling for the phone, sounding in his pocket of the trousers he had failed to remove from the night before. With a quick pull he removes the device, seeing Petes name on the caller id, "malc?" he asks, petes voice sounding rushed and panicking, "who? Matt get to addenbrookes a and e quick"" he says, "its Harvey"

∗∗∗∗∗∗∗∗∗∗∗∗∗∗∗∗∗∗∗∗∗∗

A bikers funeral procession was truly a wonder, one not always understood by onlookers but one of great spectacle and clarity, an occasion when the weaknesses and human nature of tougher men would be on show for all too see. And it was not a bad thing, in fact it was something so rare to see it was sobering to watch. Hard battle worn men on there bikes, going at a slow pace down the roads, there fallen comrade in a small urn, dressed in black ribbons in a side car of the presidents harley Davidson, fitted to his ride for just such an occasion.

It showed weakness, but not as a fighter or a battle rager might define it, to see men in tears as they slowly rode, looking solemn and in deep thought for there loved one since parted. It showed a side that made them human, for too often they tried to keep an image of something far more machine like and undefeated. And that had its purpose too, it was needed when keeping order from the chaos of the world around them, it made people fear and respect them, it made them approachable with troubles in need of addressing and made the club a force for rivals to shake in sight of, yet on this day, there greatest strength was there weakness.

For sometimes, even a greased machine, needs to show it can feel pain, reminding its creators humanity had still played a part in its construction.. And it was plainly felt, as the bikes passed the park, hundreds of people lining the roads in silent respect, police officers, near fifty of them standing among the crowds, looking frantically at the people out to mourn.

Titan had not been disliked, neither had the club, and so the hundreds at the park outstretched to nearly a thousand or more along the road to the marina, each person having there own reasons for being there, the most common that they felt a sadness, the same the club was feeling, the same so clearly on show, the bikes revving and idling to move slowly, the riders nodding as they pass the onlookers, all showing there signs of remorse and sadness.

Of the onlookers Marge and Anne and Kim had walked alongside, from the top of the road at the park they followed as Stripper lead the procession down the streets, keeping pace with them, walking at the same speed as the bikes, many doing the same, many following to the road that lead to the marina, the procession took a good half hour, the journey slow for a reason. Stripper having had given it a great deal of thought.

For the slow speed over the short distance gave the onlookers chance to see themselves reflected in the journey, each seeing a saviour slain, a friend that was no more, a biker carried to rest by his brothers, each saw and felt what Stripper had hoped, that in the urn he so proudly carried, laid the victim of a crime all too reminiscent of something that would have happened long ago. He wanted them to see the struggle for peace was still raging, he wanted them all to know each loss was felt, and above all, he wanted them to sympathise, so that they would better understand his actions when finally he caught the one responsible for titan now riding in an urn. His face was graven, his eyes ever probing of the crowds, hoping to see some glimpse of the culprit he felt was out there, somewhere.

The procession rode passed the shop, passed the priory garage now becoming a wreckage as diggers and cranes lurked by it, silent for a moment, the workers stopping to show there respects. Passed the two pubs and old post office the bikes went, the crowds lining the roads, some throwing flowers, others throwing there voices, saying "rest in peace," and "may god watch over you", the bikers hit the main road leading to the marina, all of them holding there positions perfectly.

The president at the front, ripper riding close to him, Crusher to his right, then in rows of two, the column went, there was Scruff and Boxer, two large men with large tattoos around there necks, then there was Slayer and Shiner, followed by dread and Ratchet, the two nodding and saying thanks to the crowds calls of sympathy and support, then there was gadget and ripple, two of the younger members, riding proudly behind there brothers. Behind them were fang and trench, then behind them riding a bit further back, two prospects, scooter and zoom. The two proudly following there brothers in front, hoping to one day join them in the column, hoping to earn the patch they had spent the last year trying to get.

The procession began its descent to the marina, a small hill and rise in the road leading up, then a short drop down along the road brining them down to the bridge, where at the rivers banks, waited yet more hundreds, people piled on either side of the river, standing in solemn silence as the bikes arrived to pull up outside Strippers lodge, the place where it had all began.

The lodge itself had yellow tape and boundary warnings all over it, a digger and skip parked in the driveway as over the passed days the wreckage had been cleared and new footings dug for a new porch to be built. Stripper still awaiting the go ahead from the housing officers to clear the building to be safe to enter again. The large hole in its wall from the explosion making the man believe it may yet still be a while, a thought that crossed his mind as he pulled the bike to the side, coming to a stop. His brothers behind doing the same, all dismounting, a small area on the green of the riverbank before them clear of people, save two, Titans parents, who stood in tears, as Stripper bows to them, "my sorrow for your loss" he says gently, "and ours for yours" the father replies, putting a calming hand on his wifes shoulder, the two stepping aside for the bike club to gather.

The detective inspector had watched from afar, him and Thomas wading through the reeds and thicket of the overgrown bank on the other side from where the bikers gathered, they had managed quite simply to achieve what they had been wanting to do, the two men holding the form of a young lady in dark green to the ground, an rpg laying hopelessly beside her as she struggled to break Thomas strong grip, "home wrecker!" she cried, "I'll kill you!" she shouts, her voice lost under the visor of her helmet, so to the vibrations lost to the reeds her head was buried in, "bring a car round, do it quietly" the detective said, phone to his ear, "bomb disposal to our position too" he says, hanging up the phone, quickly helping Thomas pull Mary up, "come on, quickly" he says, guiding them away from the river, leading back towards the road entering the marina, no one really seeing them, all eyes focused on the large biker, an urn in his outstretched hand,

"his name was titan, and such a label never beffited a man more, a brawler and fighter, a boxer and a champion with his fist, and ever more so his heart" Stripper says, his voice carrying to the waiting crowds, "for of us all here, he was the most beloved," he says, opening the lid on the urn, chucking the ash to the gentle breeze, the particles spreading to scatter along the water of the flowing river, "and may he rest knowing that." he says, his words falling silent for a moments respect, "he was murdered!" he says, addressing the crowd, "taken from keeping you safe, his sweat and honor keeping the shadows from creeping and his mighty legacy and that of his club ever wishing for nothing but peace!" he shouts, the parents of titan not taking there eyes from the waters of the river, watching the ash sail along it calmly,

"and so how ends such for Titan?" Stripper asks, "that he should be slain in a moments violence and noise he had so strained to surpress all these years, I am sorry to him and to you all" he shouts, honesty resounding from him, "that we have failed to allow such a thing as this to happen here, where law supersedes desires to see harm return!" he says, looking at the crowds around him, "and so maybe not just you, but the club too need reminding of what keeps the VigilanteS patrolling the streets, and it be this," he says pointing to the river, "it be the ash at the wake" he says, the remains of his brother hitting a small water fall, falling to hit the lower level of the river under it, travelling under the bridge a few hundred yards away, "let this be a reminder if a time were to return, that all of us would be Titan" he says, his voice softening a bit,

"so come join us for merriment and honor of a brother now gone, come drink at the sun and speak of fond memroies of him who we scatter, come the weeks start you are all invited to celebrate our anniversary" he says, his eyes taking everyone in before him, "five years!" he shouts, "save the day that robbed us of a great man we have had peace!" he shouts, "and so as we remember Titan today, may you join us to remember the years he brought to you, and those of his club too, in celebration on the monday", he says, "but for a moment, before we go to drink and recall his fond tales, let us have a moments silence, for the one now ever silent himself" he says softly, his head turning, watching the river carry the ash,

"safe rest my friend" Crusher says, his brothers beside him all saying there goodbyes too, none of them seeing the police car in the far distance, as a small green leather clad girl is piled into the back, Detective Bruce and fire inspector Thomas jumping in beside her. Bomb disposal carefully wading through the reeds and thickets, taking there time in disarming the rpg laying in the brush.

✳✳✳✳✳✳✳✳✳✳✳✳✳✳✳✳✳✳✳✳✳✳✳✳✳✳✳

Addenbrookes was not a hospital, well it is, but not to Matt meadows, it was a maze, or a better description a city within a city that housed a maze within a maze filled with misleading maps and unending floors and levels and elevators that appeared to go side ways instead of up or down. In short, the place was hard to navigate, and hard to get too.

Even if matt had driven, which he couldn't for his wife had taken the only working vehicle he had access too, he still would have struggled. For parking at Addenbrookes was like winning the lottery, do it enough times and still you loose, the occasional win giving you some hope but still, finding a parking space was usually a one in a million chance, so luckily at least, Matt had not driven, instead, he had cycled to Fordham, and caught a bus to Cambridge, the city being where the hospital was.

The journey had taken a lot of time, much more than intended, for firstly he had just missed the bus going form Fordham, arriving just a minute late to catch it, having to wait another hour for another to come by, then when he had got onto it, the notorious main roads to the city had become congested, an hours journey taking nearly four, the traffic blocked in both directions due to some pile up somewhere, which happened quite frequently, or so he was told by his bus driver, who tried to explain away the reason for the delays, "happens all the time" he had shrugged, "unless you want to walk there your stuck on here" he had joked, the comments making Matt even the more angry, his rage being taken out on the bus hand grips of the seats, his fingers frantically pinging a tune on the metal, until finally he had arrived.

From his diesembarkation point he then had to jump onto another bus running directly to the hospital, which had caused some annoyance as the same thing happened, the vehicle becoming bogged in traffic, the journey taking another hour or so, his feet finally happy to land on the grounds of Addenbrookes hospital, though that had not been the end of it.

For he had been told Harvey was at accident and emergency which was easy enough to find, but on arrival he had been told his frend had been moved to the cardiac ward, which the receptionsit had circled on a small map and handed to him, was at a different section of the hospital. So even with the map, Matt had found himself lost, going up different flights of satirs and asking nurses and doctors, all giving helpful directions that eventually after half an hour of searching, brought him to the correct ward.

The receptionist had guided him to the correct bed, and so after hours of trying to get to his friend, he found him. Laying in a hospital gown with large bruises on his face, a large bandage on his head, Pete sitting next to him, both looking as Matt approached them, "here he is" Harvey joked slightly, "christ don't ever come to my funeral will you, be a day late" he smiles,

"traffic" matt shrugs, looking at his friend, "what the hell happened?" he asks, Pete looking slightly worried at the question, "caught him dealing" Pete says, Harvey nodding slightly, "just like you warned" he says, looking at Matt,

"you alright?" he asks, sititng beside his friend in an empty chair beside his bed, "besides the heart attack and mild concussion?" Harvey jokes, "fine mate" he smiles, "heart attack?" Matt asks, "don't..."his friend says, "too many fags or something" he murmours,

"when you getting out?" matt asks, pete looking at him, "they said he got to stay a few days, do some scans on this" he says, tapping his friends bandaged head, "check the heart is pumping properly too" he adds, "doubt they'll find anything in there then" Matt says softly, "stupid fool" he smiles,

"yeah…" Harvey admits, his voice sounding to hold a tremble to it, "Scooter and Crusher thought so to" he sighs, Matt looking at his friend pete, the mans eyes shooting him a warning glance, "you havent told anyone?" Pete asks quickly, Harvey looking at him with a dry smile, "think im a grass now?" he says, the question hanging with no answer coming from pete, "course I havent…not going to either" he says,

"well that should keep your friends happy" Matt says to pete, his eyes accsuing as he stares at him, "you're my friends" Pete says, "and you don't look happy to me", "this is what you want to be part of though" matt says slightly angrily, "putting boys in hospital beds", "oi" Harvey says, "who you calling a boy?"

"well if he wasn't selling drugs…" pete says defensively, "then what?" Matt says, "he wouldn't be in here?" he scoffs, "well he wouldn't" pete says firmly, "I think you'll find it was the smoking" Harvey says, cutting inot the argument, "wasn't the club gave me a heart attack was the fags" the comment making pete and matt stop there bickering, "anyway…" he adds, "just did it the once, hardly merits my home being destroyed"

"well I can get that cleaned" Matt says with a sigh, "try and get it ready for you when you get back" "feed chester?" he asks, thinking of his tortoise left without any food in his garden, "yeah I'll feed the tortosie too" Matt chuckles lightly, "you might have some fresh turtle soup when you get back too" he laughs, Harvey chuckling with pete joining in,

"so your alright?" Matt asks, his voice going sincere, "yeah" his friend smiles, "good looking nurses and free meals" he shrugs, "should sell weed more often" he jests, the joke making Pete groan slightly, "well," he says, " I need to get back" he says, patting his friend on the shoulder, "need a lift Matt?" he asks, "yeah…" matt says softly, Harvey grabbing his friends hand, "I heard about kim " he says, his words gentle as he talks to his friend, matt looking at pete and his gentle shrug suggesting that had been a conversation topic to fill the hours in between scans and tests, "best thing to happen to you mate" Harvey smiles, Matt sighing and tapping his friends hand, "just focus on getting better mate" he says, standing up, "I'll have the house ready for you in a couple of days",

The two men said there goodbyes to there friend, saying a polite thank you to the receptionist and leaving the ward, taking the long and wide cooridors to the lifts, going down to the bottom floor and finding there way to the exit, the car park ahead of them filled and overflowing with beeping cars as frustrated drivers vied for parking spaces, "guess you got to get back to your friends then" matt says, as they approach Petes car, "no" he says firmly, clicking the button on his keys, the car flashing as it unlocks, "I just left him up there!" he says stubbornly, "no friends of mine" he says, opening the car door and getting in.

"but you think he had it coming" Matt says, sitting in the seat next to him, "if your going to be like this you can get out and walk" Pete moans, starting up the engine, "am I wrong?" Matt asks, his tone accusing, "he sold weed matt" Pete says firmly, "I mean you know…not in Isleham…" he says, shaking his head, " so you get a slap on the wrist and carted away by police" Matt says angrily, "not put in a bed", "you want me to defend them!" Pete says, "I mean come on mate," he pauses, "its how things are done, you never moaned of it before" "everyday " Matt says, "me and Harvey moaned about it, everyday" he says firmly, "well maybe that's why you only got me and him as a friend" pete replies coldly, "besides you only ever met once a week" he scoffs,

"you know what.." matt grunts, climbing out the car, "I'll find my own way back" he says closing the door, "oh come on Matt" pete shouts, slightly opening his car door, "don't be stupid!" he calls after him, "fine!" he maons, slamming the door shut again, reversing the car out, two vehicles waiting to grab the now free spot, a blare of horns as pete drives off, one of the cars getting to the spot first Matt walking with a huff towards the bus stop he had previously arrived at, coming to rest against the glass of the waiting area as he groans, "christ, losing friends fast"

****

The evening had been raucous, the rising sun pub filled with hundreds, its car park overflowing with people holding glasses of beer and cider, glasses of wine and different spirits. Mixers and straights of rum and coke and the odd fine malt in the hands of those wishing a more pleasant and calm sip rather than those around them, that downed there drinks with an unholy thirst, running back to the bar and waiting in the ten man thick queue for more drinks.

It was fair to say, the rising sun pub, could suitably accomadate half the number at a push and leave people waiting nor more than a few minutes for service. However with nearly a thousand descending on the place, every square inch was fought over, every seat taking two upon it and the row of cushioned benches lining the walls crammed with dozens where usually it would sit ten or less. The pub itself was divided into five main areas, the car park out the front, a medium room with a pool table greeting you as you enterd to a door on your right, the room having the usual slot machines and a small opening to the larger section of the pub, the main area. Large with a dart board and having ten tables and plenty of chairs and a small staging area for a band to play, a dining area just off to the left of the main bar area, able to house two dozen diners, a garden out back with a childs play are and more seating. Usually the place was full, and had always been accommodating to the large numbers that often drank there, however this night was the exception. With a dozen thick que for drinks and barrels running dry within moments of being put onto the taps, the whiskey and spirit bottles emptying quicker than they could be replaced.

It had been busy, and at the same time, a great night for all involved, as people sung and spoke fondly of titan, as people plied the mans parents with drinks and everyone embraced everyone, the night had gone well, although stripper certainly felt it could have done with one slight adjustment. The figure of kim hanging to his neck for all to see, was a particular annoyance. One he had tried to subtly solve, every now and then going to the toilet or sneaking off to talk to another group far from where he had left her sitting, each time his plan failing, as she would quickly find him and return to putting a loving arm around his waist, a motion that crusher and ripper had greatly enjoyed, constantly joking about wedding bells and the man most likely getting laid to the same girl for the rest of his life.

Crushers own wife, jillian had visited briefly to show her respects, as had marge, the two staying a short while before returning home, Jillian offering to pick up Kims son from school and look after him for the evening, an offer that had made Stripper wince, for he had hoped it the perfect excuse to end Kims display of public affections towards him, however, his suggestion Todd needed his mother was quickly overruled by Jillians generosity, "oh please let me have him" she had said with a kind voice, "besides his mother needs to unwind" she had winked, and the matter had been settled, to crusher and rippers laughter, and too Strippers dispair.

Marge had been quite kind really, on hearing about Kims seperation from Matt and her desires towards stripper, very little judgement had come from her, though she couldn't resist a little dig at the biker when seeing the two holding each other in the middle of the overcrowded pub, "so nice our saviours look after victims of failed marraiges" she had jested, her smile making stripper shudder slightly, "thank you" he had said, leaving the matter there, "well must be off, to busy for me" Marge had said, "my respects Stripper", "thank you" he had responded, this time his voice acknowledging he actually took what she said on board .

"you don't mind?" Kim had asked frequently, "little old me hanging around with you" she had said playfully, the question having no easy or truthful answer to it, "no" he had said for the tenth time that evening, "happy to have you" he had lied, "oh you'll have me later if you want" she had jested, the comment not helping to stem the laughter from crusher and ripper, the two following the couples conversations with great interest, "well, I just got to sort something out..." he had said, seeing Ratchet chatting up Anne in the far corner, "crusher" he had said, gesturing for the man to follow him, "ripper, keep her company for a bit would you?" he had asked, Ripper grabbing kims hand playfully, "oh don't you worry,. Pres" he had joked, "not going anything to happen to mrs stripper" he winked, Stripper rolling his eyes as him and crusher approached Ratchet,

"well the best I've had is seven inches.." anne had been explaining to a smiling ratchet, the man ever so slightly red in the face as Anne spoke quite playfully in his ear "but I wouldn't mind seeing what you got to offer" she had said, her hand moving towards his softer areas, "ratchet" Crusher had asaid, the two looking up at the approaching Stripper and crusher, "anne go" Stripper had said, "to be continued" she had whispered into his ear, walking away with a smile, pressing amongst the throng of people as she tried to get herself another drink,

"whats up pres" the Scottish man had smiled, watching annes thin body press between people as she struggled towards the bar, "your causing me problems ratchet" Stripper had said, pulling the man up carefully and leading him out the pub, the three men taking the front exit and walking a bit down the road passed the car park, to where no one was listening, "problems pres?" Ratchet had asked, Crusher looking at him with a serious expression, "you were meant to get the garage to cooperate" Crusher said firmly,

"I was going to" Ratchet had shrugged, "was going to talk to him thought id get my bike done whilst I was there" he says innocently, "man said he had an interview to do so I left them to it, was going to talk to him after but you know…" he shrugged again, "he failed ol thumper" he scoffs, "can you imagine"

"you go talk to a mechanic and instead you get an m.o,t" Stripper had mocked, "I knew I should have gone myself" he sighs, "too busy getting over that mary" Ratchet had joked, the comment not making anyone laugh, "look…" ratchet had said, "I offered two hundred to pass the bike, he wouldn't even take that" he says with a loud groan, "I mean if he wont take a simple bribe then he aint gonna want to set up shop with us" he concludes, his logic slightly falwless, yet still had been iritating to hear, "if we got no garage, then we got no income!" Stripper had hissed, the sound making Ratchet suddenly sober up, "you said he was a good lad Crusher, you said he wasn't holding onto the past" the pres had moaned,

"said he was a good mechanic" Crusher corrected him, "handy man to go into business with, obviously his son is still on his mind.." he had added, "well now that good lad needs a shaking" Stripper had said fiercely, "he's already had the police round his, who knows what he might have told them", "could just leave him" Crusher said, "he cant tell em anything that can hurt us, only ratchet here offering a bribe, stupid bastard" he had said, slapping his friends head, the Scottish man not even flinching, "yeah and now every mechanic in that shop will tell everyone

they know you can stand against the VigilanteS without repercussions"
Stripper had scoffed, "a garage openly telling one of my boys to sod off,
and not wanting to have a single chat about a business venture neither,
Titan murdered, boys selling weed on my streets" he had moaned, "I got
to get a handle on this crusher" he said firmly, "I cant…we cant let the
club become something that can be risen against" he had said firmly,
"rightly or wrongly, that garage owner poses a threat"

"could just buy a house pres" Ratchet had offered, "turn it into a
workshop", "oh yeah and you see any cheap houses for sale?" Crusher
had sneered, "cost too much now the village is considered safest place in
Cambridgeshire", "we just run it from our garedn sheds and workshops
then" Ratchet had offered, the president not looking amused, "great
fourteen different points of operations, what could possibly go wrong" he
shook his head, "we need a legitimate business lads" he had said, " forget
Fordham" he concluded, shaking his head, "we set up shop there now the
police will be our first customers" he had sighed, "but we still need to
send a message" he had declared, staring hard at the Scottish biker,

"you screwed this one up so you can be the one to do it" Stripper had
ordered firmly, "tomorrow night, you shake em but don't hurt them",
"with the police crawling around there?" Ratchet had protested, "well if
your caught you were angry about your bike being failed" Crusher said
firmly, the Scottish man just looking away, "think it's a bit harsh to be
honest pres" he had finally said, "we meant to be keeping peace in
Isleham not shaking honest men from Fordham"

"the village that neighbours ours you mean" stripper had snapped, "the
village everyone here passes through to go to work or to go to get there
cars done? Can you imgaine what chaos could spread if stories of
standing up to us spread back to our own streets? Especially coming from
Bruce jaggard" "you were up for it last night" crusher had added, "its
just.." Ratchet paused, his expression quite sad, "the funeral and
everything… maybe we should focus on this bazooka boy" he had
shrugged, "you let me and crusher worry about that" Stripper had said,
"you do what your commanded" he had added strongly. "aye pres, I will
have a chat with him then," he had said, holding his hands up, "make sure
he don't go blabbing about nothing".

And so the conversation had ended, the three returning to the pub, the
hundreds still lining up for there drinks as Kim found stripper and put her
arm back round his waste, the laughter erupting form the club members
again. The night had drawn on, until finally it had come to a close, the
parents of titan saying a fond farewell to stripper and the club, giving a
large embrace as they said there thanks and goodbyes, a taxi the club had
paid for waiting to take them back to the train station, the train they had
also bought tickets for waiting to leave the platform, ready to take

whoever aboard back on a long journey to scarborough.

The club had sent the parents on there way, and had hugged each other and said there goodbyes, each going there own way back to there homes, crusher and Stripper and kim walking back towards crushers, Anne unsurprisingly hanging onto Ratchet as he made his way home . "hell of a send off" Crusher had said proudly, as they walked towards his home, kim hanging onto the presidents arm as he agreed, "yeah hell of a turn out" he had smiled, "everyone loves you" kim had said playfully but honestly, "would you expect any less than the thousands to turn up?", "true" Crusher had agreed, looking at stripper awkwardly walk, his footsteps muddled by too much drink and the young lady holding onto him, "not the only good turn out either" he winked, Kim smiling at him, Stripper ignoring the gesture as they reached the front door of crushers home.

"well, good night then" Crusher had said, nodding at his brother and walking up the stairs, leaving stripper alone in the hallway with kim, "so…shall we" she had said, kissing the mans lips and feeling her hands up and down his chest, "another night," Stripper had replied, gently pulling away, "too much to drink…" he offered as a lazy excuse, "besides your son needs to go to school in the morning", "okay.." kim had mumbled, slightly upset, "another time then" she had said, taking the stairs and looking at him for a final glance, "just buried a friend" Stripper shrugged, "no..I understand" she had sighed, walking up the stairs, "goodnight then", "good night" the man had smiled, waiting until she had walked away, the door of the room she was staying in closing behind her, "ah titan" Stripper had groaned, rubbing his face with the palms of his hands "the hell am I going to do?".

****

Chapter 4

Thursday morning had been as it always was, another day just like the ones before it, the village awaking at different times, cars driving off to there jobs, people walking there dogs and popping to the shop, pints of milk and loaves of bread in there bags, it had been like most days, though many of the villagers were nursing hangovers from the night before, the day went as often it would, without a hitch.

For matt, it had started with awaking and feeling annoyed, for he had something he needed doing, and that was an unsual feeling for him, as his alarm clock on his phone souned an early call, his hand striking the thing and turning the alarm off, his feet hitting the floor as he rose out of bed. Walking to the bathroom and cleaning his teeth, he turned on the shower, along with the radio, a song playing as he scrubbed the whites of his mouth and spat out the remains of mint scented flem down the plug hole of the sink, "got a feeling, today goona change me" the song sang, a young ladies voice sounding with a light viloin behind her, the tune melodic and soothing, though it did little to lift matts mood, as he undressed and climbed in the shower, "for I have found my love, and it feels so strange to see" the voice sings, Matts hand finding the tuner on his radio, changing the song to something a bit heavier, the power chords of extreme metal sounding as he rinses his hair, "hail the eternal betrayal, slayer of the thing and dreams we don't sing, the total absolution as satan arises, hail the newly crowned, hail the new king" it roared, the power rift behind it unsettling him as he scrubbed, his fingers finding the raido and switching it over, a news story on.

"police have announced the capture and detainment of the one the press have called bazooka boy…" the news reporter reads out, the words meaning little to matt, "shame" he groans, running shampoo through his hair with his fingers, his beard catching the bubbles as it forms a white mass around his lips, his hand swiping it away, "a leading detective on the case that has seen the killing of a motorcycle gang member has said they are as yet unable to question the suspect, who they have yet to name, as he has stated the suspect, who can be confirmed to be a young lady in her mid twenties has needed close psychological supervison throughtout the night, the detective confirming they will begin questioning now she has been deemed stable , the questions due to beginlater today…" the radio switches off, as Matt rinses the last of his hair, turning the shower off and beginning to dry himself,

Once he was dry, he got dressed, a small red shirt and black jumper, medium blue trousers and fresh pants and socks, or as fresh as he could recall, for he seemed to remember them having sat there for a while, as he pulls them on his mind thinks on Harvey, hoping his firend was okay, hoping he was being well looked after. He walks down the stairs, looking in at the lounge as the tv still sounded, the chefing kids programme mixy airing another episode, the programme about finished as the live audience cheer, the kids presenter in all his finery smiling as he held up a batch of fresh muffins, "and so kids, no present is more meaningful than one made by your own hands, because as we say here" the pixy looking chef says, the dolphin called scrumpy walking over and joining hands with him, or flipper in this case, the two starting to sing, "I love you so I made a cake, that's how good friendships made…" matt scoffing as he walks away, entering the kitchen.

He hadn't smoked for a while, the tobacco pouch and rolling papers sitting unused on the side, in truth he hadn't had a smoke since Monday night, the urge seeming to just evaporate from him, the sight of the tobacco not stirring any strong desire to light one up. He had thought of throwing it away, of saying to himself he had so nearly killed himself that it didn't matter, "why smoke when your going to die anyway?", he had asked himself, the question more an angry admittance that he just didn't care about much anymore, smoking be the least on his mind.

Harvey however, was ever present in his brain, his friends bruised face haunting him, his promise ever looming in his thoughts, as he quickly grabbed a spare key, one his friend hand long ago lended him to his bungalow, for eight years the thing never needing to be used, until now.

And so it was he opened his front door, and closed it behind him, walking along the pavement of pound lane, passing the graves of the old church in the warm sun, the griffin pub opposite to him seeming lifeless and still, the morning still being too early for anyone to have reason to be there. Rounding the corner he walked alongside the fence of the old church, passing the main wooden gated entrance of it, walking passed an old antique dealers house, years ago a shop, long since closed and converted to a home.

The walk didn't take long, passing another church and then walking passed a cemetery, the red bricks of the outlying walls running parallel to the pavement for a few hundred steps, Matt taking the second right as he passed the grave stones, walking down a road to a group of bungalows, Harveys home being instantly recognisible, for the fact blue and white police tape was across the door, though it was slowly being romoved by two young officers, both of who watched him approach, as they piled the crumpled tape inot the boot of there car, a young blonde policewoma smiling as matt aproached, "help you sir?" she asked,

"Harvey sent mc" he said, holding up the key in his hand, "saw him in hospital last night, asked me to tidy up a bit for him" he said, his eyes not really making contact with the officers, "well, we're done here, your friend wont give a statement, says he flipped out and threw everything about before having a heart attack" she smiles, "not particualry believable is it?" she askcd, looking for a reaction from Matt, "he has his moments" he shrugs, "well we confiscated the cannabis plants too" she says firmly, "gonna be talking to him about that" she says with some authority to her voice, Matt shrugging again, "made a mistake" he simply offers,

"anything you want to add maybe? Something he might have said in hospital or…?" she smiles politely, "like he said, he flipped out and had a heart attack", "well he phoned for an mbulance but was cut off before the call could be traced" she says softly, "lucky your mate found him this morning" she says, "don't think you'll be needing that" she says, pointing at the key in matts hand, gesturing to the busted lock on the front door, the thing hanging slightly crooked from its hinges,

"must have given the door a good kicking too" the other officer says, the young man closing the boot of the car, "from the outside" he says, the statement falling to deaf ears as Matt just shrugs again, "like I said he flip.." "yeah we know" the officer says, "well we're finished here, locksmith will be round this evening to secure the place" he says, getting in the car, his colleague doing the same "give us a call…mr?" the young blonde policewoman says, "meadows, Matt meadows" he says weakly, "well if you hear anything regarding this matter" she pauses, "please give us a call" she says, closing the door as the engine starts, matt watching as the officers drive away.

He walked into the property, and as messes go, it wasn't as bad as his own home. A shattered tv screen and some scattered dvds, a broken fish tank, it wasn't that bad. The only odd thing the small chalk lines scattered around the carpet of the living room at the base of the tank, there outlines depicting various shapes and sizes of what he assumed were the fish that had once lived in the tank, shattered glass mainly sitting in the base of the thing, a few shards having fallen onto the floor, the bodies of the fish matt presumed having been removed by the inspecting police officers, though what they did with them was anybodies guess.

It wasn't bad, he had concluded, getting to work picking up the dvds, stacking them onto the shelves above the broken telly, the job took a short while, then he moved onto picking up the glass and tossing it into the tank, picking it up by its base and carrying it through to the kitchen, placing it on the worktop as he saw a shattered kettle and mircowave on the floor, a thin dust on there surfaces where he assumed the officers had been searching for prints. Grabbing a large bin liner from a drawer he put the appliances into it, then opening the back door, placed the sack into a large wheely bin, walking back and doing the same with the fish tank, ignoring the clear white lettering saying 'no household goods, general waste only"

He found a dust pan and brush next, sweeping up the remains of the mess, small bits of glass and plastic being thrown in after the sack into the bin, the whole thing took about an hour, if that. Next he went to the bathroom, trying not to scoff as he saw the floating form of a goldfish sat in the basin of the toilet, giving the handle a good flush he looked at the bath, black and grimey as though soil had once filled it, so he set to work with a sponge, cleaning the thing. bringing it back to its original colour. And that was that. The home was fit for purpose again, save the shattered tv, to which matt didn't want to move, thinking his friend would probably want a new one, he darkly mused on Harvey returning the broken one to the shop, demanding a refund saying it was faulty.

The matter now remained, of chester the horsefield tortoise. Matt coming to stare at him from the kitchen window, the creature scraping at the chicken wire mesh of its enclosure, looking hungry. "what the hell do you eat anyway?" he pondered, turning round to look in the fridge, the thing bare and empty, his eyes catching the sight of the cupboard doors, swinging them open and finding a box of hoop shaped cereal, "do torotises eat cereal?" he typed on his phone, the answer coming up with mixed opinions on the matter, the main response being they preffered a salad based diet, mainly cabbage and plenty of variety of veg and some fruit, "well…" he groans, tapping his pockets, "I got about a pound to my name" he sighs, stepping out to garden, "sorry buddy" he says, seeing the toroise clawing more energetically at the wire mesh, the creature apparently determined to break out and find its own meal.

Matt looked at the fencing, noticing to his left the fence only stood half a mans height, walking over to it and leaning over, "hey there!" he shouts, "anybody home", no answer coming, matt noticing the back door was slightly left ajar, "got a hungry tortoise" he says, climbing the fence, really not caring he was now technically committing a crime, "hello!" he calls, stepping through the neighbours garden, his hand pulling open the back door. No answer, as he steps in, "sorry to disturb" he says, "anyone home?"

The home was empty, yet it was most definitely not lacking, matt was amazed, as he stepped into the kitchen, the place holding more jars of spices and herbs he had ever seen, a gas fired cooker and an ice making refridgerator, the knives in there block looking proffessional and the surfaces of the worktop gleaming, "can I just pinch some lettuce?" he asks, checking to see if anyone was home, walking through to the lounge and bedroom respectively, quickly returning to the kitchen once he had made sure the coast was clear, "I'm just going to borrow some things" he says, opening the fridge, the thing packed with an array of meat and vegetables, matt smiling as he finds a lettuce, pausing as he sees tomatoes and a cucumber, "salad based" he muses, pulling out the ingredients and finding a chopping board, the knife cutting away at the greenery, as he finds a large china bowl and places the ingredients into it.

Now it should probably be agreed, that what was transpiring was completely illegal, it goes without saying that breaking into a home and making oneself a salad is never a lawful venture, yet for matt he had gone passed the point of caring, a marriage down the pan and a friend in hospital after a violent assualt may well cloud a persons judgement, but add to that the fact he had not long tried to kill himself, and somehow, the whole experience had made him feel free. Standing in a kitchn as fine as he had ever seen, in a small and comfy home with no visible signs of trauma, the feeling his actions were helping a friend in need and the motion of preparing a salad with fine knives he had never held before and, he felt a small burst of joy, from the thrill of it all.

Cutting the tomatoes he gladly found the phone that was ringing in his pocket, his voice quite calm as he answered, "matthew meadows?" the voice asked, "that's me" he smiled, placing the phone between his shoulder and his ear, continuing to slice the red fruit, "Dean here, from the job centre" "ah yes dean…" matt sighed happily, placing the tommatoes in the bowl and moving onto the cucumber, "I understand you didn't turn up for our chat we had arranged, the one with the gp" the voice says sternly, "any reason for this?"

"a friend of mine was hopsitalised" matt says, his voice serene as he cuts the vegteable into lengths, then slicing the lengths into small chunks, "well I am sorry to hear that" Dean says, "however you should have called to rearange it, as such my bosses have taken this as a step to far on your part" the voice explains, matt not really listening as he brushes the chunks into the bowl, his eyes scanning the fridge as he opens it again, finding some cheese and a red onion, pulling them out and finding a grater under the sink, placing the untensil on the chopping board, grateing the block of cheese,

"we have tried to help over the years and each and every time there has been an excuse for missed meetings or missed days at work, so as such.." Deans voice says, Matt humming a tune in his head as he grates, "we have conceived the only way to help you is to set an example to you, missing a prearranged appointment when we took sympathy for you is absolutely a kick to the organisation and goes against the morals and practices by which we seek to help people who find themselves in similar tough situations" the voice continues, matt finishing his grating as he puts the grater to one side, sprinkling the cheese over the salad, "so I am afraid to say we are imposing a fine" dean says, the words making Matt snap out of it slightly, "a fine?" he asks, "your next job seekers allownace and housing benefit shall be halfed, also your wife has informed us your son no longer lives at your residence so your childs suport allowance has been stopped until we receive word he is living under your roof again"

"okay.." matt says, peeling the red onion and chopping it in half, his eyes watering, "I'm going to level with you dean, I have no money" he sighs, "none, barely a pound, wife took the bank card and I have no cash" he says, chopping the onion into little bits, "so I need that money, I need the usual payment to go into the bank on Friday so I can take my son out on the sat.." he tries to explain, Deans voice cutting the explanantion short, "I am sorry Matt, the company does not enjoy doing this believe me" he says honestly, "but you have forced us, so please take the warning and use it to find some new determination," he says, "we can discuss it further on Monday" he states, "Dean I've known you a long time now" matt says, "I mean we arent friends but we seen each other every week for about five years now", "im sorry mr meadows, but my bosses have already put the block on your next payment", dean says flatly, "please come in Monday and we will work a new way to overcome this" he adds, "dean.." matt says, brushing the chopped onion ontop the salad, his fingers doing a sprinkling motion as the dark purple and white flecks drop onto the top of the cheese, his hand mixing all the ingredients together.

"I am sorry" dean says, "well before you go…" matt says, opening a cupboard door and looking through it, finding a bottle of fine balsamic vineagar, removing the lid and sprinkling a few dashes onto the salad, "I just gotta say…you're a piece of shit" he says, hanging up the phone with a joyful huff, his eyes taking in his creation. The blue and white china bowl holding in its depth the crisp colours of bright green, suculant red and juicy dark green, purple flakes and bright yellow whisps of cheddar running through it. His dark thoughts well buried below his pride, his smile rising thick and broad, "well best play the good host" he says, walking over to the sink and filling it with warm water, squirting some washing up liquid into the mix, picking up the end of the unscd lettuce and walking to the fridge to return it the sound of the front door opening filling the kitchen.

A sudden panick grips matt as he hears the voice of a middle aged man talking to his wife as the door opens, matt panicking and looking at the salad bowl, not thinking he abandons it, still holding the lettuce in his hand he darts out the back door, quickly closing it behind him, with a leap he jumps the fence, falling to look at Chester the tortoise peering at him through the mesh of his enclosure, "oh damn it" Matt curses, leaning his hand through the tortoise run and picking the creature up, "come stay with me for a bit" he says, looking at the neighbours house and quickly running inside Harveys, opening the front door and tucking the tortoise under his arm, looking both ways to make sure he isn't seen, quickly running off down the road.

****

"and so the struggle this brave bird has faced continues" the news reporter said, the lady holding the microphone as he talks to the camera, the rspca man holding the bird again in his arms as he holds it steadily, a fresh new bandage on the grey herons chest, "two more operations and now it seems, the leg that was broken has yet to set properly, is there any hope for misty?" she asks, holding the microphone to the rspca mans mouth, the herons beak almost taking out his eye as it quickly tries to peck him, the man placing it down on the floor before him, the bird limply walking off, "well as you can see when she walks, her left leg is considerably weaker then her right" the man explains, the bird walking for the camera to zoom in on the small splint around the injured leg, "the vets have confirmed she will never fly again" he says sadly, "but they will reset the leg and if that is a success, she can live a quiet life at a local sanctuary" he explained, the reporter bringing the mircrophone back to her mouth, "misty the heron, a future in doubt, questions of recovery still needing answers, so to that of bazooka boy, who we are informed shall face her questioning today, the local police reporting that.." the tv cuts off, the police meeting room with the half dozen or so officers groaining and "awwing" as they spin round to face Detective bruce holding the remote in his hands.

"back to work" he says, putting the remote down on the desk in front of him, "now" he says, gathering all eyes and attention to him,"I will be leading the questioning, meanwhile I expect vigilance to continue, keep a presence in Isleham" he says, the young blonde officer looking at him, "but sir we caught bazo.." she tries, "but not the club" Bruce says forcefully, "and they are up to something, I can feel it," he says, "now fire inspector Thomas has returned to mildenhall to carry on his duties, his liason and support have been greatly appreciated, but just because the fire service conclude the matter dealt with, the police force, does not" he says, his words filling the meeting room, "so I will get a confession so I can relase the name to the press, and you will get me something on the VigilanteS, our superiors feel if there was a time to get them, it is whilst they are on the back foot"

"well.." the young blonde policewoman says, "we believe they just put a young man in hopsital" she ventures, "though he won't give a statement to that fact" she admits, "victims name?" the detective asks, "Harvey flint…" she goes to finish, interrupted by a large Scottish lady entering the room, "ah doctor Gloom" Bruce smiles, "our suspect passed your tests?" he asks, the large lady nodding, "she has calmed from her hysteria" she replies, "I can give you this In all confidence" she says, handing a formal looking bit of paper to the detective, "a pass for her mental state, she is now legaly fit for interview", "my thanks" Bruce smiles, the Scottish doctor leaving the meeting room.

"chase all leads on this Harvey flint, see what it unearths" he says to the room, "ill see what I can get out of our bazooka bo.." he pauses, "actually that should be gril shouldn't it" he sighs, "gotta name everything now" he groans, leaving the room, an officer leaning over and flicking the tv back on, the picture of the heron walking about on its injured foot filling the screen, the officers letting out an 'aww', "back to work!" the voice of Bruce echoes into the meeting room, the offciers jumping to it and quickly going about there business.

Yesterday had been a long one, having caught the suspect and bringing her to the station she had become irratic, a madness seeming to take ahold of her, arms thrashing and spittle running down her chin, her fury at being caught increasing when she had seen her father marched into the police station in hand cuffs, the man charged with the posession of the rocket propelled grenade. It had taken all day, and all night to calm the situation, the young lady kept in a holding cell, her voice shouting to her father, crying that she was sorry, that she was a shame to the family, bust most worryingly, she had threatened to end her existence.

The checks had gone from every fifteen minutes, a police officer continually keeping an eye on her to her becoming a one to one case, an officer sitting in the cell at all times, keeping watch on her and trying to calm the situation, it hadn't worked. The night becoming later and later as finally the call was made for a phsychologist to intervene, the Scottish doctor, dr gloom arriving in her cell, working her magic and calming the young lady, Mary eventually gaining some form af rest, if only for an hour or so.

The question had then arisen, of Marys capacity to be questioned safely, without harm coming to anyone or her causing any to herself, a prcosess that had taken all morning, and though lorazcpam was on the table, a drug that could be prescribed to help the most enraged find calm and tranquillity, it had not been deemed necessary by the doctor, the Scottish lady finding mary had become more calm as the situation sunk in, and so after many tests and questions, it had finally come to pass, that the young lady was ready for questioning. A fact detectvie Bruce was all too glad to hear, keen to get some answers to nagging thoughts he had. His hand pulling the handle on the interrogation room, stepping through to sit before the young lady, her long red hair drooped across her face, her hands in handcuffs, though not too tight they were secured by a bolt to the table, a precaution the detective had had to get signed permsission for, though on seeing her so calm, he had wondered whether it had been worth the extra paperwork.

"mary" he says, sitting down on the chair in front of her, wresting his hands on the table, "I am detective inspector Bruce Turnpike, I have been leading this case" he says, looking as one of the young officers brings him a small case file, the officer leaving and closing the door, "I am glad see to you have scttlcd" he says honestly, "gave us quite a fright through the night" he says, Mary smiling at the rhyme, "so…where to begin?" he taps his fingers on the table, "what will happen to dad?" mary asks, her voice quite soft, the question full of concern,

"well, under the firearms regulations" Bruce sighs, "he's looking at life imprisonment" he says honestly, " I.m, ah..I'm sorry" he says, "we will of course try to help him, we will give full account of his co-operation in this matter," "so what?", mary smiles, "he might get a year off for being helpful, twenty four years instead?" she smirks, "mary…I'm sorry, the man had an unlicensed arsenal…" "oh please" she says, "he never hurt anyone, just kept the damn thing as a memento….still he could plead insanity, all them bloody stories he tells sure a judge will believe him", "maybe.." Bruce smiles slightly, "the fact he got them back in the country is impressive….but then airport security was slightly laxed back then" he admits,

"well, sure he will enjoy the socialising in prison" mary smiles, "plenty of people to tell stories too", "indeed…" bruce nods, "you will of course be kept informed of your fathers trial" he says, his words sounding kind to marys ears, "and me?" she asks, "what happens to me?"

"do you admit to killing a man named tobias grimwald? A man known as titan of the VigilanteS motorcycle club?" Bruce asks, "I do" Mary nods, "the bastard had it coming" she says pointedly, Bruce feeling a tingle on the back of his hands, "you meant to kill Titan?" he asks, "well I shot him with a grenade launcher so…" she shrugs, her smile somewhat chilling, "you weren't aiming for Stripper then?"

"he was next on the list, all of them were" she says darkly, "stripper especially, home wrecker!" ahe sneers, "but why Titan?" bruce asks, "why any of them? Stripper I understand the motive but…" "they think they're our saviours" she cuts in, "and I had the perfect shot to kill them all!"her voice getting angry, "lined up in the perfect row"

"you killed titan so you could have a shot at all of them?" bruce asks, the surprise in his voice making mary smile and calm from her growing rage, "he visited strippers every night, same time, same place" she chuckles, "it was an easy mark"

"but why?" bruce asks, leaning in and softening his tone, "why kill the VigilanteS? What had they done to you?", "to me?" she laughs, "besides ruin my village and ride out the VendettaS" "the VendettaS? You knew them?"

"everyone knew them, scum to a man" she sighs, "but if you knew them like I did, they were friend to anyone who wanted to be", "you were..in a relationship? With one of them" he asks, "not everything is about sex detective" she smiles, "no, I was one of the few, that felt home was home with them around, then the VigilanteS came," she sneers, the detective opening the file before him, a picture of a young man being pulled out, a bearded man, with long ginger curls and a broad smile, his waistcoat identifying him as a VendettaS member, "Karp," he says, pointing at the name tag on the mans chest, "so called for his love of fishing, "went missing a month or so after the VigilanteS turned up, case was never solved" he says gently, "was the son of your uncle, a Bruce jaggard, your cousin"

"oh the pieces are falling together for you arent they?" Mary says, looking the detective in the eyes, "been a long time coming, cost me my relationship, every night obsessing how to get even for karp" she says, her voice softening at the mention of her cousins name, "he was a good lad, never harmed anyone, had a thing for older women but that was his only fault" she cries slightly, "my uncle didn't understand the life, tried to get him back on the straight and narrow"

"the owner of Fordham garage, his son rumoured to be killed by the VigilanteS," he sighs, "no wonder he wont talk to us" he says, putting the picture of karp to one side, "so why sleep with Stripper? If you hated him so much?", "I was going to kill him" she says plainly, "took me back to his and I was going to slice his throat, but…I couldn't have gotten a chance at the funeral, not to take them all out together" she sighs, "I had secretly hoped it had been stripper at the lodge, but it was titan instead, didn't matter was going to kill him anyway" she shrugs softly, "if you had killed stripper the night you slept with him, you would have been the prime suspect" bruce nods, "but all this" he says, showing pictures of the body parts of Titan, "on the hope for a shot at the club gathered" he sighs, "seems unbelievable" "you got me" Mary jokes, no humour to her voice, "im a jilted lover, told she would have her hearts fancy and betrayed once her precious flower had been taken" she laughs, "or at least that's the more believeable truth I dare say the papers will print"

"all this for your cousin?" Bruce asks, avoiding rising to the foul joke, "not just for karp, but for Isleham, and Klaxon, and your own officer killed in the masacre of pattersons pass" she says calmly, "klaxon?" Bruce asks, looking at the notes in the case file, "the VendettaS member stabbed in the brawl" he sighs darkly, "suppose you knew him too?", "was going to be my lover…I had hoped " she smiles, remembering the tall mans manner and wit, "was a joker that one, a kind heart, before they arrived of course"

"so this is why your uncle said you had family problems" bruce states, "his son disappears and your boyfriend killed" he shakes his head, "wasn't my boyfriend, would have liked it, but klaxon needed working on first, wasn't the sort just to sleep with anybody" she says fondly, "uncle Bruce never understood Karps choices, but me and dad did, dad blaming himself for his disapearance" "blames himself? Why?" Bruce asks, "would help him fix his bike, helped him when he got in trouble, gave him a place to stay when he fell out with his father, never pressured him too much to leave the club, he knew it was a losing battle" she shrugs, "then one night he just…vanished, dad never forgave himself, never spoke to his brother again after a while, he just couldn't answer his questions, none of us could, but we knew…we all knew the VigilanteS had something to with it"

"these rumours? you believed them?" Bruce asks, "people don't just dissapear detective, you must know that," "but another rival gang?, there were a few in Isleham at the time…""ha." Mary scoffs, cutting in quick and sharp with the remark, "they shit themselves at my cousins club, none of them had the balls" she sneers, "it was the VigilanteS" she says, stating it as fact.

"all this time to get revenge, why wait five years?" Bruce asked, the question nagging at him, "Harvey" she smiled, "Harvey flint?", "yeah, Harvey flint.." she says, the fond memory of the mans face coming to her, as she spoke the name, "after klaxon and karp, I was..I was messed up, even thought of ending it all, but he, well he has a humour about him that is just too adorable" she muses, "he helped me through the tough times…but, it lasted only a few years" she sighs, tears coming to her eyes, "every joke and prank reminding me of Klaxon, and with his memory karps…" she trails off, "I tried to make a go of it…but I couldn't, night after night hearing the saviours patrol the roads, there bikes sounding like thunderous righteousness through our windows" she groans, "Harvey tried…he tried to help me best he could…but" she shrugs, moving her hand so the handcuffs rattled, the message read clear to the detective,

"did he know? Your hatred for the club?" Bruce asks, "he knew bits of it" she nods, "but not how far I would go…he never knew about dads weapons he is innoccent in all of this" she says quickly, "relax" Bruce says, holding up a calming hand, "he's got to answer for some cannabis found in his property, but…" he pauses, "he's not a part of the case against you" he smiles, "gone back to smoking it again has he?" she asks playfully, "I must of messed him up bad" she says, her eyes seeing a worried look in bruces face, "somethings happened to him" she says leaning forward all of a suddden, the movement making the dtective recoil slightly, "whats happened!" she demands,

"I suppose it is a duty to inform you, " he sighs, "Harvey is currently in addenbrookes hospital, after having a heart attack and aquired minor head trauma" he says, looking at the notes in the file, "we believe the VigilanteS are somehow involved", "bastards!" she yells, spitting on the table, "setting there own laws and thinking themselves judges!" she spits again, "bastards!"

"I promise you mary" the detective says, pressing a button under the desk, three large officers coming in to unlock the hadcuffs from the restraing bolt, helping her to leave the room as he kicks and thrashes, "bastards!" she spits, "I promise you I will keep you informed on Harvey" he says, the womans legs disappearing from the room as she is escorted out, her profanity filling the hallways, her screams too. The young blonde police woman coming into the interview room, "sir?" she asks, "you believe her?", "I do" he sighs, "I do, wait until she has calmed down, then charge her with the murder of tobias grimwald, and the conspiracy to commit further acts against the VigilanteS motorcycle club", "yes sir" she says, "and you sir?" she asks, bruce looking at her with an unhappy grin, "I'm going to keep at it" he says pointing at the phot of Karp, "cause this tale is far from done" he said, the long day drawing to a close.

A bloody salad, that was what the excited and confused mrs Finch had
ran over to crushers house to say, finding Stripper first thing in the
morning and insisting he come look at something terribly urgent. A
bloody salad. Browning and the leaves crumpled, the food looking near
ready to be chucked away, the blue and white china bowl sitting on the
kitchen side, as mrs Finch and her husband Nigel pointed at it frantically.
The conversation having taken about half an hour to get some form of
sense from,

"well I had rang July Dean and asked if she had been round doing
some of her cleaning again" mrs finch had said, "and she said she hadn't
been in at all yesterday, so we rang up our boys didn't we Nigel" she had
said, her husband nodding as his wife spoke, and spoke fast, "but of
course it wasn't them cuase they are trekking across Zimbabwe at the
moment, which in my panick I had totally forgotten" she had explained,
the large biker leaning against the kitchen worktop and folding his arms
as she spoke, "well you know, we had only popped out for Nigel to buy
some of his films, you know the big booby ones and the ladies that
scream when they getting a good curdling" she carried on, Nigel going
slightly red, "oh don't be embarrassed love" she had laughed, "ol stripper
seen it all before, used to do some yourself I hear" she said, playfully
poking the biker, the man giving Nigel a knowing look, Nigel avoiding
the conversation, "point is we were out an hour, maybe two" he said,
bringing the conversation back on track,

"so what?…" Stripper had asked, his hands stroking his face from the
tediousness of the conversation, "what is your point" he had said,
pointing to the salad, "well we didn't make it" mrs Fich said quickly, "I
mean night before last was ham night, we had some left over and were
going to do some eggs with it, oh and some nice home made chips too",
"sounds lovely mrs finch" Stripper had smiled, "but clearly you made a
salad" he suggests, "no don't you see dear?" she asks, her smile slightly
grating to Strippers eyes, "we been burglarised" she says, Stripper
laughing at the statement, "well that's just what marge did too" mrs finch
sighs, folding her arms, "you told marge?" Stripper asks, his tone
suddenly becoming concerned, "well I thought she might have popped
round, I mean she used to bring us fresh cakes and the like, a passion for
dining that one" she says with a wink, "but when I told her why I was
asking she laughed, I told her someone had obviously broken in and
mixed up a salad"

"and what did she say?" stripper smiled as he asked, "well she just
laughed, saying that we should forget the bazooka boy because the mixer

was loose", "the mixer?" stripper sighs, "everyone gotta have a name now" he groans, "well that's why I came to find you" mrs finch continues, "I have narrowed every possibility and all I can reasonably conclude is someone broke in, " she says,

"and mixed up a salad" he sighs, Nigel looking at the biker, a knowing glance being exchanged between them, "well…" stripper says, unfolding his arms, " I'm glad you brought it to my attention, the club is always here in times of need" he says, looking back at the salad, "you asked the neighbours? They see anything, didn't pop in to help themselves or anything like that?" he ventures, "well we asked Darren next door and he was out courting all day, although he didn't get very far, he's got a thing for that Anne of yours I'm told.." she says, Nigel coughing and prompting her to get on with it, "well I mean we could'nt ask Harvey anyway" she says, "what with the break in and his heart attack and all"

"break in?" Stripper asks, suddenly interested, "yeah happened couple of nights ago, apparently hes told the police he flipped out but we heard a tremendous banging and shouting didn't we Nigel, told the police as such too, they reckon it was a break in of some kind", "in hospital you say?" Stripper asks, his head shaking at the thought of it, "well…could be linked couldn't they" mrs finch says, "man tries to steal something from one neighbour then makes a salad in the next" she says, Stripper smiling as he steps away from the kitchen counter. "well, I will keep an ear open mrs finch" he smiles, planting a kiss on her forehead, "rest assured you will be protected from this…mixer" he smiles, giving a nod to Nigel as he walks out the kitchen, stepping through the lounge, the tv on the news channel, the reporters words catching his attention,

"so the identity of the Bazzoka boy has been confirmed today, moments ago the police releasing this statement" the man reading from a ledger as he quotes the report in his hands, "a mary Jaggard, from Isleham village Cambridgeshire has been charged with the murder of a tobias Grimwald, also receiving a charge for conspiracy to commit further acts of murder…" Stripper standing still in shock as the news fills his ears, "well you must be relieved" mrs finch says, patting the biker on the back, "caught your would be assasin" she says warmly, "a bit of good nes hey Nigel" she says, her husband nodding his agreement, "yeah..good news" Stripper mutters, the reporter continuing to read the ledger, "the details as to why mary jaggard killed the club member known as titan has not been released by the police, however certain papers and press representatives have said they have revealing facts from indpenedent sources saying it was most likely due to a love affair gone wrong", "oh god" Stripper sighs, stepping out the lounge and going through the main door, stepping out onto the small front garden path, "you will keep us informed, about the mixer?" mrs finch shouts after him, "as soon as I can mrs finch, good day" he says as politely as he can

His feet couldn't carry him fast enough, his legs going at all speed, his anger boiling as he raced down the road, his momentumn quickly taking him passed the red bricks of the cemetery walls, turning right at the old shop on the corner, passing the rising sun pub and charging towards crushers, his breath not leaving his body until finally he comes to the open garage door, Crusher and Scooter inside, both looking over the greeves motorcycle now on a small jack at the rear of the garage, "you bastards!" he roars, his face going red as crusher and scooter look up from there tinkering, the prospects face going red and his legs shaking, "whats up pres?" Crusher asks casually, unphased by the outrage before him, "Harvey flint?" he asks sourly, "was that who you roughed up the other night" he says, "yeah, you told us too" Crusher said, "you said youd leave it with me, so I sorted it, scooter too" he says, Stripper biting his lip as he points a dagger of a finger at them, "so that's why hes in hosptial then!" he roars, "when I said shake him you heard break him!"

"hey guys" marge voice says, the three looking at the garage door, a box of freshly made cakes in the ladies hand, "just come for a tea and a chat with the grils" she says, her smile causing Stripper to control himself, "oh lovely" Crusher says quickly, "jilian will love that, there just indoors, kims got a day off so Anne popped round too" he says, "I know" Marge says carefully, "that's why I popped round" she winks, "well leave you to it" she says, stepping away from the garage door, Stripper looking at the two men before him,"you stay low" he says fatly, "keep on that greeves" he says pointing at the bike, "do nothing but get her running til this blows over" he sighs, "god damn day!" he huffs, kicking a bucket beside him, all manner of soot and ash and sand falling out, "here pres" Crusher smiled, trying to lighten the tone, "you catch the news?", "don't you bloody tempt me crusher" stripper roared, walking towards the man, "everything going on my name is going to be a joke, the mans who ex lover tried to blow him up" he scoffs, Crusher smiling, scooter looking away and staying quiet,

The sound of a motorbike roaring and coming to stop at the garage door turned there attention away from the sure to ensue punch up, Ripper quickly jumping off the bike and running in, his face worried as he looked at the president, "what is it?" Stripper asks, hardly believing his day could get worse, "its Ratchet pres, he's in a coma" the men looking at each other in confusion, as the voice of crushers wife echoes through the open doors of the house

"marge!" jilian smiled, embracing her friend in her leopard print coat, the big blonde kissing the ladies cheek and joining anne and kim in the garden, the grils settling down for a nice pot of tea between them, "brought the muffins" she smiles, placing the box of freshly baked cakes on the centre of the table, "you seem a good mood there marge" kim smiled, kissing her friend on the cheek, anne doing the same, "well, just got me a burst of inspiration" she says, her voice all a flutter, as she grins, "just came out of nowhere on my way here, god be praised" she laughs, "oh another art piece then Marge" Jilian says warmly, "still havent seen the last one yet" she smiles, pouring the lady a cup of tea, "well, I shall have to get to work on it soon" marge smiled, "ooh the thought of it has made me all tingly" she laughs, "in all the right places too" she winks, the grils joining in the giggle,

"well keep us posted then darling" Anne says, winking back at the large lady, "oh I will" she smiles, "don't you worry about that", "so did you hear?" jilian asks, leaning in to speak in a slightly hushed voice, "mary was bazooka boy", "oh to think it" Kim sighs, "heard it on the radio, couldn't believe it" she says, "well ladies standing up for themselves helps create a fine portrait for artistic minds to consider" marge jokes, the ladies rolling there eyes, for they knew her mind was now permanently fixed on her new found project, "well stripper best watch himself round our kim" anne jokes, "mary had a bazooka but she got nothing on that temper of yours" she jests, the ladies sharing a giggle again, "well talking about tempers, I was talking to that mrs finch…you know the one who acts a saint but puts her husband in that leather garb with those pulleys and dildos" she says, kim almost coughing on her tea as she sips, "well she rang me yesterday, and you never guess what she told me"

****

The photos of the accident sat on the reception desk of the Fordham garage, the detective inspector Bruce Turnpike making sure the garage owner bruce had a good look at them, the pictures showing a twisted harley Davidson, the legs of a biker protruding from a recycling bin, his body seemingly submerged in its hold. The pictures weren't pretty, but the dtective wanted the owner to look at them all the same,

"why you showing me" bruce the garge owner said, looking away from the photographs, "well," the detective said, "looks like an accident to me, lost control or was speeding" he ventures, "coming to crash into the bins", "outside the chequers pub," Bruce pointed out, using his finger to point left of his own garage, "so it happened outside theres I would imagine"

"I think the person responsible would want you to think that true" the detective nodded, "but for a thing called basic investigation the culprit would have gotten away with it" he says, pointing at another picture, this one of the helmet removed from the riders body, "looks like a blow from something long and metal, funny to think the helmet showed no sign of indentation" he mused, "no brake marks either, nothing to indicate the bike had lost control"

"so?" bruce asked, his demeanour not changing at all, his voice and body language completely calm, "told that man to get his tyres and brakes checked, only a matter of time before he had an accident", "yeah.." the detective smiled, "strange to happen so late at night though, almost as though he was on his way to see someone, found a lump hammer in his saddle bag, strange thing to carry around wouldn't you agree?" he asks,

"you'd have to ask him" bruce shrugged, "I would" the detective said plainly, "but for the fact he was induced into a coma a few hours ago" he says, his voice filled with accusations, "your security cameras, working I presume?" he asks, pointing at the cameras, "we checked the petrol garage ones, somehow they weren't recording between twelve and one", "same problem here" Bruce shrugs, "must be a technical fault", "indeed" the detective smiles, "let me just float a theory" he says, leaning in on the desk, "this ratchet whos club you have somehow offended, comes to do what they like to call a 'shake up'" he quotes, "only to find you arent as unprepared as what he was hoping for", "good theory" Bruce smiles, "just needs some proof though"

"I know about your son" the detective says, the words making the garage owner flinch slightly, "bit strange, his rumoured killers now visiting you and ending up unconscious further down the road" the detective ventures, "my son, has nothing to do with this" he pauses, calming himself, and smiling, "if this ratchet, were to theoretically have come to shake me up, then why dump the body and make it look an accidnet" he asks, "why not just claim self defence"

"you come from a bikers family" the detective says, "you knew your sons ways well enough to know how to send a message, we might not be able to prove it was you, but the VigilanteS" he sighs, "they will know your meaning well enough"

"I have never done anything illegal in all my life, I could dare say the same about my son up to a certain point" Bruce says firmly, "now I built this place from a scrap heap to a legal and thriving place of business, and none…no matter there passed will take it from me" he says, leaning in to the detective, "so get your proof for your theory" he says boldly, "and good luck with it", "you may start a war here" the detective says, "if my theory is right that is, I would ask you to think on that before you submit your statement" he says, his voice genuine, "start one, I haved lived in one since my son joined…" he stops himself, looking away from the detective, "I give jobs to young boys and teach them a craft" he says, "I take them away from the easy streets and teach them something that will shape them to be greater men, and they…what do they do?" he shakes his head, "claim self defence?" he chokes on the comment, "so people will think they are untouchable? That they can threaten honest livings and still ride the roads free of the chains of trial and sentence?" he looks at the detective, "I submit my statement sir" he says, slamming a piece of paper down, "the mot report for ratchets bike, faulty brakes and worn tyres, advised to get them seen to as soon as possible" he scoffs, "the reason he crashed, was he didn't pay attention to the law!"

✳✳✳✳✳✳✳✳✳✳✳✳✳✳✳✳✳✳✳✳✳✳✳✳✳✳✳✳

"add some eggs and some flour, tis the time for mixies hour, chocolate chips and coconut, time to see what the chef is cooking up" the television sang, the live audience cheering as mixy the chef walked onto the stage, "see that" Matt said, staring at the tortoise chester as he roamed about on his lounge floor, "that's mixy, we like mixy," he says, staring at the toroise as its little head raises from the ground, seemingly staring at him as he speeks, "todd likes him too, that's my son by the way you'll get to meet him" he continues, as mixy starts singing a song, "what ingredients shall we use today, what's in the box we gonna bake?" the children sing and clap, the childrens chef pulling out a large box covered in a massive question mark, "I know what your thinking" matt says, watching the torotoise crawl towards him, "you're a grown man" he says in an exaggerated high voice, presuming if tortoises could speak theat is what they would sound like, although there voice would most likely be deep and slow talking, "what you doing watching kids shows"

"well mr tortoise" matt sighs, lifting the creature up and holding him with his palm resting under his body, his little legs sitting happy on the sides of his hand, his head raised towards matts nose, "that is a good question" he smiles, "I have no money, and I cannot change the channel" he says, pointing the torotoise to look at the snapped in half tv remote, "so what do I do on a Friday night without money or the means to watch what I want?" he asks the torotoise, the little green and yellow head slightly bobbing up and down, his claws starting to dig in matts hands as he tries to move away, "I watch this crap" he groans, using a finger to stroke chesters head, then popping him back down on the floor,

"oh we got some eggs" Mixie the chef cheers, the audience doing the same, "some butter too, oh and some milk and flour" he pauses, rifling through the mysterious box, pulling out items ten times the size they ought to be, "oh and some maple syrup" he cheers, pulling out a massive bottle from the box, "cant lie chester" matt sighs, "riveting stuff", his eyes watching as the tortoise crawls towards the tv, his head seeming to raise as his eyes reflect the light from the show, "sounds to me like your bored" the high squeek voice says, matt looking at the torotise with a nod, "oh you said it my friend, fed up too" "why not go out and enjoy yourself? it's a Friday night" the voice of chester says, the torotoise quite eerily turning round to look at Matt, his eyes filled with questions, "I havent got any money" matt says, watching mixy jump and down, "oh I got an idea" mixy cheers, "I know just what to make, I'll take what I got, and I'll make you all pancakes!" the audience cheering, "my god, pancakes! What a surprise" Matt mocks, pretending to clap,

"you could go out" matt says, doing the high pitched voice and looking at the tortoise, the creature turning back to roam around the lounge, "need money to have fun round here" matt scoffs, "a pound aint gonna buy me squat" he adds, "didn't stop you yesterday though" the high pitched voice says, matts eyes connecting with the tortoises, the creature seeming to hold the gaze, "you had fun then didn't you?" he asks slowly,

It was true, the tortoise was right. It had been fun, an unbridled peace and the rush to be in someone elses home, away from the clutter of hanging wires and reminders of a failed marriage, away from everything, just to be able to forget yourself and your cares, Matt knew what the creature was saying, though at this point it is doubtful whether matt knew the tortoise couldn't actually speak or not, the man seeming to descend into some kind of depression based lunacy.

"well, I got no food in the house" matt admits, looking at the clock on the wall, the time showing nine in the evening, "and most will be out for a drink or two" he smiles, "treat yourself" the high pitched voice of chester says, Mixy jumping up and down with a novelty frying pan as he throws and cathes large pancakes, the live audience laughing and clapping, "oh what a treat!" the chef laughs, catching the pancake in the pan, "oh what a treat I will have for you all to eat"

"whos most likely to be out though? I mean they could come back any minute" he sighs, putting a hand to his head, "stay there chester, don't eat the tv" he says, standing up and finding his shoes, pulling them on and going out through the back garden, opening the garage door at the side and throwing the switch, the garage filling with the flicker of the tubular bulbs, as he looks for his old work bag, finding a massive heap of old and failed projects of his on the shelves, different locks and door handles he once fitted, different mechanisms in there housing he had once practiced prying open, his work as a locksmith some years ago inspiring his hobby of lock picking, though it had only lasted a year or so. His father always having a massive panick attack when his colleagues asked him "so what is your son up to these days?"

Finding a small patch of fleece with a band around it, matt finds what he Is looking for, opening it up to find all manner of different sized picks, his head racing with the idea of what he was about to do again, his eyes resting on his fathers motorcycle bumper sticker, "when you care you are

chained, when you don't you are free", his smile to read it again
confirming to himself the words held new meaning, his mind racing as he
leaves the garage, closing the door behind him, "whos got the best
kitchen I wonder.." he asks himself, pausing for a moment, was that the
right question, he was hungry, he needed time to cook, so the question
was, who will be out the longest, "VigilanteS" he says to himself,
walking back into the kitchen and grabbing his door keys as he closes the
back door, the question had seemed dangerous when he pondered it, but
in truth it seemed the most logical.

They were always out on patrol, finishing at the rising sun at ten and
never leaving before eleven on a Friday night, it was the logical choice,
one of them would have to suffice, but who?, Matt pondered, walking to
his front door, Zoom was the obvious answer, the young prospect lived
quite close by but he lived with his mother and she was probably still in,
crusher was close, but matt had heard that was where kim was staying
and for the time being he didn't much care to face his wounds. So with a
thought he thinks of a name, one quite close to him, one only a short walk
away, "Rippers house" he nods, quickly opening the front door and
sleeking into the evening darkness, looking at the lights of the pub in the
short distance.

He had hoped not to be seen, so he took a route that would optimise
that wish, turning right from his house and walking down a little way
until coming to a small path, quickly taking the route he travels along a
wall, cutting into the village and across a field of horses, he quickly takes
to the end of the field, climbing a stile and cutting down a few more
paths, turning left at a small cross section, his feet bringing him to a small
house at the end of the path, the driveway offset slightly form a small
road that a few yards away joins a main road passing the local shop.

The house seemed empty to matt, the lights were off and there was no
sound either, save the odd car or bike that travelled the road a few yards
away, matt looked carefully, knowing ripper lived alone, his wife leaving
him a year or so ago, he knew ripper had a good kitchen, ,Marge had
spoke fondly of it every Friday night over the years, saying "oh you
should see rippers wifes new worktops" and "oh her oven is just simply
divine" the usual marge quotes, they had been annoying at the time, but
now, now they gave Matt the chance he wanted. And so with a quick
look, making sure no one was watching, he sprints to the front door, the
lock picks in his hands going to work.

****

The night had been a blur, his head throbbed and his vision was far from
normal, his sight flickering as his heavy eyelids fluttered open and shut,
his head barely moving as he tried to sway side to side, the momentumn

trying to help him fully awake. His hands felt like fire across the wrists, his eyes finally opening for the briefest of seconds, looking down to see black cable ties drawn tightly around them, his mind suddenly realisng he wasn't laying down at all, instead his posture and position indicated he was sat.

What brief moment his sight allowed confirmed to him his hands were bound, the cable ties, two on each wrist, restraining him to what appeared to be a wooden chair, the arm rests to which he was tied, seeming to be painted white. His mind willing his body to wake up, as suddenly scooter realised, he was not in a safe place.

With determination he rocked his head back and forth, the motion helping to gain some bearing and slowly his vision his returned, as he fully opened his eyes, the situation around him became no less apparent. He was dressed in his prospects waistcoat, but he quickly realised, that was all he was wearing, the garment hanging lossely over his back and parting at his chest to reveal he was topless underneath, his trousers and pants and socks to which he had been wearing the night before, seeming to have vanished, his bare naked form underneath the table before him, the chair he was sat on slid under the table, the wood of the structure covering his knees and nakedness underneath.

He felt his feet below as he thought on it, feeling the same as was on his wrists, reasonably guessing they had been bound in a similar fashion, his mouth too felt odd. Realisng he had a leather gag tied around it, feeling the knot at the back of his head that bound it to him, a solid piece of leather slightly thrust between his teeth, the leather stopping the tongue from moving freely, as he noticed with a muffled, "what the hell is going on?", his words barely legible, the volume muted and lost to the gag.

He looked down at his crotch, not being able to fully see it for the table in the way, but something felt odd there too, something familiar. The twinge one would normally awake to after a night of passion, the gentle throbbing coming from his manhood confirming he must have had sexual intercourse at some point during the night. He paused as he thought of it, trying to remember it.

He had finished patrol with the others, first drinking at the griffin and speaking to Ripper and Crusher, the president stripper having been absent that night, the man travelling to Addenbrookes hospital to check on Ratchet, who so far as he knew was in a coma, though the circumstances surrounding that fact were still unclaer, reports saying it had been an accident. Scooter could rememeber the conversations well, him and crusher had been laughing about the presidents ex lover trying to blow him up, they had laughed about the so called mixer making salads in peoples homes, the whole pub talking about it in fact, and Harvey, scooter could recall his shame when the conversation had turned to him,

He had not wanted to harm the man, but with everything going on he had felt his frustrations pour into his dealings with the weed dealer, he had recalled how he felt about the death of titan, a friend he had known for a few years, the one who had nominated him to start prospecting for the club. His anger over his murder spilling out at Harvey, he had not meant to put the man in hospital, and yet to his shame, it had happened. Scooter had felt bad, he recalled vividly his wanting to leave as the conversation down the rising sun pub, focused on the mixer and Harvey, his patrol finished, Crusher telling him he could leave if he needed too. "But then…then what?" he asks himself, his muffled voice says aloud, his thoughts trying to retrace his steps, as his eyes catch sight of the unsual lay out of the table,

A plate was set before him, a fine green and white china plate, with the green a fine circle around the edge, with leaf patterns on its rim. Beside it three different knives, the other side three different forks, all different sizes and slightly different shapes to one another, to the top three different sppons, one a soup the other a dessert, the other scooter really didn't know, his eyes taking in the array of glasses, lined up in a perfect row, a champagne glass, a wine glass and a water glass half the height of the wine glass beside it, everything laid out before him, in perfect symmetry to each other. The table set with a fine woven green and white table cloth, depictions of small leaves flowing around the outskirts of the table, two large silver candle sticks centre place in the table and, too Scooters surprise, a camera perched on a large tripod in the far corner, it looking old, as though it still used film rather than digital, a small slither at its front suggesting it would automatically print the photos on there taking. The situation was all very confusing.

As he groaned at his confusion, he felt something strange below, his testicles seeming to not be comfortably sat, in fact he could swear they were hanging down, a shuffle of his behind and he confirmed the chairs seat had a cut out in it, his manhood freely hanging in the gap, his realisation that he could make the outlines of a bucket underneath him as he leant his head to look, he was getting worried. And for good reason too, his eyes scanning the area, the room itself was small, a single light with a silk woven lampshade and small pearls hanging from it, the walls a gentle cream colour and all that resided in it was the table and the chair he was sat on. A small cupboard built into the wall with green doors rested near a set of steps leading up to a small wooden door, thick sound proofing fabric mounted to it, a couple of small heaters mounted near the door. And that was it, a well laid out and presentable small room, though he felt the humming noise of something behind him, leaning back as far as he could, the chair not moving much as it was undoubtley bolted to the floor, Scooter was able to make out the sight of two extractor fans, the old machines whirring away with a gentle hum,

"what the hell did I get up to last night" he cries, his mind racing with ever impending thoughts of danger, not helped by his sudeen realisation he wasn't alone, a chair sitting next to him, a frightening occupant sat a yard away from him, a skeleton, his arms bound with aging cable ties and a leather waistcoat on him, the frayed and aged patch on his front naming him as 'karp', his bare naked skeleton only covered by the waistcoat, his bones semming odd, for they were painted a bright shade of gold. "oh sweet jesus!" Scooter yells in a low muffled voice, "help!"

****

"mum when's aunty marge coming round?" Todd asked, the young boy running into the garden to join Jilian and anne and kim in the garden, Stripper sat outside too, crusher sat beside him, both looking graven and forcing a smile as the kid runs up to his mother, Kim smiling and planting a kiss on her sons forehead, "I told you, the film isn't until seven" she says, "that's four more hours darling", "I cant wait" he says excitedly, "oh we can tell" Crusher winks at him, the ladies having a little chuckle at the boys enthusiasm, "a good film is it?" stripper asks, putting a cup of tea down on the table, "the best one, theres a man of metal and a Viking and a man in blue…" he excitedly lists, the boy counting them on his finger, "they gonna fight a big purple guy" he says, pretending to pucnh the air, "and the heroes shall prevail!" he shouts,

"sounds good" stripper smiles, "go and play with your cards or watch some tv todd" kim says politely, brushing her sons hair with her hands, the boy smiling and running back in, pausing before he goes through the door, "im still going to see Scrumpy tommoorw aren't I mum?" he asks, his mother forcing a smile, "well your father is sorting that one" she says, "so im sure you can count on it" she says, the lie not feeling great as she says it, "is he any better then?" Todd asks, "can we see him again soon?", "soon darling" kim smiles, "mum and dad just having some time away from each other" she explains to him again for the tenth time since staying at Crushers, "he's been ill so we needed to give him some space" she says again, "now go and play"

"bless him" jilian sighs, watching the boy run into her house, "hard for the little ones" she says, picking up her cup of tea, "a night out will do him some good" crusher says quite sincerely, "needs to go out and play with kids his own age" he adds,

"how you been doing?" anne asks kim, "I'm okay" she sighs, looking at stripper, "a lot going on at the moment" she offers, Stripper nodding his agreement, "aint that the truth" he groans, "sorry strip" kim says, rubbing his shoulder fondly, "hows ratchet?" she asks, "still in a coma" he grunts, "reckon he will be for a while" "an accident I heard, came off the road" Anne says, slightly prying, Crusher laughing at the statement, "if you believe the papers" he says, "anyway" Stripper says, changing the subject , "Ripper phoned me last night , said he got back home and someone had made a chilli" he laughs, though not with any sense of humour to it, "even left him a bowl of it on the side, a thank you note attached to it", Anne smiling at the news, quickly loosing the grin as she sees the expression on crushers face, "the mixer?" she asks,

"swears down he didn't make it himself" Stripper huffs, "did he eat it?" jilian asks, the question making her husband roll his eyes, "well what kind of question is that" crusher groans, "someone breaks into your house to make a chilli and your first thought is to eat it?", "I don't know" stripper answers, " didn't think to ask him"

"well who is he?" kim asks, rubbing strippers shoulder, "havent a clue" he admits, "no one saw anything last night, no one has spotted this guy yet" he shrugs slightly, "need to find him though" Crusher adds, Stripper nodding his agreement, "is he causing that much harm?" jilian asks, "with everything else going on is he really that big a concern"

"if nothing else were happening right now he would be an annoyance" Stripper says firmly, "but because of everything he is a threat, a man breaking into peoples homes in the middle of all this is not something we can just allow to carry on" he says, "already two homes on our patch and word is spreading that this rebel is breaking into homes, unchecked and unchallenged, imgaine the implications it has"

"you'll find him" Kim says softly, sensing stripper growing angrier and angrier, "oh you can count on it" crusher smiles, finishing his cup of tea and placing it on the table, "where has scooter got to?" he sighs, looking at his phone, seeing no missed calls, "meant to be here helping with the bike" he says, putting the device back in his pocket, "probably sleeping off a hangover" jilian smiles, "anyway" she says, looking at Anne, "care to help me clear the table dear" she says, her eyes gesturing at kim and Stripper, the young lady sensing the message, "of course" anne says, standing up and collecting the empty cups and pot, jillian picking up the tray and piling the small empty plates that had held some biscuits on it, "go get on with your tinkering dear" she says to Crusher, the man nodding and slapping a hand on his presidents shoulder, "leave the loved ones to there discusions" he jokes, the presidents eyes going slightly wide at the jest, the three clearing off, leaving kim and stripper alone in the garden,

"so..." kim says softly, "any news on your lodge?" she asks, seeking a conversation starter to break the tension she felt growing between them, "be ready in a couple of weeks, insurance is stalling for a moment, apparently there is some discrepancy about bazookas being covered or not" he says, a forced grin on his lips as Kim strokes his shoulder playfully, "should be fine though" he adds,

"how you…how you handling this thing with mary?" she asks, the question feeling awkward as she asks it, "I'm not" he says honestly, "not handling anything, truth be told im glad the police got to her first" he says, "would have been…unsettling having to deal with that through the club" he says, his words holding tuer meaning than his tone implied, in fact he had been greatly relieved she had been captured, he had never had to kill before, and that was what he would have had to do had he found her, the face of a young lover scorned ever to haunt him, he had been relieved the police had been involved, it saved him from the worst thing he would have had to do.

"did…did you not love her?" she asks, the question nagging at her, the overwhelming thought that he had only recently been in a relationship before becoming involved with herself, it was a lot to take on, especially when the guy wouldn't openly talk about such things amongst his brothers, and he was usually always amongst his brothers. "love?" Stripper says with a slight scoff, "mary and I shared one night" he says plainly, "was just an easy lay"

"so is that what I am?" kim asks, the real question she wanted answers too coming to the forefront of the conversation, the inquiry making Stripper nervous as all hell, "I mean…we havent even slept together yet" kim says, "but I feel something between us" she says softly, stripper grabbing her hand from his shoulder and gently kissing it, "kim…" he sighs, "you got to understand…"he stutters slightly, "you know im stripper" he smiles faintly, "the seven inch dick on a muscley stick" he jokes, kim not smiling as the conversation gets even more awkward, "I just, I just sleep around…" he says gently, "I'm not saying you and I don't have a shot" he says, the admission making kim feel slightly relieved, a small smile forming on her lips, "but…" Stripper says, "with so much happening at the moment" he says softly, "we just need to get things back to normal, I need to get back in my lodge, the club needs to recover, the village needs return to peace" he says softly, "and I cant think about us, until I have sorted all of this out" he says, kim taking her hand from Strippers grip and stroking his face,

"todd is out tonight, Crusher and jilian are going to the merry monk for a meal" she says fondly, "gives me chance to help you….relax a bit" she whispers sweetly, "maybe explore how we are feeling" she says, Stripper feeling his primal desire taking over his sense, "well…" he sighs, melting into her soft touch, "maybe I do need something to help take my mind from things"

****

Now it could be said, that throughout the week so far, there has been a lot of smiling, everyone seems to smile, even in the darkest of moments a dark grin seems to form, and so with everything going on, it was unsual to see the smirks, the chesire cat like smiles, the cheesy grins. But it was no more apparent than in the evening, when at last Matt had thrown caution to the wind and decided to venture out to the griifn public house, his joy at seeing people a strange shock to any that knew him, his 'hellos' and 'how are you' seeming to be misplaced on the man they all thought miserable and incapable of such a thing, and yet, on his journey to the pub, he was pretty happy, the biggest smile he had shown on his face, for he had found a new freedom, and he had revelled to hear the village alight with talks of it.

The local shop had apparently offered a sweep stake at guessing the name of the mixer, the local restaurant the merry monk offering a mixer special, a side salad next to a vegetarian chilli, matt had heard. And it felt great to think everyone was talking about him, the feeling echoing his popularity the years before his fathers demise. His smile large, as he walked into the pub, to his surprise, it was busy, with nearly twenty patrons sat inside, pete looking miserable as he worked tirelessly to serve the waiting customers, matt walking in, sitting beside mrs finch and her husbad Nigel, both in deep discusion with a large Scottish lady, a woman named doctor gloom,

"well in your proffession you must have some idea of the sort to do this" mrs finch said, speaking to the Scottish woman, the lady sipping at a pint of lager, "I mean you work with the sort all the time" mrs finch adds, her husband Nigel nodding to the conversation, "well…" doctor gloom thinks aloud, "it shows a need for acceptance, if indeed the mixer is doing it for recognition, or perhaps a lost soul just in need of some form of self expression, something they cant find the art of in there own homes" she suggests, mrs finch smiling at the conclusion, "well my thoughts exactly, weren't they Nigel" she says tapping her husband, "didn't I say exactly that"

"alright matt?" pete asks, tearing the mans prying ears from the conversation, his former friend staring at him with an empty glass, "pint?" he asks, matt nodding, "yes please " he says, reaching into his pocket and pulling out three pounds fifty, the coins having been so welcoming on the bikers side board the night before he just had to take them, he didn't much care at the theft, it was only a couple of quid and he had already broken into the home and made a chilli so there was little harm in adding the theft of three pounds fifty to the growing list of crimes he had committed, the coins being placed on the bar, as his former friend pours him his ale,

Matt looked around him, he had never seen nor heard of the pub so busy, for at least five years the business had barely managed to keep five patrons a day, the odd traveller coming in for a lunch or dinner, but all these people, matt mused, all these were local. There was garth the ex boxer, owned a farm down little London, drinking with his wife Sheila, a large but very striking brunette who ran her own small hairdressers from her own lounge, there was Michael and roy, two lovers who used to sell palm trees as an exotic rarety to the local homes that could afford them,

There was ted and bill, who many joked once got stuck in a phone box, the fireservice once having to cut the two out after being stuck in it for exactly eighty nine minutes, the two apparently getting stoned and trying to make some calls, the two somehow getting stuck and phoning the fire brigade to help them, in fact matt recalls, he hadn't seen them for quite a few years, he was genuinely happy to see them. There were others too he recognised, farmer karl who grew cucumbers and wouldn't stop talking about them, farmer trey who raised horses, all the old faces matt had forgotten were here, even doctor gloom the large Scottish lady everybody thought was secretly a witch. He was amazed, as his pint was placed on the bar, pete taking the coins and opening the till

"well everyone's talking about it aren't they Nigel?" mrs finch continues, Matt listening intently with a huge grin, "get so used to a way of things, something like this comes along after that business with bazooka boy and well.." she says pausing to take a quick breath, her husband trying to keep pace with the conversation, doctor gloom patiently waiting for her to finish, "I mean people are saying you know, maybe the club isn't what it used to be" she says, Nigel coughing a warning, "well its not just me, whole village is talking about it, Nigel!" she slaps his arm., "coughing in the middle of my sentence well…" she huffs. Doctor gloom nodding in agreement to mrs finchs words, "well add a bit of unexplained chaos to an uneasy peace" she sighs, "exactly, exactly what I said wasn't it Nigel"

"unusal to see you on a Saturday" pete says, closing the till after putting the coins in, "rare treat" matt shrugs taking his attention away from the conversation beside him,, taking a sip of the ale, "been alright?" pete asks, matt looking at him, "yeah, you?" he replies, "im..ah..im sorry about the other night" pete says, the appollogy coming out of nowhere, "me too" matt nods, putting his pint down, "quick smoke?" pete asks, keen to get Matt outside for a private chat, "havent smoked for a while" he shrugs, "watch me have one then" pete says quickly, Matt sensing the urgency in his voice, "alright" he says, stepping away from the bar and walking through the door at the back, walking out of the porch area and out to the smoking area, pete joining him,

"busy tonight?" matt asks, pete lighting up a smoke and inhaling, "has been since Harvey" he pauses, checking to make sure they were alone, "people arent so happy to go down the sun at the moment" he says quietly, "people starting to feel the VigilanteS aint all that, know what I mean" he says, Matt not really responding, "since they learned what stripper did to mary and what she did because of it, they feeling a bit less than pleased with the whole thing" pete says, taking another drag on his smoke, "still business here been improving because of it"

"so you still hanging out down there?" matt asks candidly, "nope" pete admits, "thought on what you said…Harvey and you are friends" he says honestly, "was different when its people you hate, but when its someone you know, makes you realise.." he pauses, " and now the mixer is loose" he grins, a knowing glint in his eye, "people laughing saying they cant even catch a theiving cook" he shrugs, "makes you question wether the club is even a good idea"

"a salad and a chilli does all that?" matt laughs slightly, "what a world, where some lettuce can undo a vigilante state", "a bazzooka too" pete adds, "and bikers ending up in comas" , "well," matt says, "I couldn't care less" he grins, "with everything going on I just wanted a pint" he says, stepping back towards the door, "you know its strange, the mixer striking first next door to harveys house," pete says, stubbing out his smoke, "the same day you went to tidy up" he adds, Matt laughing, "strange world" he says, stepping back into the pub, pete following him and quickly grabbing his arm, "you need to stop mate, VigilanteS aint impressed and they are looking for you" he says, sincere warning to his voice, "no idea what your talking about" matt says, wriggling his arm free, "just came for a pint mate" he lied. As he steps back through the door.

In truth he had come to see what people were talking about, and to his joy it had been the subject he had hoped it would be, and so he just left, taking another sip of his pint and slipping out the front door, nobody really noticing him leave, all too busy in there own conversations, pete watching him go, a concerned look on his face as the door closed.

The dark sky of the night had a slight chill to it, but not a shiver came to matt as he walked, for he had truly hoped to confirm to himself whether Marge had been in there, he knew she was due to go out, she was taking his son and hers and a small group to see the latest superhero film, the fact she wasn't in the pub confirmed she would have gone to the cinema as planned, for marge was a thing of habbit, always popping in for a quick drink so far as he could recall around seven on a Saturday, though it had been many years since this was the known case, the possibility arising that she may have changed her habit, or indeed was in the rising sun instead, the cinema being canclled for whatever reason, but these were just brief paranoid thoughts, quickly swept aside.

He walked with a purpose, for he knew his next target, he knew his next fix and where to get it. Walking carefully so not to be seen he passed the local shop, walking down the road passed the small road he had used the night before, walking and seeing nobody, presuming on a Saturday evening everyone was out, he passed nobody, and came to stop outside marges house, his hands keenly finding his fleece pouch of lock picks, setting to work on the mechanism, a few clicks and the door opened, which considering the lock wasn't very modern, didn't really surprise matt as he entered.

He didn't randomly pick this house, he had planned it through the day, firstly because he knew marge and her son Kieran would be out, secondly because he didn't really like her all that much, and thirdly, above all else, she had always bragged about her kitchen, and on stepping through the lounge to enter it, he could see why.

Spices in jars and herbs lined in alphabetical order, large jars, small jars, an array of pickles and different flour, white flour dark flour, plain and self raising, sugars too. Icing, demera, sugar lumps and the kind for tea and the kind for coffe, caster sugar, and all manner of cordials in green bottles in order of size, running along a small shelf above the back door to the garden, elderflower, raspberry, all manner of tonics and cooking brandy, cooking wines and different vinegars. The place was a heaven for the chef minded, and Matt knew he had chosen well.

A gas fired oven with not four but six different hobs, a fine kettle in dark green and knives too numerous to count, all in dark green blocks, long knives, bread knives, steak knives, butter knives all the kinds that existed were here, and matt just didn't know where to begin, "well, ive done a side and a main" he ponders, looking at his phone and pulling up mixies website, the happy looking chef pinging onto his phone as he searches the website, "a pudding maybe?" he wonders aloud, typing in desert in the search bar, a recipe for carrot cake pinging up, "that'll do" he says, clapping his hands together, seeing a dark green chefs hat neatly hanging from a peg with an apron of the same colour, his hands quickly picking up the hat, placing it on his head, the thing siting comfortably as he looks around, finding a mixing bowl and a large spoon, looking at his phone he searches for the ingredients, pulling out carrots from the fridge and pulling down jars of sugar and flour, finding a bottle of vegetable oil from the small chef, finding some eggs too. "marge my darling" he says mockingly, "your in for a treat tonight"

****

Chapter 5

He awoke at full mast, the phone beside him blaring beside his head, his body aching quite fondly, as the young kims arm was outstretched over his chest, her fingers still and unmoving, her hair tucked behind her ears from the sweat of the night before, her chest lightly rising and falling underneath the covers. Stripper looking at the feint lips and sweet face, her eyes closed, trapped in the wonderous dream he thought she looked to be having. It had been a good experience, Stripper thought to himself, perhaps even one of the best, he had never had sex with someone so frustrated before, years of forgoing the pleasure due to a collapsing marriage seemed to make the young lady more hungry when releasing her pent up desires upon him, and lord how she had unleashed them.

Stripper had had second thoughts about her advances during the day, thinking he needed to get out of this tangle he was weaving for himself, thinking of a way to find her a safe place to stay, taking her son with her and then forgetting about her and finding someone far less needy. But for all the excuses he could think of, for all the scenarios he had ran in his mind, she had at last won him over, with a simple bit of seduction, but one that had worked a charm nonetheless. She had showered, and stripper had kept himself downstairs, trying to avoid the fact they were alone together in the house, he had thought her evening shower would take her mind from it, but it had in fact been a most sensual ploy, for minutes after the water had stopped running, she had come downstairs, wrapped in a thin pink towel, the fabric barely clinging to her, her wet hair flowing as she stepped quietly to him, grabbing his hand and running it along her forehead. "to the bedroom" she had whispered, taking his slightly shaking finger, and sucking on it playfully,

Well that had been it, Stripper was a man after all, how could he say no to such an advance? Following her up the stairs and into the room he was staying in, she had undone his belt and let the trousers drop, helping the man to kick them aside, her hand removing his waistcoat and pulling his shirt over his shoulders, stripping him bare for all but his boxer shorts and socks, leaning into him and planting a tongue into his mouth, her hands clawing at his back as she put a leg behind his, tripping him gently onto the bed, her towel rising slighty as she pulled it up, her other hand undoing the buttons on the boxer shorts, a mighty lust taking her, as she mounted what was protruding from him,

It had been slow at first, but quickly it turned to a rampage of moans, becoming louder and louder as she thrust herself harder and faster, Stippers eyes wide and his hands gripping the duvet cover, as his nuckles turned red from squeezing harder and harder, she had then taken to remove the towel, keeping the same length of it either side of her, letting it drop so the middle was forced against her lower back, grabbing strippers hands and giving him each end of the towel, the man pulling it back and forth, the momentum of it making her thrust with each tug and pull, stripper in control, as she gave herself to his directions.

It had been frantic, as he pulled and released, pulled and released, her body coming down so her bare breast were ontop of his, her tongue dug deep into his throat, her moans echoing and filling to his ears, as he pulled the towel harder and harder, her groans and whimpers becoming louder and lasting longer, it hadn't taken long, but both had been reaching there end, Kim sensing the same as him, had wrapped her knees, tightening hard across his side and putting an arm under his head, she rolled, the sudden weight going to the left of the bed making stirpper spin too, coming to a stop and finding himself now on top of her, as she moaned and kicked her legs out wide, her hand finding the pink towel, raisng her lower body so he went deeper, pulling the towel out and throwing around strippers behind, pulling on it hard, burying him as deep as he could get inside. His breathing uncontrollable, as she pulled and relased on the towel, over and over again, pulling and leaving it taught for a few seconds then letting go, pulling again and releasing a few seconds longer each time, the two panting with each deep thrust, stripper almost howling as his groans had told her he was ready, as was she, a final release of the towel and she had let go completely of it, grabbing his lower back with her hands and massaging the flesh, pushing hard and wrapping her legs around him, it had eded with a roar, the sweat covering the sheet and the limp body of stripper laying loose ontop of her, as she kissed him all over his face, biting his ear and licking the lobe, the two laying there for hours, eventually falling asleep.

And so, it had been a good night, one with a happy ending. The morning seeing her cuddled against him, his manhood seeming to stand to the moment, it sticking up creating a great mound coming from underneath the covers, her arm gently resting on his chest, it was a good morning, save the phone ringing on his bedside, "yeah" he sighs, picking it up and answering it, "marge?" he asks, bringing himself to sit up on the side of the bed, " I've tried ringing you all night" the voice says frantically, "sorry, " Stripper says, "phone on silent, was…busy" he sighs, looking over his shoulder to see kim slowly start to wake up, "he was here! Last night in my house!" marge says, her voice not sounding angry, more like the tone of someone fancying spreading some gossip, "two cake tins and a mixing bowl on the drying rack and half a bloody carrot cake with thank you written in flour next to it" she says quickly, "what?…" Stripper asks, "who was there?" he asks, not really waking up fully and the woman's voice was particualry jarring to say the least, "the mixer, love, I been telling everyone to keep an eye for a man in a green chefs hat, cheeky bugger nicked that an all" she says,

"you been telling everyone?" stripper asks, his voice getting angry, "well of course darling, people need to know don't they" she says, "anyway you needn't worry love, just thought I would let you know as a common curtesy" she says, hanging up the phone, "oh that bloody woman!" he groans, taking the phone from his ear, "I swear she hates me really" he scoffs, standing up finding his clothes, "whats wrong?" kim asks, sitting up in the bed, "this bloody mixer" he maons, "half the village will be talking about him now to the other half thanks to your friend"

"marge?" kim asks, "why was he at hers last night?" she asks panicked, "oh todd, was he with her when…" she says, shooting up and running into the next room, the door flying open as she sees her son sleeping soundly in the large bed, a small smile on his face as he snores, "don't be stupid" Stripper says, through the door, pulling on his trousers as he speaks, his shirt and waistcoat back on, "he strikes when no ones home" he says, "todd was safe at the cinema"

"morning pres" crusher says, coming out of his own bedroom door, his eyes taking the sight of kim wrapped in a loose sheet, a knowing glance to his brother making him chuckle slightly, "downstairs now" Stripper says to the man, "get dressed mary" he says to kim, suddenly realising his mistake, "kim" he corrects, the young lady looking shocked, slamming the door closed, leaving stripper and crusher in the hallway, the two looking at each other, "have a good night then?" crusher asks, the president slapping him and dragging him down the stairs, Crusher laughing as he goes down.

"any word on scooter?" Stripper asks, the two entering the kitchen and putting the kettle on, "hasn't been seen since Friday night" crusher says, "I mean you said lay low so.." he ventures, "you find him" stripper says firmly, "get him back here and sorting that greeves out, needs to be ready to be shifted by tomorrow, got a buyer coming to collect it,"

"yes pres, if I cant I'll get zoom to come help" he says reassuringly, "scooters probably just panicked a bit, probably found some bird to take his mind off it", "maybe" Stripper nods, hitting the radio on the side of the kitchen counter, the news coming on, "police have announced that alongside mary jaggard her father gus jagard has been detained, the man is charged with the possesion of the arsenal the so called bazooka boy had used in the incident that claimed the life of a tobias griwmald, also know as titan" the finger flicks the news off, stripper looking at Crusher. "means a cheap house going to come available pres?" crusher grins, "our own workshop maybe"

"no one else lives there?" he asks, crusher shaking his head, "just mary and the old man, it'll be put up for auction I would imgine, what with them having no more use for it, big enough to be converted to a workshop" "keep an ear out, I want to know the moment it hit's the market" stripper says, crusher nodding, "we leave old bruce alone for now, build our own shop and once evreythings settled, we can always revisit Ratchets wounds" he says, a plan forming in his mind, a smile hitting him as he sees a clearing through the mist of it all, things starting to fall into place, a happiness almost grabbing him, until Kim comes thundering down the stairs

"mary! Fucking mary!" she yells at him, full dressed and raging she storms into the kitchen, "is that all I am! Another lay!" she shouts, "you know what!" stripper yells, bringing himself to her face, his temper flaring, "I have enough shit without some tart adding to it!" he says, "so get yourself gone!" he yells, pointing at the front door, "don't you worry" she spits, "you wont be seeing me again!" she yells, disappearing out the kitchen, moments later her son todd following behind her, his mothers hand grasping his hand tightly as she pulls down the stairs, "mummy!" he cries, "mummy please!" he shouts, "come on todd we're leaveing" she says, pulling open the front door, jilian racing down the stairs at the commotion, "Kim!" she yells, racing to grab her and clucth her crying face, "whats going on!?" she asks with a fire to her, turning her head to bare daggers at Stripper, "I've had my fill of her!" he shouts, pointing at the door, "you got what you wanted!" Kim spits, "sorry jilian" she says to the lady, pulling todd out the door, "where are you going to go?" jilian shouts after her, "kim please"

"let her go!" stripper shouts, walking over and slamming the door closed, jilian slapping him hard on the face, "disgusting!" she says sourly, "poor girl like that going through what you put her through," she says again slapping him, "you get out of my house!" she yells at him, Crusher stepping in between the two as stripper reddens from each blow, "Jilian!" crusher roars, "no!" she snaps back, "he is out of our house! Let him go stay with another of his gang" she shouts, "your not welcome here, you disgusting pig!" she says, throwing another slap at the man, crusher catching it, "calm down!" he says, holding her as she struggles to free her hand, stripper leaning hard on the wall behind him to avoid the coming blows, " you get out!" she shouts, pushing back against Crusher, "pres get going" Crusher says, "she needs a bit of time to calm down" he advises, stripper opening the door and backing out of it, "oh crusher" he says seeing the waiting police car outside the house, the small silver micra of kims car roaring off the driveway, "crusher" he says with more sand to his voice, "the jagard house" he says quickly, "perfect target to watch tonight, no one there, just like our mixer likes" he says, quickly closing the door. The police jumping out the car, the detective inspector and the young blonde officer approaching him, "Stripper?" bruce asks, "a domestic going on?" he asks, hearing the shouting coming from inside,

"lovers tiff" he shrugs, "well, no matter, need you to come with us" bruce smiles, "a few questions for you", "questions, you caught her didn't you?" stripper says icily, "oh not about bazooka boy" the young blonde officer says, "about the murder of Harvey flint"

The news, late the night before, had come as a blow, if by the term it was meant a thousand pound hammer falling onto a single shard of glass, the momentum smashing what resolve and hope remained in the thin and delicate fragment, the shard turning to attoms and spreading for thousands of miles, no longer any resemblance to the from it once was, to put it short, the news pete had phoned matt to say, had killed whatever was left of him.

There wasn't anger, or sadness, just destruction and a swift nothing to the news, the phone call had ended, and matt had fallen to the lounge floor, the torotise hiding somewhere under the sofa, quite where he didn't know, and right now it was the last thing he cared about. His mind trying to imagine his friends face, a friend who though beaten, had seemed in good enough health when he had left him in the hospital bed. However, as pete had relayed the message from the hospital, all had not been whet it had seemed, the bandage on his friends head masking a far more sinister problem than even the doctors could not have foreseen.

It was called intracranial hematoma, so pete had explained, the blow to harveys head slowly causing bouts of dizziness and vomiting over the coming days, putting pressure on the skull as blood lined the brain tissue, the doctors had spotted it, and the surgeons had operated as soon as they could, yet the anesthetic and the stress of everything combined on harveys weakend heart, had caused complications, and unfortunately, they had proved too fatal to overcome, a rare case, the hopsital had admitted, but it had happened nonetheless, the cause of the bleeding, the injury he had sustained during his self reported destructive episode, or at least, that was the hospital had put as the determined cause.

Both matt and Pete knew differently, they knew now he was a victim of manslaughter, if not murder. The news coming to matt via pete had come as beyond a crushing blow, the man trying to work out how to get himself and his son to Cambridge at the time, to see the live scumpy show. All thoughts of that vanishing, as he lay on the floor motionless.

Harvey may not have been the best of men, but to matt he was the best of friends, the only one who had truly stuck by him, though he saw him as little as once in a while, each encounter had always felt as though they had never been apart, he was a friend, and now he was phantom.

So he had done what any in his position would do, something which pete agreed as well, they had both phoned the number of the ely poilce station, and told of Harveys confession he had been attacked, though matt knew he was now a grass, as the streets would probably call him, he really didn't care, he had in his darkest moment thought of a plan, and pete had offered very little resistence to it on the suggestion, perhaps seeing the ploy and agreeing it was for the best, or simply he too was too greif struck to offer much argument against it, so they had rang the number independently of each other, and said Harvey had confessed stripper had been the one to attack him.

It wasn't the greatest plan, it certainly had its dangers but matt had learned to over think sometimes is to fail. He pictured the president of the so called saviours being bogged and harassed by all measure of questions and pressure, the past catching up with him as often it did, the man being forced to give the real names of the attackers, if ever he had the slightest hope of avoiding a sentence, matt hoped the man would be forced to sell out his precious club. Even if he didn't and the police had nothing on him, pete had agreed to spread the word the VigilanteS had killed Harvey, there hold on the village slipping as anger, betrayal and shock seep through the cracks they had created for themselves. It was of little comfort though, none in fact. for his friend was phantom.

He lay on the floor, the dolphin called scrumpy singing a song on the television, the noise a blur and the words a garble, as Matt thought on Harvey, thought on what he would do now, now he had no one in the world to call a true friend. There was always pete, but he sensed they had never truly got on as he had with Harv, the man never really seeing Matt as a friend, more a better option than having no one at all. Matt didn't know, nor did he much care to think upon it. For his only friend was gone.

The floor seemd to vibrate slightly, as little claws emerged from under the sofa, pulling along the fabric chester came out, the tortoise coming to stare at Matt, there eyes connecting, "your just going to lie there?" the squeaky and high pitched voice says, matt unaware he was talking to himself again, "I failed him…I failed as a friend…" he sobs, "I should have been by his side" he weeps, "you couldn't of known" chester says sadly, "no one could have"

"what do you know!?" matt shouts, the voice making the toroise pop into its shell, "your just a damn frog in a box" he sighs, turning his head from him, "and you're the mixer" the voice says softly, "and your friends been murderd" it squeeks, "so what you going to do about it?"

"oh I'll make the bastard a cake of course" he scoffs, rolling back over to stare at chester, the tortoises head popping out of its shell, "not all vengeance is violent" he says, his eyes catching matts again, "and the village is ready to rise", "im not a symbol, barely a dream three days old" he says sourly, "my friends body rots in a bed I cant afford to get too and all I am known for is making a bloody salad! Even then I'm not known, not at all by any, my wife hates me and my son is ashamed of me" he cries, "what can I do to make a village rise?"

"where are all eyes looking to now?" Chester asks, his voice trailing as his claws drag him to turn round, his small body sliding back under the sofa, "don't leave me" matt cries, "chester!", "see where the eyes linger, and see your answer" the voice fades, the tortoise slipping fully under the sofa, Matt grabbing his phone and dialling, "yeah" petes voice says glumly, "pete, do me a favour, find out where the VigilanteS will be tonight", "what…matt I cant.." petes voice says, "I cant face them at the moment…" "I know mate" matt says, rubbing his head with his hand, looking underneath the sofa, the darkness under it hiding the tortoise from sight, "just a feeling mate" he says, "tell them you heard the mixer was planning on robbing the jagards place tonight" he suddenly thinks, remembering hearing it on the radio that both its occupants were currently locked up, "the perfect place for him to strike…" he says, pausing as he hears his front door slowly open, "please pete" he asks quickly, "be careful" Pete sighs, the phone going dead as he hangs up.

Matt rolled to look at the approaching footsteps, readying himself for a fight, fearing he had been discovered too soon, rising up to a sititng position then jumping to his feet, his fists clenched, his hands quickly hanging by his side in shock, as the red eyed kim and todd slowly walk into the lounge. "daddy!" todd screamed, running and grabbing matt, the mans arms flinging round his sons as he kneels down, "oh my…" matt weeps, "what a sight I needed to see" he says kissing his sons head, "daddy are you better now?" todd asks, his voice cracked as he cries into his fathers chest, "can I come live here again?" he weeps, "of course," matt sobs, "course my little man can, the tickle monsters been lonely without you…" he says, his fingers gently tickling the boy, todd looking up and kissing his dad on the cheek, "I missed you tickle monster" he smiles, his tears slowing, matt looking up at kim, "does the monster need another victim?" she asks softly, her eyes filled with regret and longing, "no" matt says looking away from her, "hes got eyes only for his son" he says kissing his boy, "you sit on the sofa todd, watch your show"

"what happened to the lounge?" todd asks, seeing the mess of cushions and dvd cases scattered about, holding up the broken half of the tv remote, "the monster got carried away" Matt smiles lightly, kissing his son, "theres a surprise for you under the sofa too," he adds, "just let him come out in his own time though" he says, todd instantly dropping down to the floor to stare under the sofa, "Matt…" kim pleads, following him out of the lounge, into the kitchen,

"I'm sorry" she cries, trying to stroke his shoulder, matt batting it away quickly, "you are my wife!" he hisses, "that is my son!" he points towards the lounge, "don't you ever fucking apologise" he says, grabbing kim and embracing her, the young lady going limp in his grasp, "it was a fathers fault, not the families" he cries, holding her tightly, "stipper.." she cries, "he wasn't…he wasn't the answer.." she sobs, "and neither am I" he says, waiting a moment and releasing his grip from her, pulling away slightly, "not as I am" he says softly, "not as we are"

"I'm sorry" she says again, matt rubbing away the tears from her cheeks, "you need to go kim, todd too" he says quickly, instantly realising the danger before him, he had forgot about his family in his madness, not thinking for a second how his lunacy could have endangered them so, if they found out he was the mixer, if they found out he had grassed. "go to Cambridge" he says quickly, "take todd to the show", "no… that's your time together" kim sobs, "I cant get in the way of that" she shakes her head, her eyes red and her lips quivering, "your not in the way of anything" he kisses her, "but I cant take todd tonight, but you can" he says firmly, "please kim, do it for todd" he says, his voice pleading, his wife nodding gently, "okay," she says, "okay I can take him", "show him a great time, spend whatever you got and don't worry about a thing" Matt says, "we're not alright kim" he says honestly, "but we will get there, as a family, just this one night, is all I ask, I have something I have to do"

****

The interrogation room was silent for a while, as stripper sat in handcuffs, the metal of the chain bolted to the table, his posture firm and fixed, his demeanour giving nothing away as the detective inspector entered the room, this time a collegue of his, the fire inspector Thomas checker coming to sit in on the interview, the two men sitting down and placing a large file before them, Thomas looking at his colleague with a broad smile as he sits down, happy to be involved in the case again.

"I'm not under arrest you know" Stripper says, holding up the handcuffs as far as the bolt on the table would allow, "no you're right " bruce says, "I forgot that bit I am sorry, you are under arrest" he says plainly, "there happy" he smiles, the president lowering his hands and staring at the detective, "for what?" he asks, "well for the murder of Harvey flint for a start," Thomas says with a slight sarcastic remark, "oh I'm sorry I didn't introduce my friend here, Thomas checker of the Cambridgeshire fire service, acting liason on the case involving your friend titan and the so called bazooka boy" he smiles, "a case already solved" Stripper grunts, "well, do you admit to the killing of Harvey flint?" Thomas asks, "no comment" stripper grunts, "oh here it is" bruce smiles, undoing the elastic from the large case file in front of him, "my favourite two words" he jokes,

"anyway we will come to Harvey flint in a bit" Bruce says, pulling out a photo of a group meeting of the VendettaS motorcycle club, "because when it comes to the case of the law against the VigilanteS, we really need travel back a few years don't we?" he asks, "no comment" Stripper scoffs, Thomas smiling at the words as his colleague continues, "I didn't see the family resemblence at first," he says pointing at the picture of the VendettaS club, "but this man here" he says, finding a blown up version of the young man he was pointing too, "I mean he was nothing really, apparently he lasted a few months or so prospecting and then one day…" bruce says softly, "stabbed in a turf war, one of the local drug runners had gotten in a fight with him, and as usually happens, someone came the worse off"

"you were a medic, serving in the army at the time" Bruce says, pulling out a picture of Stripper from years ago, wearing an army uniform and looking a lot happier, "called you strip didn't they? Your comrades?….we phoned your old commander, said you got the name because you used to get naked everyday during basic training and run around chasing after everyone" Bruce smiles, "said you turned out to be one of the best recruits they ever had, got a commission too, you were going to be an officer weren't you?" bruce asks, "no comment" stripper says, looking away from the photos, "hard working and honest military man like yourself" Thomas adds, "cant imagine hearing your son was trying to earn his colours for an outlaw club was welcomed news"

"I think you tried…" bruce says gently, "In fact I know you did, I phoned the prison the former president of the VendettaS is serving a life term in" he says, "and he told me you had asked him to keep your son out fo it, said you offered him money, threatened to destroy his club if he hurt your boy" bruce shakes his head, "did what any parent would do" Thomas adds, "but he wouldn't listen would he?" "no comment" stripper says, his tone beginning to sound angry, "said the boy is his own man, then..a few weeks later, he died" bruce sighs, "well you just lost it, your commading officer said you just walked, threatened to leave the ranks by force so they gave a swift discharge to save face, in honour of the man who had served, and saved so many brave souls for all those years" Thomas says, his voice sounding respectful, "so what did you do?" bruce shrugs, "no comment" stripper says firmly, "left your wife, well she didn't understand this new rage within you, moved to the village your son had died in, found like minded souls that didn't like the VendettaS, recruited from rival gangs and clubs, trying to stand above the rest all the time, making it clear you would clean up the mess, that you would have peace in a place only knowing war",

"but it wasn't easy was it?" Thomas asks, "all those different opinions under a banner yet to merge and galvanise to your dream, you might have hoped for a peaceful solution, but your members were yet to learn the extent to which you wished your ideals to be enforced", "you couldn't control them back then" bruce says, "for all your show of control you had little, a new club far different from any before, your members betrayed you, tried outing you, some even siding with your rivals" the words making stripper just stare at the two men, "revenge" Thomas adds, "people so often think killing is it in its basest form, but you didn't want to become like them, you wanted the club that robbed you of your son destroyed, not dead, but destroyed, as you had so threatened to do"

"no comment" stripper scoffs again, "so the brawls were petty, went on a while with no one winning ultimately, you had people desert for not delivering on your promises, someone even tried to kill you at one point," bruce says, reading an old file note from the desk, "went wrong though, the man losing his nerve before pulling the trigger, reports best guessed it to be a man known as Karp, the former president wouldn't give us any enlightenment on that matter I'm afraid, you two are very similar in that regard " he says, the comment making Stripper look away in disgust,

"well you were on the rocks, you were losing and down to what? A dozen or more members, where once you had thirty?" Thomas asks, "then Karp disappears, and none can explain it, the whole village searched and questioned, the rumour spreading the VigilanteS had finally turned the tide, the VendettaS losing a member, it was enough to get an upper hand" Bruce cuts in, "his body never found , yet your clubs name always going where the legend of it does" he says, seeing stripper roll his eyes, "had nothing to do with it" he scoffs, "quite, unfortunately we cant prove otherwise either" bruce admits, pulling another old file note to read, "but what you did do, was intensify the fighting, soon streets buckled to you, gangs running scared for fear the same fate would befall them, you used that mans 'disaperance', as a means to mobolise and assualt the rivals into a corner" Bruce says, "and after a few weeks, pattersons pass came about"

"we looked into it" Thomas says, "two of your members swore the VendettaS member known as klaxon was holding the knife, that they tried to wrestle it free from him, a police officer patroling at the time saw this, running in to break up the fight" he says, bruce looking at the case note he was holding, "according to other witnesses at the scene at the time, they saw the vendettas member strike wildly, stabbing the officer in the lower abdomen" bruce says, "the two members regaining control of the knife and returning to tussle with the rival member, the knife becoming lodged in his right lung, " he pauses, "but this sounds familiar doesn't it?" he asks, "no comment" Stripper says, "a terrible accident" Thomas says, "officer Meadows and Klaxon losing there lives, your two members getting seven years a piece for involuntary manslaughter"

"well that was that, the VendettaS were done, nowhere for shelter and public opinion had changed, they weren that well liked anymore, and so you helped to run them out, your thirst for revenge sated" Thomas says, "of course we know that isn't how it really happened, a few forth coming accounts coming to us of a different tale, a few lads who were until recently scared of you claiming they too had seen what had happened, saying one of your men had had the knife, and that you were there too, the wrestling had ensued as Klaxon fought for his life, the officer coming over to break it up, but hey you know the rest, and you made out the VendettaS member had been the one responsible for the local policeman's death, a fact that helped the village see you as the righteous choice, the locals saying enough was enough and bought your promises of peace, helping to drive out the VendettaS" he says leaving the thread of the conversation there, Bruce reading from a freshly printed witness testimony in his hands, "sound about right?" he asks, "no comment"

"anyway," Bruce sighs, "moving on, you had some busy years, clearing the streets of gangs," he says reading from a sheet of paper, "twelve accounts of young males ending in intensive care, each one reportedly returning and casting away there wicked ways, two counts of assualt, one member sentenced for it, getting four years for actual bodily harm, his victim apparently known to steal cars, of course he served only two for good behaviour, a man you call crusher I believe" he smiles, "no comment" stripper smiles back, his eyes tired and his tone shifting, "you ruled with an iron fist" Thomas adds, "and whilst some may respect you for it, none of them are here in this room" he says, leaning forward, "you clear streets by making confused boys into men and give them a future they can work towards" he says, "not inflict your own ideals upon them and call it law" he says, leaning back as Bruce pulls another paper from the file,

"so that leads us up to this passed week" Bruce sighs, "we know about bazooka boy of course, no elaboration needed on that I don't think, but if not for Mary jaggard, we would never have started looking into you or your club, thinking the cases were old or unsolvable" he smiles, "you know she wanted to destroy you, all of you?" he grins slightly, "no comment" Stripper says, looking away from the detective, "well she might have just managed it, it really bothered me" Bruce says leaning in, "this whole thing with the priory garage closing down, I mean you just walked from it, and the rumours surrounding it" he says, "rumours you no doubt tried to squash, unfortunately fuelling the fires more, the rumours becoming louder and louder," he adds, "then this fascination with Fordham garage, well it peeked my interest, I mean, what could a motorcycle club that modelled itself as lawful and pure, occasionally dabbling in misdemeanours where it suited them, really want with a garage?" he shrugs, "drugs? Money laundering?" he guessed, "no comment" stripper says again,

"your boy ratchet goes in to make first contact, course he's an idiot so

the thing doesn't go well, so you go and sniff the area out" Thomas says,
"doesn't go well either, I mean the owner is the father of the VendettaS
member that disappeared that your club was rumoured to have had a hand
in,, of course it wasn't going to go well, but you were running out of
options, having him say no to you must have been like the French
resistence to the Nazis" Thomas says, "all you wanted was some work
benches, but old wounds" he shrugs, "your rule couldn't face someone so
openly defying it, especially not someone related to an old and bitter
rivalry, but you made a mistake didn't you" bruce adds, "Fordham is a
few miles from Isleham, and we call that expansionism, something your
wonderous empire is far from being able to achieve" Thomas adds., "so it
just raised flags to us, you had to be desperate, especially to try it with the
father of man you are rumoured to have killed"

"so why the garages? If not for smuggling or nefarious gains?" Bruce
asks, "a simple answer" he says, "one I needed my colleague here for" he
says, looking at Thomas, "you see I needed to search your lodge Stripper,
but with nothing to get a warrant for, or at least not a warrant I could get
very quickly" he shrugs, "and without alerting you to it too…" he pauses,
"well being the victim of a recent explosion, my capacity as a fire
inspector allows me to enter the homes of anyone I feel poses a fire risk"
Thomas says casually, "and bruce here told me just what to look for"

"titan, or tobias Grimwald, moved from Wales to ely to Isleham,
joined your club a few years back, " he says, producing a picture of the
man, "you see like most organisations you got structure, crusher and
some of the others your muscle, then you got movers and grifters if so
inclined to have them, but you also have accountants" he pauses, "the
reason Titan was outside your house that night, as most nights before,
was reported to be because he feeds your cats for you" he says, "so?"
stripper says, his voice slightly nervous, "well that's the thing Stripper,
we called your neighbours, you don't have any cats"

"I reckoned, like most bosses, you liked to keep an accurate account on
finances" Bruce says, "and so your accountant would fill in the ledger
every night, making sure you were constantly aprised of the clubs funds
and earnings" he smiles, "and guess what I found, when I looked among
the bookcases?" Thomas smiles, bruce producing photocopies of sheets
and sheets of numbers, "you weren't up to anything at all" bruce sighs,
"you really were just doing up old motorbikes and selling them, a few
parts here and there but all legit, we ran the numbers too, looking for
discrepancies, all legit" he huffs, his voice sounding disappointed,
Stripper smiling at the two men, "well I could have told you that" he
smiles,

"ah yes, but heres the thing" bruce says leaning in, "Harvey flint, was at
an interview at the garage when your boy ratchet was there, he was a key

witness you might say to that first interaction between your club and the garage, a witness to something that set in motion a chain of events," Bruce smiles," and it is odd your brother, Ratchet the very same man Harvey witnessed, seems to have been planning some form of assualt a few nights later, possibly going to shake up the Fordham garage owner, who has finally admitted Ratchet had threatened him that night there had been an altercation and he acted in self defence, Ratchet ran away, got on his bike and crashed further down the road" he shrugs, "good enough for me, wont be digging to much further into that one I don't think, he would of course need a witness to help back his story up, not only his own employees but someone totally impartial, the young Harvey flint, " bruce says holding his hands up, "so whats that got to do with me?" stripper sighs, not understanding at what they were getting at,

   "I got a book of accounts showing your only source of income is through fixing up motors, I got proof your last venture with a garage went down the pan and proof you sent a man round to try to get Fordham garage on board, i got proof that there was a wintess to the whole thing, where the whole thing began and now he has died, following an assualt we have proof your club committed" the detective says, his words coming heavy, "I got a witness who's soul testimony could have supported the case that you were trying to get business back as uasull by using Fordham garage by which to do so, resorting to illegal tactics and threatening behaviour and bribery, all could have been verified by Harvey Flint if we had known to ask him 'were you there when ratchet tried to bribe the owner of Fordham garage?' The first piece of the puzzle that solely explains the rest of what has transpired, and now.." he says his voice filling with a stone cold tone, "I have a key witness I have proof your club killed!" he says icily, "for fear he would expose you or for the fact he was growing a bit of puff, it doesn't matter, the judge will see the same thing I do, The same thing this sequence of events points too," he says, Stripper looking away ,

   "we got two calls saying it was you that assaulted the boy" Bruce calms himself, sititng back in his chair, "I got finger prints from the scene, I'm sure will match up, so you will go to prison stripper, at long last you will go to prison", "I wasn't there" he spits, "your prints wont match mine", "we know" Thomas nods, "commanders rarely carry out there own orders," he says, "small time player like Harvey flint" he laughs, "no, you would have sent someone else, who?"

   "no comment" he spits, "you tell us the names and we don't lock you up in a cell block with all those old friends who are dying to see you one last time" bruce says, "you can say they acted without your go ahead, you could walk out of here stripper" he says, "no comment" the man spits again, "well no matter, we will arrest all your club on suspisicon anyway,

see who's prints match up" he says, "and to think, none of this could have
been possible, if bazooka boy hadn't chosen your lodge as a target place,"
he sighs, "the vital piece to the story on your shelves all along", he says
pointing to some wording on the papers he was holding, the account
ledgers saying "need action on establishing a new garage fast, the club is
haemorrhaging money" , he smiles, as he shows him,

  "president in prison, one in a coma, at least one more to join you in the
cell" Thomas clicks his tongue, "one missing as well our officers seem to
think, lost sight of him not so long ago" Bruce says, "still, sure he will
turn up, if he hasn't ran already," "the collapse of a club can make a man
think to get out" Thomas says, the two men standing up, "well I suppose I
can't arrest you for the murder of Harvey flint" Bruce says, "so I am
arresting you for threatening behaviour, and suspicion of orchestrating the
assualt that lead to the death of Harvey, also" he adds, "this mixer fellow,
seems to have helped make a few tongues wag a bit more, our officers
have been having a great time, plenty of cups of tea talking to those
dozen or so men you had beaten up during your rise" he says patting the
president on the shoulder, "apparently no one fears a club that cant even
catch a thieving chef," he says, "and I am sure your list of charges will
grow the greater for it, the case of the murder of Klaxon and officer
Meadows surely being reopened, I might not get you a life term, but at
least I can get you off the streets for a good long while, just think " Bruce
smiles stepping towards the door," Mary started all this trying to kill you
but your own clubs actions are what's going to be what buries you ", he
smiles once more, leaving the interrogation room, "how far a king falls
for the faults of his subjects" Thomas smiles, walking out the door too
"oh piss off you horrid fireman, go save a cat out a tree" he spits, "still be
more pussy than your going to be getting" Thomas smiles walking out,,
Stripper left alone, his body shaking slightly as he bites his lip, a massive
roar coming from him as the door closes on the room.

****

Chapter 6

The evening hadn't darkened yet, in fact it was more late afternoon than
any other time, when at last Marges ex came to pick up there son, the
man knocking on the door and hugging the boy, his manner quite cordial
as he promised he would take good care of him for the coming half term
break from primary school. Kieran telling him all about his fun filled day
at the cinema, his dad laughing as he helped his son into his car, waving
goodbye to Marge and driving off, the large blonde lady watching as they
go, a fondness in her heart to have seen Kieran so happy, for he did often
like spending time with his father, and that was enough for Marge, she

could forgive his tresspasses against there marriage for a small short
moments, each time letting go of the past as the husabnd came round to
pick up and drop off Kieran, and today of all days, she had been
especially happy to see Kieran go with his dad, for she had a burning in
her blood, and her artwork was calling.

She had left the project to sit a while, a good day or so to let exhaustion
work its course, for she had found on her first attempt, to try to prepare
the canvas too early, resulted in difficulties. She had thought a lot over
the last few hours how best to capture her vision, thinking the best way to
move the project along so it was ready for her artistic flare, and she had
had also considered her needs, and that was why she had chosen scooter,
for Anne had often talked about the mans talent, and she hadn't been
wrong.

Seducing the man had been easier than she had thought, capturing him
in an unusual and self loathing state, which had helped her to get him to
willingly come back to hers, making sure of course they weren't seen, if
they had been, she would have had to forget the idea, and try again
another time, but fortune had smiled, and she had got him to come for
drinks, then one thing lead to another, and she had seen for herself the
talent Anne had spoken off, she had lasted a good long while, scooter had
too, until she chlorophormed him. The young man going limp on the bed
then dragging him down the stairs she was sure she would wake her son,
but luck again had been on her side, and she managed to get him to the
door of her basement, the door that only she was ever allowed to use, the
door swinging open and the rest was simple, putting the man on the chair
and putting his waistcoat on him, tying his wrists and feet into place, so
the man would awake, sat at the mostl perfectly set table she had made
over five years ago.

She recalled the night fondly, as he closes her front door, and grabs
half a carrot cake from the kitchen counter, munching on it hungrily as
she opens the basement door, stepping down it and closing it behind her,
a thick mass of sound proofing fabric lining the door. Slowly she walks,
enjoying each salivating taste of the cake in her hand, scooter looking at
her, his eyes going wide.

The picture had been perfectly set, with the plates all exactly as they
should be, her guests sat in exactly the position they should be too, the
cutlery all aligned in exactly the manner she wanted, the lighting in the
room too, was perfect, she bore the scene with amazement, picturing the
perfect creation still needing to be made, her nose sensing a smell in the
air, as she looks at the bucket under scooter, stepping along and ignoring
his muffled cries, pulling it out and opening the small green doors of the
cupboards, emptying the bucket into a composting bin and putting the lid
on it, returning the bucket under the terrified man.

The extractor fans did there job well,keeping the smells under control and keeping the room the perfect temperature, the heaters near the sound proofed door keeping the place at an ambient temperature, she looked around her, smiling as she leans down, unlocking the restraining bolt attached to scooters chair, pulling it and her captive slightly backwards, enough room for her to sit on his lap, the last of the cake going down her gob, as he chews and looks into the young mans eyes, "its not easy you know" she says finally, "this love of mine," she says, tilting his head to look at the skeleton of the VendettaS member, "first you got to wait for the life to drain away, then you gotta leave the room for about a few months or so, " she says, "nature taking its course until everything is nice and…tender and easy to scrape off" she says, scooter screaming in muffled bursts, "then you got to clean every last millimetre, sand out any imperfections, got to drill little holes into joints and tie loose bones together, bit of gluing too, process takes another good few weeks, school days and kids outings you know, get in the way a bit" she says, "then you get to the painting, two coats of base white, takes about a week to dry, then four coats of your chosen colour" she smiles, "mine being gold of course" she laughs, "process takes another few weeks, and then.." she sighs, "the perfect picture" she says, plonking the terrified man on the nose, with a playful finger

"well I mean choosing the right person for it takes a while too, a few years in your case" she says playfully, "see I don't consider it murder, no, that is just a nasty word, more…a service" she smiles, "old karp here, Mary thought he was saint but no…no he tried killing your president and well I had had enough of gunshots and stabbings lining my street" she says, staring into Scooters eyes, "see I have always loved the human body," she says rubbing his chest, "or at least what is underneath it" she chuckles, "might say I see the form of skeleton painting, a release from ones worry and strife, the rush when you create from a death something more beautiful than what it was when it was living…well its just other worldly" she explains, rubbing scooters terrified face, "I tried to get help, I did, but all these lectures on the internet on suppressing ones own artistic license, " she sighs, "well its enough to make you question who's telling you these things, and question if law really aides development…or hinder its evolution" she says playfully, "because Marge doesn't like it when people screws with her things" she says plonking him on the nose, "and Ilseham is my village too you know" she says, rocking herself back and forth and swinging her legs round to satnd up beside the biker,

"he was a good lad, until he tried to resort to murder" she says, tapping her golden creation, "as were you, until you assaulted my friend, who died by the way" she adds, "did you know that? No. no matter, I didn't like him much, but what he did for mary and that humour of his, he deserved better, so imagine my joy, when finally I have found a subject, a blank canvas for my craft, who I heard talking about harming dear harv, well my desires just tingled love" she smiles, "and another biker too, so you will fit perfectly with my scene, the perfect photograph, still working on a name but I was thinking the golden supper?" she ventures, "well, I will have plenty of months to think on it" she says, pulling down her trousers and nickers, mounting the terrified Harvey," everyday and every hour I can spare, I'm going to help you slip away" she says, feeling his manhood and pulling it up into her, "helps move the process along you see" she says, gasping as she achieves what she wanted, starting to thrust hard and slow, "a shame that my friend dies from the cruelty of dread and fear, only for you to die in agonising and constant ecstasy" she says, groaning as her rythym increases, "and it will be constant scooter" she says, "for my art demands of me great sacrifce and patience, and so my golden supper shall near its completion, and we will see what new peace reigns from it, just like your predeccessor before you," she sighs sensually, "oh yes, Scooter, my golden boy, you are going to be my masterpiece"

****

The night was dark, as the shower water flowed, the form of matt basking in the stream of hot and steamy water, his eyes closed as he recalled his farewell to his wife and child, embracing and kissing, wishing his son a good night at the live scrumpy show, Kim promising to find a hotel for the night, her kiss on his lips before she left stirring fond memories of a time he had long forgotten, a time when he had been happy, when he had been in love and his son had been conceived , sure he had been only a teenager, his father shouting at him as any good parent did, his anger subsiding swiftly to turn to support and calming words, his father ever reassuring he would help in way he could, offering for kim to move in during her pregnancy, helping to craft a crib for the baby to come, matt recalled it all, as the water fell onto his hair,

   His father had been a policeman, a proud one too, tinkering with motorbikes and painting pictures in his spare time, helping to teach nappy changes and feeding routines for the newly born todd, he had been nothing short of the model citizen, he had often kept the peace between the gangs, and helped bring them down when they stepped out of line, he was a man of morals, Matt fondly recalls, the only time he let go of them was when he was on his bike, when no one was around and no one to judge but the open road, that had been the spirit of being a biker matt knew, that was what the freedom he cared for was, that was it purest shape. And too have such a man taken from him, by a group claiming to have a superior law than the one his father had so proudly enforced, well. For matt that had been the greatest blow. And the world was a sadder place without the likes of officer Meadows, a rarety of a man that could keep peace and obey the law, and let go of his worries at a safe place and time, to return from a ride out and paint something so wonderful, and to offer nothing but love to a teenage couple who had made a mistake, matt loved his father, and though at first he knew he had brought shame to him, he knew it was fleeting feeling, one his father ever regretted having.

His father was loved, matt knew, by the people of Isleham,and that was all he needed to know when it came to the measure of a man, for if the community can love you, even though you enforce its laws, then truly you are an example of what should be set for others to follow, and matt knew, his father never once enjoyed handcuffing or restraining or enforcing tough laws, he had told him as such many a time, instead, he had simply done it because that was what the law demanded, to keep the peace, and to keep the morality and value of the community at a meaningful measure. The man had flaws, as all did of course, he would sometimes forget to buy things or forget to set an alarm clock once in a while but if you were to ask anyone, he was respected, he was tough, and he was loved.

His passing had created a spiral, matt knew, one his father would frown upon, one his father if he were still alive would have dragged him to one side and said "enough! Time to man up a bit", matt knew his passed years were caused by the death of him, but it had never truly dawned that it should have been lived, in fond honor of the man his father had raised, showing the world that his father had instilled the core values and morals to help him overcome his hurdles, and yet, he was ashamed to admit, he had instead betrayed the mans memory, and become something far removed from the son he once was. And it pained him, as the water fell, to think of the things he had done, the things he had let happen, the poor choices, the lazy attitude to life, his descent to the depths of depression and his foray into crime. He knew his father would be biting his lip, watching from the heavens wanting to shout all manner of curses at him, he knew well, his father would chuck lightening bolts of advice if he could, he knew well, he had failed, but so too, he knew, just as his father had taught, that even the most hopeless and lost, could still turn something rotten into something of beauty and merit.

The shower poured onto him, and this time he needed no music whilst he bathed, for the list had gone of things to help him through the day, a new mechanism now put into place, revenge, not as it was often coined but still very much the same thing , as his mind raced with how to do it, he settled on a plan, and that was that, he needed no music, for the calm had taken him, and he feared tonight was his last night on this earth. As he steps out onto the bathroom floor, turning the water off, he picks up the towel and dries himself, looking at the sink where chester the tortoise splashed about, a warm wash for him too as his head bobs up and down, "did you ever speak?" matt asks, as he begins to pull on his pants and socks, the tortoise not answering, seeming content in the water as it claws move back and forth, its head dipping below the surface and returning again, "my madness I speak in a toroises voice" matt laughs, pulling up his black trousers, pulling on a black short sleeve shirt, stepping to the mirror and grabbing a load of talc powder, smearing a load onto his face, then a load more, and a load more still, the powder forming some form of white and ghastly makeup effect, his black beard standing dominant amidst all the white, his hand grabbing some hair gel his son liked to use, running it through his dangling strands of hair, making sure it keeps long, wiping the remains from his hands on his towel and throwing it to the floor, picking up the dark green chefs hat and folding it at its centre, placing it on his head to sloop to the right.

He looked in the mirror a short while, his white face and black beard and eye brows and dangling wet looking hair, he looked a spectre arisen from drowning, and he was content. Picking up the tortoise and giving him a quick dry, walking down the stairs and plonking chester on the carpet of the lounge, the tv playing Mixies show, "add some eggs and some flour, tis the time for mixies hour, chocolate chips and coconut, time to see what the chef is cooking up" the theme tune played, matt walking to the back of the tv, "nope" he says, pulling the plug out of the socket, the tv shutting off instantly, "not this time" he says, looking at the tortoise before he leaves, "please don't shit on the carpet" he asks, walking out the room, opening the front door, walking into the darkness beyond.

****

They had gathered in force, the group walking down the road of little London, the large house crusher hoped would soon be converted to there new garage, the house of gus jaggard, the group of men walking, all of the VigilanteS had turned out, save scooter, who was till absent without leave for some reason, the large form of crusher turning to stare at his force, all dressed in black with there waistcoats proudly worn, all of them looking to make an example of there prey, hoping they could regain the control they had felt they were losing. looking to reset the balance this dark night.

There was ripper, Scruff and Boxer, Slayer and Shiner, dread gadget and ripple, fang and trench, with the young prospect zoom at the rear, and all were armed, very heavily so. For on crushers orders, who still awaited news of his presidents release, he had decided subtlety had no place here, he felt this mixer needed making an example of, and the village would once again learn, that the VigilanteS could amass a mighty response to whatever threat may dawn. Most held a bat, the solid cricket equipment held firmly in there hands, two held large crossbows, the things designed for hunting and the love of the hobby, the weapons now coming to bare against there enemy. One had a small axe, the other a lump hammer, the prospect had a stick with a small knife celotaped to its end, the steak knife reflecting the light of the moon, Crusher had no weapon, he didn't need it, his fists would do the work for him.

The party arrived at the house, just stopping short before entering, quickly peering into the windows, everyone of the members talking, "no lights on" Ripper said, "sure he's in there?" he asks, "Pete says he heard he'd be here, the pres said it was a good target too" Crusher said, walking up to the house, "could be hiding, saw us and cowering somewhere" he says, trying the door handle, putting his shoulder into the door, the thing not budging, "be ready" he says, his brothers lining up behind him, a hefty kick from crusher near the handle and the door flies open, the VigilanteS piling in, tossing over furniture and yelling away, each member searching a different room, Crusher waiting at the the kitchen door, Dread calling to him, "might want to see this" he shouts, Crusher following his voice to the kitchen, the man pointing to the worktop, the thing covered in flour as he stares at a message inscribed into the powder, "thank you, you made it too easy" it read, crushers face draining of colour, "get out!" he shouts, racing for the door, a sudden flash of blue erupting from all sides of the house, dozens of armed officers screaming and shouting in there high viz jackets, "down!" they yelled, "screw you!" one of the corssbowmen yelled, Boxer raising the weapon as he ran outside, a bullet taking him in the leg, the shot echoing from one of the officers rifles filling the air, boxer falling to the ground with a scream,

Tasers and batons coming to bare, as the club members we forced on by one on the ground "shot fired control!" one of the officers shouts into his radio, "taser taser taser!" one of the officers shouts, the young blonde policewoman bringing Shiner down with the electric prongs, his body vibrating wildly as he fell, the bat falling from his hands, her body piling ontop of him as other officers helps restrain him. All was commotion, as one by one the members were pinned down and restrained, "I got knives, bats, crossbows" the officer on the radio was shouting, "come in control these men are amred and dangerous" he says, watching as a member called gadget raced at one of his colleagues with an axe, the frustrations of the clubs demsise seeming to pour out of him in his rage enduced charge, "firing!" the officer shouts, squeezing the trigger, the shot sounding loud, ringing through the air with a thunder as blood erupts from the mans thigh, the man hitting the deck hard, the axe flying from his grasp, all were captured and pinned, there screams and shouts filling the air, Ripper swearing and kicking wildly as five large officers piled on top of him, one of the last members to be subdued in the ordeal, all of the VigilanteS accounted for, all save for Crusher.

The man had managed to slip away, quickly hugging the long garden wall of the property and in the turmoil managed to escape, his fist knocking one officer unconscious with a single blow as he ran passed him, the biker quickly running, his feet taking him up little London, a look behind him and he saw no one was following yet, quickly he ran, turning left and running passed the local shop, running faster and faster to pass the old church and the graveyard, turning left and passing the rising sun, his feet racing as he passed the old post office, his house coming closer as he ran, in absolute exhaustion he managed his front door, piling into his hallway as quickly a she could, and that is when he saw him, standing in his kitchen.

It had started with some eggs, and a glass mixing bowl, some flour and some milk, the whisk gently whisking away in his hands, as he stared at the exhausted form of Crusher, now limping towards him, "you!" he yelled gasping for air "would you like a civilised conversation?" matt asked, the man looking ready to pucnh him, "very well" he says, pulling out a long and sharp kitchen knife from the counters rack of knives, Crusher too exhausted to try anything, his eyes seeing the glint on the blade, "now sit" matt said, gesturing with the knife for crusher to take a seat at the table, the man doing as he was told, if only to gain a few moments to recover his breath, "and keep it down" matt tuts, "wouldn't want to wake the wife" he winks, Crusher looking at him as he breathes heavy, his face a mass of rage and longing to cause him harm,

Matt grabbed a frying pan, and placed it on the hob, placing the knife down beside it, making sure Crusher could see it was still very much in reach, he put some butter in the pan, and quietly waited for it to melt, "do you know?" he says, looking at crusher, his white face and black hair making his expressions stand out ten times stronger than ever, his loping green chefs hat tilted to the right as he spoke, "it was so easy to fool you" he smiles, his big grin annoying the brute at the table, "just had to tell you where I was going to be, and tell the police the same thing," he laughs, "over thinking things sometimes" he tuts, "it's the simple things that prevail" he sighs, "I thought of so many ways too"

"how did you know I would be here, I could have been caught to?" the large biker spits, his breath still lost and his colour not returning to his face, "knew?" matt laughs, "what you talking about silly I just wanted to make some pancakes"

"if you've hurt my wife" he says, his voice filled with warning, "well think you done that yourself my friend" matt shrugs, "I mean your going away for the rest of your life" he says, clapping his hands together as he see's the butter has melted, pouring some of the mix into the pan with a single hand, keeping the other near the knife, "you know your problem crusher" he says, pausing quickly, "I mean the VigilanteS problem" he says nodding his head, watching the pancakes begin to whiten and form, "your not outlaws" he says, throwing his hands wide, "not the one percent of bikers, you aint the clubs that know how to do things" he says, letting out a little "ooh" as he sees his pancakes start to brown slightly, grabbing the knife and starting to pry the baked mixture from the suface of then pan, little motions helping it unstick, "your just a bunch of boys playing at being cops" he says, "we kept this place safe!" Crusher sneers, his voice being caught short by matt holding a knife up to his own lips, making a 'shushing' sound, as he points at the pancake, "the fun parts the flipping" he smiles, grabbing the pan with his free hand, a slight wiggle and a flip, the pancake flying in the air with a single turn, landing on the gooey uncooked mixture on the underside, landing perfectly in the pan,

"them boys, maybe not the VendettaS I mean they were as helpless as you are" he concedes, "but them boys know how to keep order, those men know how to earn respect" he says, shaking the pan slightly, resting it on the hob, turning the dial to a lower heat, "if your going to make your own laws then become an outlaw yourself" he says playfully, "otherwise when you go to do the cooking, your going to burn yourself" he says, the knife hanging down at his side, Crusher watching it carefully, "me well I don't dabble in crime, I accept it, it has become this person before you, this spectre you once hunted now making you a treat" he smiles, "but you and yours, chose when to be lawful and when not to be, worse still when to enforce your rules, and when not" he laughs, "and that is why I am the one making the desert, and you are not" he smiles, seeing his pancake brown to a perfect colour, "so what now? Now this lecture is over?" Crusher spits, his breath coming back to him, "who said it was over?" matt smiles, "now any maple syrup?" he asks, looking at the top cupboard,

"you mother fucker!" Crusher roared, seeing his moment and leaping from the chair, his body coming to bare into matt, the thin man able to step aside and leap out the way as the large hulk of the biker stands up straight, his fists balling up tight as he closes the gap, Matt looking at the long knife in his own hand, "woops, " he says, dropping the thing on the floor, "shouldn't be holdoing it like that anyway" he jokes, ducking to the side a large fist narrowly misses him, his legs leaping to the hallway and his hands grabbing the door, "shame you didn't want desert, not after the main course was so scrummy" he laughs pulling the door open and closing it quickly behind him, Crusher yelling as he chases him, barely a second behind him, matt pulling his chefs hat off, using it to wipe the white from his face quickly as he runs, blue flashing lights reflecting along the road before him, sirens blaring as Crusher emerges from the door "was a chef that bested the saviours!" Matt laughs, not looking back "what kind of law is overturned by a two course meal!?" he laughs again, Crusher screaming "come here!" and yelling all manner of profanities as he gives chase, "help!" matt shouts, seeing the police cars screeching around the curve of the road, coming to stop just in front of him, the man tucking the hat into his shirt, "help! Theres a mad man after me!" her yells, passing the cars as the officers pile out, "hey you!" one of them shouts towards matt, "stop!" he yells, "madman!" he shouts back pointing at Crusher racing at them, his eyes white and his teeth barred as he runs, "go go!" the officer shouts to matt, waving his hand to indicate the man to run, "stop!" a half dozen officers warn, "fuck you mixer!" the enraged mans voice yells, tasers taking him down, all six in fact, before finally he fell to the floor, the electric shocks making him jolt around on the ground.

Matt looked back, before he disappeared into the darkness, the officers not watching which way he went, so with a run he passed the rising sun pub, taking a right and passing the old church, passed the graveyard and second on the right, he made it home, the door closing behind him as he fell to the floor, breathless and shaken, but victorious all the same, his eyes seeing the tortoise in its shell in the hallway, a lump of brown poo beside it, the thing spreading in a puddle in the fabric of the carpet, "don't worry buddy" Matt he laughs, "you aren't the only one to shit the bed"

****

Chapter 7

Monday had come and the bustle with it too, the school holidays were upon the village, and the sun was out, the morning breeze had welcomed the dog walkers and the garderners and the people tending there chickens on the allotments, the day had dawned, and life had kept on going, despite the news on the radios and televisions constantly talking of the impending release of misty the heron to a wildlife sanctuary, other smaller stories reporting the arrests of an entire motorcycle outfit, charged with an array of different offences, the charges being made public brought against Crusher for the manslaughter of Harvey flint, the charges too against Stripper the president, facing a heavy sentence for his part of various assualts and acts of threatening behaviour as growing amount of new charges continued to stack against him. The trial too filled the airways, of the notorious bazzoka boy and her father.

The car radio was filled with such things, each making both kim and

Matt smile, and too they felt sad, for mary and her father, the mention of Harvey flint bringing them sorrow, the decleration of the manhunt for the man known as scooter bringing them some confusion, but alas they were happy, or at least the happiest they had been for a long time. In the back of the car in the middle seat sat Todd, telling wonderful tales of the live show he had watched with his mother, his voice giddy and filled with joy as he recalled some of the funnier moments, Anne sat beside him, feeling a mix of emotions that the people she had known so well were most likely to be locked up for a long time, Pete sat the other side of the boy, staring at Anne the whole journey, the young lady encouraging his looks, winking at him and saying things he wanted to hear.

They had passed the rising sun, where the owner apparently still felt people would attend the anniversary celebration of the VigilanteS, and he had been right to keep to the time and date, quickly adjusting the banner that once read "VigilanteS for five years and counting", to a more befitting sign, "VigilanteS, hopefully rotting for five years and counting", half the village had turned up for it, toasting and drinking early in the summer glow, enjoying the barbeques and eating the cakes and drinking the ales and lagers,

They had driven for a while, taking the road to ely down pound lane connecting onto prick willow road, a mass of green fields and tall tress going on for ten miles as they drove, the car filled with conversation, each occupant recalling fond memories of Harvey flint, each guessing who the mixer could be, though Pete and matt obviously lied with there guesses.

They arrived at Ely, and matt had entered the pet shop, walking up to the pecked and featherless form of destiny, the large canary he had always dreamed of owning, telling the young girl at the shop he was ready for her, his wife by his side confirming they truly were. They too bought a small glass tank for the tortoise, for it had proven a slight concern having him loose, roaming about the floor all the time, Kim almost tripping over him on her return earlier that morning. The couple agreeing he could sleep in the tank, and wander the garden during the day, and so it was they bought the tank, and in a small white box the bird was put, handed to matt free of charge as promised, matt smiling and leaving the premises,

He had walked into the job centre and seen dean his case worker, the man smiling as he entered, his smile turning to a frown as matt told him to go fuck himself, leaving the building with a massive grin, saying he would never again step into the place, and so they had returned to the car, Pete and Anne staying behind, agreeing to grab a meal together and perhaps go see a film.

They had driven back along the Soham road, taking the large

roundabout and passing through Fordham, coming to a stop outside the garage, Matt kissing his wife and his son wishing him luck, matt walked with a purpose, the small white cardboard box in his hands, the young lad at the reception greeting him, "hello sir" he had said, "boss about?" matt asked politely, "one moment" he had replied, the young man scuttling off into the workshop, a voice coming through the door, "looks like he's got a bird in a box. Looks like trouble" the comment making matt smile as Bruce Jagard the garage owner steps through the door, smiling at Matt as he enters, "can I help you?" "heard you keep an aviary mate" Matt says politely, "I do" Bruce says, "room for one more?" he says handing the owner the box, "well this is unusual" he grunts, clasping the box carefully, "needs a good home mate, one suited for it" matt smiles, "well not everyday I get given a bird" Bruce admits, "I mean I can take it" he nods, "how'd you know I got an aviary?", "your kitchen overlooks it" Matt says, the answer making the man nod, a sudden concerned look coming to his eye, "I found a chocolate cake by my washing machine this morning" he grunts, "a letter saying thank you on it" he says, his voice sounding accusing,

"sounds good" matt smiles, tapping his fingers on the reception, "you still hiring?" he asks, "yeah…for an apprentice " Bruce says somewhat confused, not believing the boxed bird in his hand or the implication this young man before him had somehow broke into his place and baked him a chocolate sponge, "why you interested?" he asks, matt smiling, "well…"

✳✳✳✳✳✳✳✳✳✳✳✳✳✳✳✳✳✳✳✳✳

" a job well done" detective bruce declared, holding up a glass of champagne, Thomas checker beside him doing the same, the small police meeting room filled with the young officers, there glasses raised as the detective inspector leads the toast, "some may say we weren't exactly by the book, some may say we were harsh when we should have been fair, and fair when we should have been harsh, some may say the job is still unfinished, that the rascal scooter is still on the run" he says happily, keeping his glass raised, "but to all of them I say but one response, in my slightly slurring and drunken form as I stand here now" he says cheerfully, "we are but people after all!" he says proudly, "as are those we live to protect" he says, "cheers", the officers and fireman joining him, the room sounding with a resounding "cheers"

"oh sir" the young blonde officer says, turning up the tv as the reporter talks live from a local sanctuary, "well it has been a tough time for misty" the young lady says holding the microphone to her mouth, the picture showing the wetlands of the vast reserve behind her, "and as the mystery of the last week come to the light, so to do we hope our dear misty, can finally find some peace of her own" she says, the camera panning to the rspca man, "mr creek?" she asks the man, as he puts the heron down on the floor, the creature limping quite gladly towards the pools of water beyond, "as you know, animal rights activists have become heavily involved in this ordeal, a time when vets said it would be more humane to put her down, some agreeing, some professionals saying the bird would never survive its wounds, even on a sanctuary such as this, the topic becoming the most hotly debated across social media platforms, what do you have to say to the supporters of this choice, to persevere and see misty given another chance?" she asks the rspca man his name badge finally on his chest, reading j. creek, the man looking behind him as he watches the bird find its stride,

"well, I mean personally for me, having worked so closely to her for the last few days, seeing her out here now I got to agree with the attitude that all life, no matter how far away from hope of survival should be allowed to be given a chance to thrive, given another chance to live " he nods, the camera zooming in on the heron, "and what do you say to those that believed the nicest thing to do was put misty down?" the reporter asks solemnly, "well have a look, see what a bit of optimism can achieve when levelled against so called reason and thoughts of humanity" the rspca man smiles, a small red cloud seeming to make its way towards misty, "hang on" he says, the camera zooming in on the heron, a fox coming at it, taking it swiftly by the neck and dragging it along the wetlands, the body going lifeless in its jaws, "but then nature does have its say in these things too" j. creek adds, the camera following the reporter as she drops the microphone, her feet racing in the direction of the fox, "misty!" she yells as he runs, "misty no!" the screen going black as the young blonde officer hit's the red button, the room filled with the shocked faces of the officers,

"well" detective inspector Bruce says, sharing a smile with his colleague Thomas, taking a sip of his champagne as all the officers turn to look at him, glum faces on each and everyone of them, "maybe you shouldn't have named it" he laughs, his friend beside him sharing the joke, there faces going red, "fucking heron!"

THE END…..?   .

Authors note.

All characters in this book are purely fictional, any resemblence or similarity is purely coincidental, I do not condone harm to herons or the

use of foul language unless used in a suitable environmnet, I recommend looking up the needs and making sure you areable to meet them before aquiring a tortoise and understand that they most definitely cannot speak the human dialect. Motorcycle clubs are awesome and so too the police force and the extoadinary work they do keeping the public safe, any situations that have have been described that have affected you personally I would advise to reach out and discuss with a proffessional, physchologists are most definetly not witches though they may wear the odd black cape and pointy hat and breaking into anyones property without there permission is indeed a serious crime, I would personally like to thank the great work the RSPCA do as once they helped remove a giant terrifying owl from my premises and they do stand up work, my apologies to have misrepresented you slightly but all for the sake of good fun I assure you. Also I know very little about policing or the fire service and I am unsure as to whether you would have collaborated as described but it goes without saying that firefighters are total bad asses and you have nothing but my respect.
All characters are purely fictional…oh I already said that,

Thank you for reading, and god bless.

If you liked this and want to read some of my other crap, then here are some of other titles,
A collection of madness (volume 1)- by s.j tasker
A collection of madness (volume 2)- by s.j tasker
The riddle of World- by s.j tasker